CW00419908

OXFORD
TRINITY

David Matthews

SCRIPTORA

Published in Great Britain by

SCRIPTORA
25 Summerhill Road
London N15 4HF

in association with SWWJ (Society of Women Writers & Journalists)
www.swwj.co.uk

© David Matthews 2019

All rights reserved. No part of this publication may be
produced or transmitted in any form without the prior
permission of the publisher.

This is a work of fiction. Any resemblance between the
fictional characters and actual persons, living or dead, is
coincidental.

ISBN: 978 -0-9500591-4-3

Designed, printed and bound by Witley Press Hunstanton PE36 6AD
www.witleypress.co.uk

To Mum and Dad.
The world seems a less kind
place without you.

To Uncle Bill Fewster
1929-2019
Forever grateful for your lifetime
devotion and friendship.

ACKNOWLEDGEMENT

Many thanks to
Mary Rensten, Vice-President SWWJ.
For her unwavering interest,
encouragement and editing expertise.

CHAPTER ONE

HAPPY ANNIVERSARY

It was a miserable Monday with a light persistent rain drizzling down from the grey, wintry sky. The tall angular figure of Detective Chief Inspector Joe Loxley stood disconsolately on the pavement outside the Old Bailey Law Courts. The court case had proved a frustrating one, with the accused getting off with a much lighter sentence than Loxley would have liked. With his hands thrust deep into his coat pockets, he silently cursed the defence barrister who had successfully reduced the charge from attempted murder to actual bodily harm. Not for the first time defence supremo Rupert Buxton had prevented him from securing an appropriate jail sentence for someone who was a particularly nasty piece of work. Through a masterly combination of working the juries and highlighting minute technicalities, young Buxton had swiftly built a formidable reputation as one of the finest defence barristers in the land. At that precise moment, a distinctly deflated Joe Loxley found it difficult to join in with the admiration. He was soon joined on the pavement outside by his junior sidekick James Cumber, who after a look of commiseration led him swiftly to the nearby *Viaduct Tavern* in Newgate Street for a spot of lunch.

*

Just across the road from the Old Bailey, Marcus Varney stood staring at the law courts. The busy thoroughfare of Old Jewry was teeming with people going about their business but he had no interest in them. The object of his attention was still inside the building. Though he had been standing there for some time, he was oblivious to the chill breeze and relentlessly falling rain. With his eyes fixed intently on the law court entrance, he could feel a growing sense of excitement; but he also felt something else. Something that went much deeper; a malicious, raging hatred that could, and would not be denied.

*

Comfortably installed within the confines of the pub Loxley's spirits gradually began to lift, helped appreciably by a tasty jumbo pasty and a pint of Guinness. Loxley looked around the interior of the pub approvingly, for the recent Eighties fashion for trendy wine bars held little appeal for him - a good old-fashioned pub had always been much more to his taste. After a disgruntled conversation between the two men, referring to liberal judges, clever barristers and soft sentences, DS Cumber moved the discussion on to the subject of cars - always one of his favourite topics. As his junior detective enthusiastically expanded on the relative merits of the

Porsche 944 and the Saab 9000, Loxley's mind began to wander as he relaxed with another large swill of his Guinness. The *Viaduct Tavern* was a popular pub in the immediate vicinity of the Old Bailey; as a consequence it was well frequented by all sides of the law. The melody of the Communards *Don't Leave Me This Way* could just be heard above the hubbub of noise generated by crowds of animated solicitors' clerks, office workers, and relatives of the accused.

The date was the 3rd of November 1986 and it was Loxley's rare intention to leave for home early that day, as it was his 21st wedding anniversary. He had booked a meal in a newly-opened restaurant near to his home in Broxbourne to mark the occasion. The twenty-one years had flown by in the blink of an eye, but he had never lost sight of the fact that his wife Janet had been the sustaining rock upon which his successful police career had been built. She had tolerated his long hours and delayed arrivals home through all those years with stoic resignation while raising their daughter Clare. He still found it hard to believe that his daughter was now twenty years old and away studying English at Exeter University. Where did the time go? Loxley was suddenly snapped out of his thoughts by DS Cumber drawing his attention to the tall elegant figure that was Rupert Buxton. The barrister had entered the pub accompanied by two junior clerks, still displaying the cool confident air of a man who was at the top of his game. To the surprise of both Loxley and Cumber, he nodded to them in recognition and paused briefly as he passed their table. With a charming smile that seemed almost apologetic he asked them, 'No hard feelings I hope, gentlemen?'

Before Loxley could restrain his more headstrong younger partner, Cumber replied, 'How can you stand there with a clear conscience after that pathetic sentence? You do realise that evil bastard has a legacy of brutal crime as long as your arm?'

Buxton looked totally unmoved by the young detective's strident expression of injustice, as he steadily looked Cumber in the eye before replying in his fruity melodious tones, 'I can only work with the information my client presents to me. If he tells me he is innocent of the charges then it is my job to represent his case to the best of my ability. I wish you both a good day, gentlemen.' Cumber could not help muttering to the barrister's retreating back, 'He's far too clever by half that one.'

Loxley agreed. 'He certainly does not make our job any easier that's for sure.' Thinking that Cumber could do with another pint of Carling to calm him down, Loxley rose from the table and made his way over to the crowded bar. As he waited to be served, Loxley glanced back at the handsome features of his junior partner, which at that precise moment were marred somewhat by an indignant scowl. It was the fact that Cumber cared so much and felt so strongly about injustice that he both liked and valued him. Indeed it was that part of Cumber's character that so reminded him of himself when he had first started out in the force. That they had both begun their careers as 'Beat Constables' before eventually moving on to DS status also endeared him to Loxley, as he felt that they shared a solid bond born of common experience. He also saw Cumber as one of a diminishing breed at New Scotland Yard, someone who had grown up and played on the same streets as many of the criminals. As a consequence Cumber shared their hard edge and life experience which in turn gave him a valuable insight into their criminal mentality. On a more personal note, Loxley also appreciated the fact that Cumber shared his interest in the fortunes of Tottenham Hotspur Football Club and that pretty much put the seal on their relationship. A good five minutes elapsed before Loxley eventually returned to the table with the drinks. 'With this level of custom there's not much danger of this pub being closed down through lack of profit,' commented Loxley. Cumber hardly acknowledged Loxley's observation as his head was buried deep in the sports pages of *The Sun* newspaper. The focus of his concentration was an account of Spurs surprise home defeat against Wimbledon the previous Saturday.

Looking up as Loxley sat down with the drinks Cumber voiced his verdict, 'Not sure about this new manager Pleat, he's even talking about selling Graham Roberts.'

Loxley shook his head disbelievingly. 'I thought the big idea was to team him up with the new signing, Richard Gough.'

Cumber tossed the newspaper on the table before declaring, 'Time will tell if he's the right man for the job.' As Cumber gratefully took a gulp of his chilled pint of Carling, Loxley contented himself with a small glass of orange juice as he was already thinking of the drive back to New Scotland Yard.

Cumber suddenly raised his glass and announced, 'Happy Anniversary,' before gleefully burying his nose into his pint pot once more.

Loxley smiled before enquiring with a hint of sarcasm, 'Can I trust you will be in a fit condition to hold the fort tonight?'

Cumber was quick to reassure him. 'Don't you worry yourself, sir, I will be fine, you have a great evening.'

They both left the pub soon afterwards and made the short walk back to Loxley's car in Limeburner Lane. The red Audi 5000CS Turbo Quatro stood out impressively amongst the small group of tightly parked cars along the kerb. The car had been purchased earlier that year and was Loxley's one real indulgent luxury. Modified with a two-way police radio, Loxley appreciated its all-round comfort, speed and anti-locking brakes. The car moved smoothly away and turned right into the Strand, before Loxley switched on his intermittent window wipers and let out a contented purr as he remarked, 'When will the world acknowledge that this car is the most sophisticated four-door sedan on the planet?'

Realising that this observation was designed purely for his knowledgeable response, Cumber laughed. 'Probably for as long as it takes car makers like Jaguar, BMW and Mercedes to stop making proper sedans.'

Loxley adopted a pained expression. 'Ouch, that hurts.'

After Cumber had finished informing headquarters back at the Yard that they were returning, Loxley asked him if he had any progress to report regarding his investigations into a spate of recent house burglaries in the Bethnal Green area. Cumber had been put on the case for a couple of weeks now but had so far drawn a blank. It was especially annoying to him as he had been hand-picked for the case because of his local knowledge, having grown up in the neighbourhood whilst still living close by in Shoreditch. 'It's a strange one, sir. So far none of my usual informants in the area have come up with any gen whatsoever. All ten burglaries have taken place in the late afternoon with all the houses being empty at the time.'

'So we have a premeditated burglary by someone who knows the movements of the household,' ventured Loxley.

'No doubt about it, sir, that's what makes it unbelievable that he's not been seen hanging around snooping.'

'Maybe he has been spotted but could well be a familiar figure in the neighbourhood who lives local, someone who no one would suspect. I would suggest taking a look closer to home.'

'I will run a check on the local addresses, sir, see if any known burglar could be working their own patch.'

They continued west through Trafalgar Square before heading left down Whitehall and hitting the usual traffic around Parliament Square.

'What time are you planning on leaving for home, sir?' Cumber enquired.

Loxley glanced briefly at the digital car clock. 'I hope to get away around four o'clock, just got to square it with the 'Super' first.'

They turned right into Victoria Street and it was not long before they found themselves entering the high security underground car park in Broadway, directly underneath the New Scotland Yard headquarters.

After exiting the lift on the fifth floor, the two detectives took their separate routes through the two main corridors that led to their respective rooms. As Loxley entered his office, he could see the slight figure of Detective Sergeant Steve Harmer hunched over his paperwork through the glass partition that segregated their offices. Now nearing retirement age, Harmer had been a part of the furniture at New Scotland Yard for as long as Loxley could remember. Though not the most physically tenacious of detectives, he made up for it with his meticulous attention to detail and insatiable appetite for processing paperwork. Loxley tapped on the window loudly, causing DS Harmer to jump before he looked up and waved a slightly startled greeting. As Loxley grabbed a coffee from the machine, Harmer rose from his desk and shouted through the glass, 'Bill wants to see you.'

It came as no surprise to Loxley that his Chief Superintendent, Bill Kemp, had requested his presence in his office before he left for home; he knew that his chief would have been fully aware that it was his wedding anniversary that day. Taking his mug of coffee with him, Loxley strolled along the corridor to the Super's office. Knocking on the door, he heard the familiar gruff voice of his Super instructing him to come in. Loxley entered the room and was greeted by the portly figure of Bill Kemp, now in his early fifties. Though he was on the phone his face lit up in friendly acknowledgement at the sight of his favourite DCI, before motioning for Loxley to sit down whilst he finished his call. The two men went back a long way. When Loxley was first patrolling the London streets in the Sixties, Bill Kemp was heavily involved in curtailing the gang crime that so notoriously existed at that time. He had earned his much-esteemed reputation when helping to deal with criminals like the Kray twins, and the Richardsons, whilst also playing a key part in the investigation of the shocking Shepherds Bush shooting in which three policemen lost their lives in 1966. In the Seventies, when Loxley had been promoted to a DS, they had been teamed together, with one of their early cases being the murder at the home of Lord Lucan and his subsequent disappearance in 1974. Their relationship had been so close and productive back then, it was not long before they acquired the nicknames in the force as Regan and Carter from the popular television series of the time *The Sweeney*. As Loxley watched his old mentor across the desk, he was reminded once more of what rewarding days they had been and how much he had learned from the great man. Unlike many of their working-class colleagues from those early days when the lines between criminals and the police were much less defined, Kemp and Loxley had probably adapted better than most to the changing police culture. They were now leaving behind those days when it had been accepted practice for some officers to turn a blind eye to a criminal offence, in return for material or financial gain in a spirit of give and take. Though the police force was still far from squeaky clean, the emphasis was now increasingly on correct and ethical practice, with many of the more recent police recruits graduating from higher education.

After finishing his phone call Superintendent Kemp said, with a wide grin, 'Congratulations, Joe, I still remember the wedding as if it was yesterday.' Before Loxley could respond Kemp raised his hand, 'Of course you can go off early, you don't see enough of Janet as it is. Ann was only saying this morning that I must go easy on you today.'

Loxley felt slightly awkward as he answered, 'Thanks, Bill, I was just about to ask if it was all right.'

'Well there's your answer, Joe,' Kemp replied benevolently.

Not accustomed to asking for many favours at work, Loxley still felt faintly uncomfortable. 'Thank Ann for us, we shall all have to have a night out soon.'

When they had worked together in the Seventies the two men would socialise quite frequently with their respective wives, but after they were both elevated in rank the relationship had increasingly become much more about their work.

Bill Kemp smiled nostalgically. 'Yes that would be good, a bit like the old days.' There was a brief reminiscent silence between the two men before Kemp inquired, 'How did you get on in court today?'

Loxley grimaced. 'Young Buxton got in the way again; he's beginning to make a habit of it.'

Kemp sounded exasperated. 'Yes, I make that about the tenth time this year he has managed to dilute your charges.'

Loxley grudgingly went on, 'It pains me to say it but the smooth bastard is really quite brilliant. Unless he changes to prosecution or retires early and takes up gardening I am afraid to say we seem to be stuck with him.'

Kemp let out a deep sigh. 'Why is it that it always seems to be the clever ones who are on the wrong side at the Bailey? It never ceases to amaze me. Is young Jimmy Cumber covering for you tonight?'

'That's the plan.'

'Is he up to it?'

'He's a good lad, I could not wish for a more promising sidekick.'

Bill Kemp grinned. 'Surely not as good as us two?'

'Now that really would be something.'

Kemp cheerfully nodded his agreement. 'That vacancy for a DI is still waiting to be filled, do you think Cumber's the man?'

Loxley did not hesitate with his response. 'I do.'

Kemp opened his drawer and pulled out a file. 'That's good enough for me, I will set the wheels in motion.'

Loxley rose from his chair to leave. 'Thanks once again, Bill.'

'Oh I almost forgot, Ann wrote out a card.' Kemp rummaged in his drawer once more before retrieving a white envelope and handing it to Loxley. 'Have a good night.' The two men exchanged a warm handshake before Loxley retreated to the door.

*

DS Cumber had wasted no time in digging out his case notes on the Bethnal Green burglaries after returning to New Scotland Yard. He realised now that he had been too complacent in relying on his small network of local informants to crack the case. Working diligently he went through the facts once again. The burglaries had been committed over a small area measuring about a mile, consisting of older houses that nestled between Columbia Road, Old Bethnal Green Road and Gossett Street. All the burglaries had been committed late in the afternoon as dusk fell, with forced entries always being at the rear of the houses when they were empty. There had obviously been a significant amount of agility and climbing skill needed for most of the break-ins, whilst the narrow windows the burglar had managed to squeeze through on some of them suggested someone of slim build. The vast majority of the property stolen so far consisted of cigarettes, jewellery, cash and the odd videotape. Cumber thought to himself that though there was certainly no sign of big-time criminality here, he had been made well aware by his parents who lived nearby that the crimes were having an unnerving effect on the local neighbourhood. Acting on his chief's advice he began compiling a list of young men who lived in the area using a combination of police data on known burglars and the recent census. He went for the age range of fifteen to thirty to start with and ended with a list of fifty-eight. The burglar had so far been careful to leave no fingerprints and there had been no suspicious sightings. Clearly this was going to entail some good old-fashioned coppering, requiring much knocking on doors and checking alibis. The more he thought about it, the more likely Loxley's theory seemed. The suspect could easily live in the immediate vicinity and arouse no suspicion, whilst handily placed to keep an eye on his neighbour's movements. It looked like the answer even though he had to concede that it was unusual for a burglar to operate so near to his home patch. When compiling his list Cumber had been amused to see one of his best mates come up on the screen. Bobby Collins had been a close friend from childhood and still lived with his parents in their original house in Baxendale Street which nestled snugly in the area under scrutiny. Cumber still met up with him quite frequently for a pint and they occasionally went to see Spurs together when time would allow. Cumber grinned to himself at the thought of telling him he was on his suspect list. Cumber was certainly familiar with some of the other names listed, with quite a few of them being on record for known misdemeanours in the past. After filling in a form requesting uniformed police from the Bethnal Green police station to assist him at some stage in the house calls, he glanced at his watch. The digital timepiece told him it was 15:45, just in time to ring DCI Loxley for an update and to wish him a good evening.

Loxley was putting on his coat when the phone rang. He recognised the familiar voice of his junior partner. 'You just caught me going out the door', he replied.

'Sorry, sir, this won't take long.'

Loxley sat down on the edge of his desk. 'Go on.'

'Just to tell you that I have compiled a list of fifty-eight on the Bethnal Green burglary list, obviously means a bit of house-to-house over about six streets.'

'Have you requested some local uniform?'

'Done. By the way, do you remember the mate I brought with me when we met you at the Spurs training ground in Cheshunt last year?'

'I certainly do.' The Spurs training ground was a short drive from Loxley's house in Broxbourne. It was one of his rare treats when he had a spare hour to pay a visit to watch the players train. 'Wasn't he the one who asked Glenn Hoddle what would be the best football boots to invest in?'

Cumber laughed as he recalled the occasion. 'That's him, a bit embarrassing.'

'Just a bit.' Loxley's toes curled at the memory.

'Well, he is on the suspect list. That will be an interesting conversation when I see him in the pub this weekend.'

'Better take the cuffs with you. That will get him worried.'

Cumber chuckled. 'Have a good night, sir.'

'Cheers.' Loxley put the phone down and briskly left the office.

As Cumber ended the call he heard the sardonic tones of DS Brian Parrish over his shoulder. 'A little bit of crawling to the boss never does any harm does it, Cumber?'

Cumber smiled to himself ruefully. Brian Parrish never failed to score a point when the opportunity arose. Young and ambitious like himself, Parrish chose to climb the career ladder in a different, less pleasant, way. Cumber began to whistle the opening bars of John Lennon's *Jealous Guy,* as it was his standard response to Parrish's tiresomely envious barbs.

Parrish went over to a tall metal filing case and opened a drawer. Pulling out a folder he was unable to resist another dig. 'He won't respect you for it, all that arse licking.'

Cumber felt his hackles rising but he kept himself calm. 'Perhaps you should try being more civil for a change. You know, try a bit of common decency instead of going about rubbing everyone up the wrong way.'

'I would not be able to look at myself in the mirror if I carried on like you.' Parrish sneered.

With a conscious effort to control his temper Cumber rose casually from his chair and turned to face Parrish. Meeting his eye with a steady stare Cumber quietly stated, 'That's because we are so different, Brian. It may surprise you to hear this but many of us don't quite see the world as cynically as you do.' A slight smile bordering on a smirk played around Parrish's lips, but he made no further comment before retreating from the room.

*

Loxley was relieved to see that the A10 was conveniently free of its usual build-up of traffic. The persistent drizzly rain from earlier in the day had finally cleared and the

Audi moved smoothly under his guidance. Driving had always come easily to him. It was something he was good at. That ability had certainly served him well throughout his police career, particularly in the Seventies when his involvement in car chases seemed to be an almost regular occurrence. He slipped in a cassette tape that contained the latest Genesis album, *Invisible Touch*. The plaintive vocal chords of Phil Collins began to work a relaxing spell on him. He was enjoying the novelty of driving home in the early afternoon. His thoughts turned to the evening ahead. He had booked a meal for two in a newly opened bistro in Broxbourne. He had told the owner it was an anniversary celebration so he was hoping that they would get some special treatment. He thought it was always worth a try. Thinking of Janet he was surprised at a slight feeling of nervous anticipation. He almost felt like he did before one of their early dates when they had first met. The feeling reminded him that it had been a long time since the two of them had last dined out alone. On the rare occasions they went out nowadays it was usually in a crowd. With the long and unsocial hours that went with his job, they would too often find themselves just interacting briefly between their individual projects. Janet herself was always kept busy with her Jane Fonda aerobics classes and coffee mornings, in addition to her part-time job in the city as a secretary in a solicitor's office in Fenchurch Street. Loxley turned into the expansive drive in front of his spacious four-bedroom house. Situated in a much-sought after avenue in Broxbourne, he had to acknowledge that his successful career in the force had brought him a sufficient financial reward. But it had come at a huge cost in terms of lost time spent with both Janet and his daughter Clare. Though he cherished them both dearly, how could he ever explain to them that his love for chasing criminals was even stronger? Noting that Janet's Ford Escort Cabriolet was absent from the drive, he glanced at his car clock displaying 17:00. It had taken him one hour, not a bad run home considering the time of day. Once inside he noticed a note from Janet on the kitchen table. She had gone shopping at the new giant Tesco Superstore in Cheshunt. A convenient food outlet situated just beside the A10, it occurred to Loxley that these vast out-of-town retail centres were becoming an increasing feature in Thatcher's Britain. The bistro was booked for 7.30pm so there was no rush. After swallowing a long tall glass of tap water, he made his way upstairs to shower.

*

Janet parked her white Cabriolet next to the Audi before retrieving the shopping from the boot of the car. She was pleased to see that Joe had made it home and that there appeared to be no disruption to their plans. Too often through the years whenever a special arrangement or occasion had been organised, there had been far too many apologetic phone calls and rushed departures. Hopefully tonight would be different. After calling out to Joe as she unpacked her shopping bags in the kitchen, Janet could just about hear a muffled cry of acknowledgement coming from the upstairs bathroom. Somehow the novelty of knowing that it was to be just the two of them going out for a meal had put an extra spring in her step. It was just after she had finished packing away the shopping and making herself a quick coffee that Joe eventually appeared in the kitchen. He greeted her with a big bear-hug and kiss before saying, 'I hear you're going on a big date tonight, any chance I can come along?'

Janet laughed. 'Only if you are on your best behaviour. It did not go unnoticed by the way that you only chose to come downstairs after I had put the shopping away.' With that comment she playfully pushed him away while complaining that his damp hair was dripping down on her face. Picking up her coffee she walked through to the lounge before saying, 'I booked a cab for ten past seven so we can both have a drink.'

'Good thinking, that's what I love about you, so organised'. Joe followed her into the room.

'Someone has to be.' she replied, before pulling an envelope from behind the clock over the 'Adam' style fireplace and handing it to him. After opening the envelope Joe made a big show of reading out the loving sentiments in the card, before presenting his own envelope which he had earlier secluded behind the cushion. Janet looked genuinely pleased, as his track record for remembering special cards through the years had been patchy to say the least. Joe then went to his coat pocket and produced the Superintendent's envelope.

Handing it over to Janet he said, 'Bill and Ann send their best wishes. I think it was Ann bless her who helped me get the evening off.'

Janet opened the envelope. 'We must find the time to see them both. It's been so long.'

'That's just what I told Bill.'

Janet propped the cards above the fireplace alongside a few others received earlier in the day. After taking a leisurely wistful look at the collection, she returned her empty coffee cup to the kitchen before going upstairs to get showered and changed.

Loxley went to the fridge and took out a can of Castlemaine XXXX, before turning on the television. He wondered how DS Cumber was managing in his absence. There was a part of him that still felt he should be at New Scotland Yard. He consciously made the decision to stop thinking about his work and took a long deep swig of his Aussie Lager. He reminded himself that this evening should be all about him and Janet. The man on the early evening news bulletin was saying something about a US hostage who had been freed in Beirut the previous day. His eyes wandered to the small videotape collection stacked beside the television. Nestling amongst Janet's Jane Fonda aerobic tapes there were feature films like *Witness* starring Harrison Ford, *Pale Rider* with Clint Eastwood and *Back to the Future* with Michael J Fox. He had already seen them all so after taking another mouthful of his lager he closed his eyes and allowed himself to drift into an enjoyable doze.

*

In a house somewhere in Central London, Marcus Varney sat on his bed shaking uncontrollably. He grabbed a pen and notepad and started to write. He scrawled down the same two names repeatedly, as if finding this irrational process strangely soothing. He uttered the names to himself as he wrote: Buxton, Galton, Buxton, Galton. Finding no pages left to fill, he hurled the notepad violently against the wall. He then reached over to a tin box he had placed on the bedside table. Opening it up, he selected a large scalpel.

*

As Loxley and Janet entered the doorway of the Bistro, they were greeted by the owner who gave them a warm and exuberant welcome. He led them over to a quiet, secluded table, nicely laid out with a red tablecloth and fresh flowers. Asked to select their drinks from the menu, Joe ordered a Grolsch lager and Janet went for a large glass of Australian Shiraz. As Janet studied the menu, Joe looked around the restaurant. It seemed to be a good choice. The lighting was just right, not so dark that you could not read the menu, but sufficiently dim enough to be flattering to people who were in their early forties. Some of the other tables were already occupied by couples talking softly, whilst in the background a Lionel Ritchie tape added its own unique ambience.

Janet peeked over the menu and looked around approvingly. 'I had heard good reports about this place. What do you think?'

Looking equally satisfied with the surroundings, Loxley replied, 'Well, if the food matches the presentation we should be in for a good night.' They discussed the menu for a little longer, before Joe eventually ordered leek and potato soup, followed by a medium fillet-steak with frites. Janet, who was always more adventurous with her food, went for calf's liver in smoked bacon, with pan-fried prawns to start. As the evening progressed and the food, drink and conversation flowed, the two of them became enclosed in their own personal bubble, increasingly oblivious to the outside world. Joe gazed affectionately at his wife in the seductive light. He was reminded of how attractive she still was. For the first time in a long time he noticed how her lustrous fringe of dark hair fell casually to one side of her forehead, seeming to accentuate the blueness of her sparkling eyes. He watched fascinated as her full lips moved sensuously as she talked, set off by just the correct shade of crimson lipstick. As they refilled their glasses, Janet talked of Clare's somewhat erratic progress at university. Since she had been at Exeter Clare's focus had blown hot and cold, but there were now encouraging signs that she was beginning to knuckle down. Joe was quite content to listen as Janet talked more animatedly, her inhibition no doubt loosened by the wine. She talked of her work at the solicitors' in Fenchurch Street. It was where she had worked when he had first met her in the Sixties. She updated him on the office gossip as he knew quite a few of her work colleagues from both past and present. After Clare was born the company had allowed Janet to work part-time. It seemed like only yesterday. Janet then went on to mention how her monthly jaunts to see her ageing parents down in Bournemouth increasingly took up so much more of her time. It surprised Loxley to be reminded that it had been ten years since Billy and Jenny had left Hertford to move down to the South Coast. Unlike his own experience of being a war baby who had never known his father, Janet had enjoyed the type of childhood full of affection and security which he could only try to imagine. Because of his own emotionally deprived upbringing, he had very much come to see Billy and Jenny as the loving parents he himself had so starkly missed out on. It was after another glass of wine when Janet revealed to him philosophically how she now regretted not having more children. He had always suspected that this might be the case, but it was the first time he had ever heard her express it to him directly in conversation. She laughingly spoke of how she longed for the day when he retired and was able to take up something less risky like tiddlywinks. To Loxley's surprise she suddenly reached across the table and locked her fingers in his. In the background the music had changed to the George Michael song *A Different Corner*. Janet fell silent and they sat there like that for some time, just gazing contentedly at one another. They were brought back to sharp reality when their mini-cab arrived on time and they found themselves hurriedly paying the bill. Soon after returning to the house it was not long before they were locked together in a long meaningful kiss. When their lips finally parted Joe felt Janet take hold of his hand, before leading him somewhat unsteadily upstairs to the bedroom.

*

Intruding repeatedly into his hazy dreams, Loxley was rudely awakened by the persistent trill of his bedside phone. Gently removing Janet's arm that was draped across his chest, he turned on the lamp and reached across to answer it. The luminous green clock-face on his bedside cabinet told him it was just approaching two o'clock in the morning. He was greeted by the familiar voice of Superintendent Bill Kemp.

'So sorry to disturb you at this hour, Joe, but I have put off this call for as long as I could.' Loxley thought that his boss sounded unusually agitated.

'What is it?'

'Well, you know we were talking about the young barrister Buxton this afternoon and you wishing he would retire?'

'Yes.'

'Well, he kind of has. He has been found murdered in Temple Gardens.'

Still groggy from being abruptly woken up, Loxley initially had trouble processing the information that his boss had imparted. 'Christ, that's a shocker. How? '

'Sounds like a knifing, pretty messy. DS Cumber and DS Parrish are at the scene along with DC Norton. It was first reported soon after midnight.'

Loxley began to get the stirring of excitement that he always felt at the beginning of an intriguing case. He felt his heart beating faster which in turn made his heavy head throb. 'I will get down there straight away, Bill.'

'I thought you would be interested. Touch base when you have the full facts.'

Janet was stirring as Loxley put the phone down. She mumbled, 'I take it you have been called in.'

Loxley sat on the edge of the bed rubbing his eyes before asking, 'Has anyone ever told you that you would make a good detective?'

Janet sat up and answered sleepily, 'Am I to assume that I am correct in my deduction?'

He leaned over and kissed her cheek. 'When are you ever wrong?' Loxley went for a shower to clear his aching head. As the falling water worked its magic, the full impact of the news began to sink in. Why Buxton? A young man at the peak of his powers struck down so tragically. Could it have been a random attack? Of course a successful barrister will always make enemies. For every winner there has to be a loser. Returning from the bathroom he noticed that Janet had already gone downstairs as he dressed quickly. He put on several layers of clothing knowing that he would probably be standing around in the cold for some time. The Embankment in November would be both breezy and chilly. Janet came into the bedroom with two mugs of coffee. Loxley took one gratefully and sat down on the side of the bed before remarking, 'It was a good night. We shall have to go out for a meal for two more often.' Janet nodded her agreement, but her expression suggested more in the way of hope rather than expectation. She knew him and the demands of his job only too well. The hot coffee was firing Loxley up nicely. It was time to go. Just as he put on his zip-up bomber jacket, Janet came from the kitchen and handed him a travel mug filled with more coffee. 'Be careful, darling.' It was the first time in a long while that he could remember her addressing him in such affectionate terms. Loxley gave her a big reassuring hug before going out of the door. It dawned on him that through all the years, he had probably totally underestimated the daily anxieties that she had felt about his vocation. As he got in the car he smiled wryly as he found himself saying under his breath, 'You are indeed a lucky man, Joe, she really does care.'

CHAPTER TWO

A KILLER STRIKES

Loxley first set eyes on the crime scene as he drove by on the Embankment. The area was brightly lit as the space-suited Scene of Crime Officers were already well into their forensic inspection. He was thankful that it wasn't raining, as the SOCOs' painstaking job was made considerably more difficult in wet conditions. Parking his car in Temple Place, Loxley went to the boot and took out some protective clothing. Though he was late on the scene and the area was being examined, he still hoped to get close enough for his own inspection. Approaching the murder site clutching his travel mug of coffee, he saw DS Cumber, DS Parrish and crime scene co-ordinator DC Bob Norton huddled together in a group. Standing outside the crime scene which was ringed by blue and white police tape, the three of them seemed to be comparing notes and engaged in animated discussion. Inside the tape the SOCOs were examining the area with their technical equivalent of a fine tooth comb.

It was James Cumber who was first aware of Loxley's arrival. 'Who would have seen this coming when we spoke to him in the pub yesterday, sir?'

Loxley looked towards the spread-eagled body of the young barrister. He was lying on his back with his eyes wide open. Just beside his head a large stream of blood had oozed away into the grass verge that bordered the path. Loxley noticed that his briefcase lay on the ground close beside his right hand. He had obviously been holding on to it as he hit the ground, his grip gradually loosening as he breathed his last. Loxley enquired, 'I take it both the photographer and doctor have done their stuff?'

'Yes sir, the doctor is still here. He has just gone off to find a public loo.'

'He could be gone sometime then,' Loxley quipped. He himself had many uncomfortable memories of being taken short when hanging around crime scenes in the freezing cold. You could never seem to find a public convenience when you needed one. 'Who found the body?'

Brian Parrish looked at his notebook. 'A fellow barrister, a Jonathan Davis. His chambers were quite near Buxton's in Kings Bench Walk. Like Buxton he'd been returning home after working late in the office. He says he left his chambers at 11.55pm and discovered Buxton roughly a minute later. He recognised Buxton immediately and was understandably quite shocked. He says he didn't see anyone or anything remotely suspicious in the immediate vicinity, yet according to the doctor he could only have missed the assault by a minute or so.'

'Where is he now?'

'We let him return home. I said we would be in touch.' Parrish closed his notebook.

Loxley nodded. He was well aware that there was no love lost between Cumber and Parrish. The situation disappointed him, and sometimes caused a difficult dynamic within the team. In his experience he had always found Parrish intelligent and hardworking, if a little lacking in both warmth and humour. He made a mental note to address the issue of their relationship in the near future. Over Parrish's shoulder Loxley caught sight of the doctor returning to the scene. He was glad to see it was the familiar figure of Tom Conway. The two of them had worked together on countless cases for many years and Loxley greeted him genially. 'Feel more comfortable now, Tom, hope you did not have to walk too far?'

Dr Conway retorted, 'Far enough,' before rubbing his hands together and adding, 'I am getting too damn old for this game in the winter; I think I will have to emigrate to Australia.'

Loxley grinned. 'Can I come with you?' Looking towards the dead body Loxley went on, 'What can you tell me, Tom?'

Looking thoughtful, Dr Conway gave his first impressions. 'It's a very efficient killing, ear to ear cut with a very sharp blade, possibly a straight-edged razor or even a scalpel looking at the cleanness of the cut. The cause of death would have been massive loss of blood, due to the severing of both his jugular and carotid artery not to mention his windpipe. It would have been over very quickly.'

Loxley was a little surprised at both the 'modus operandi' and the competent nature of the kill. This clearly was no routine stabbing. 'Poor sod. Was he attacked from behind?'

'Judging from the blood spatter I would say yes. The wound slopes downwards ever so slightly from right to left making the killer left-handed, if I am right in my assumption.'

James Cumber had been listening intently before delivering his own input, 'It appears that he was then lowered backwards onto the ground and left to bleed to death.'

Loxley glanced towards the briefcase. 'I take it we can rule out robbery?'

Cumber was again quick to voice his opinion. 'Definitely, sir, this has all the hallmarks of a premeditated hit.'

Loxley nodded in silent agreement. 'Next of kin been informed I take it?'

'Yes, sir, DC Norton went to Richmond earlier on to inform his wife.'

Bob Norton had only recently returned and was in discussion with one of the SOCOs. Loxley called him over. 'How is Mrs Buxton?'

'Not good, sir, I said I would return later when she felt she was able to come and identify her husband at Bart's Hospital'.

'Is somebody with her?'

'Yes, sir, WPC Saunders.'

Loxley looked towards the eastward sky. He could detect the first chinking shafts of light beginning to pierce through the inky blue horizon. The SOCOs needed space to complete their inspection as the area would soon be teeming with Tuesday morning workers all curious to take a look. As he watched them meticulously searching the area in a grid pattern, he realised that there would now be no chance for him to take a closer look at the victim. There was nothing more he could achieve at the scene, and he had seen enough to be able to make his first report to the 'Super'. After informing DC Norton of his intentions, he and Dr Conway left the scene together. As they made their way back Dr Conway turned to Loxley. 'It's a nasty one, Joe, cold and clinical.'

'I can't disagree with you there, Tom, but thanks to your expertise we already have something to go on. We will get the left-handed bastard.'

The doctor added one last observation. 'Add lucky to that description; the attack could only have taken place a minute or so before the body was discovered by the other barrister.' Arriving at their cars, the two men said their goodbyes and Loxley was soon driving westward towards New Scotland Yard.

*

'It has the distinct look of a contract killing.' Superintendent Bill Kemp was giving his thoughts on the young barrister's murder. He took a big swallow from his coffee cup and went on, 'Very possibly his reward for upsetting one nasty person too many in his highly successful career.'

Seated across the desk from him, Loxley felt inclined to agree. 'Obviously we will look into his historic cases and see if anything stands out regarding a grudge killing or even a Northern Ireland connection. I will get Steve Harmer on the case; he loves a dig in the archives.'

Bill Kemp responded, 'Good idea, the old bloodhound does not miss much.'

Loxley had already made up his mind that he would visit Mrs Buxton in Richmond, after paying a call to the barrister's chambers in Kings Bench Walk. He liked to get a feel of the personal life of the victim in cases of this type. It was the method he had always used.

'Excellent,' Kemp said, after Loxley had told him of his intention. 'I will handle the press and the appeal for witnesses. Obviously we will keep the murderer's apparent left-handedness to ourselves at present. You know the score, Joe; unfortunately this is a front page case, meaning there will be pressure to get an early arrest.'

Loxley sounded almost excited at the prospect. 'I will do my best to give them what they want.'

Kemp leaned back in his chair. 'Luckily for me, Joe, you usually deliver.'

*

It was around nine o' clock in the morning when Cumber, Parrish and DC Norton returned to New Scotland Yard. Buxton's body had eventually been removed and taken to the morgue at Bart's Hospital, soon after the SOCOs had satisfied themselves that there was nothing more to examine regarding Buxton's corpse. A murder tent had been erected at the scene of the crime at Temple Gardens and was now being manned by constables appealing for witnesses and information. With a part of the walkway open to the public, thousands of morbidly-curious commuters could see the SOCOs going about their work. The murder had already been widely publicised on both radio and breakfast telly, with there being little doubt what front-page story would be dominating the midday edition of the Evening Standard. DCI Loxley, accompanied by the Superintendent, had held a meeting with the murder team, which at that stage gave priority to comparing notes and delegating tasks. One hour later both Loxley and Cumber were sitting in the Audi chewing hungrily on their bacon sandwiches and washing them down with tea in cardboard cups. They were parked in Tudor Street near the Inner Temple, enjoying their brunch before paying a visit to Rupert Buxton's chambers in Kings Bench Walk. Loxley was crystallising his strategy. 'I want to make sure that we don't miss the smallest detail or clue that could crack this case while it is still hot.'

Cumber was already convinced that the murder was a grudge killing. 'The clue is bound to be in his historic court cases; it just has to be.'

Loxley felt inclined to agree, but he had been in the force long enough to know that it was folly to convince yourself of a theory too early into the investigation. He thought it wise to urge caution. 'Word of advice, James, always keep your mind wide open until the facts prove otherwise.' They left the car and made the short walk to the chambers. Not surprisingly in view of what had happened, there was a subdued atmosphere within the Temple, with bewigged officers of the law speaking in hushed tones as they bustled through the echoing alleys on their way to the law courts. They entered the grand entrance of the chambers and introduced themselves to Reception, before being shown into an expensively furnished office of dark wood with well-stacked bookshelves. The room had a distinctive aroma that was not altogether unpleasant; a combination of polish and cigars is how Loxley would have described it. An elderly clerk entered the office and introduced himself as Gordon, before explaining that the Head of Chambers, a Mr Cecil Ferguson QC, had not attended the office for some months due to poor health and was recuperating at his home in Weybridge. He also informed them that there was also a junior partner, a Mr Simon Ashley, who was presently engaged at the Courts of Justice. Cumber duly scribbled down the names in his notebook. Loxley noticed that the clerk looked somewhat drained and nervous, as in a croaky, slightly tremulous voice he told them that he had worked in these particular chambers for almost 40 years. A young woman entered and served tea and biscuits on a silver tray, as Loxley and Cumber gladly accepted the invitation to take the weight off their feet and sit down on plush leather chairs. On the fine mahogany desk Loxley noticed a closed folder lying central to the empty chair. 'How long had you worked with Mr Buxton?'

The clerk almost seemed to wince at the mention of the murdered barrister. 'About four years. I cannot believe what has happened to him. I left him here last night.' Almost as an afterthought he added, 'He was quite brilliant, you know.'

Loxley thought back to the times in court that Buxton had frustrated and demoralised him. He needed no reminding of his brilliance. 'Was it in this office that you last saw him?'

The elderly clerk looked across to the desk. 'Yes, I can see him now as he was last night, sitting there.'

Loxley rose from his chair and walked over to the desk. 'I take it this desk has not been disturbed?'

'No, not to my knowledge.'

Loxley opened the folder and browsed its contents. It contained detailed information on a fraud case that was coming up in December. Loxley took some brief notes before turning his attention back to the clerk. 'What time did you leave him last night?'

'It was about half past eight. I know this because I had waited for him to come back from *The George* pub in the Strand. He would often meet his clients there.'

'Do you know who he met last night?'

The clerk thought for a while before answering. 'No, but he came back in good spirits. Not drunk you understand, just cheerful.'

Loxley looked at Cumber as they silently confirmed to each other that another line of enquiry was opening up. 'He must be well known to the staff at *The George* then?'

'Oh yes, very much so.'

They finished off their cups of tea quietly contemplative, before Loxley asked one final question. 'On your way out of the Temple last night did you see anyone or anything suspicious?'

'No, mind you I walked up Mitre Court towards Fleet Street, not towards the gardens.' He seemed to visibly shudder at the thought of the murder site.

Thanking him for his assistance the two detectives left the chambers to return to the car. As they walked out of the Inner Temple Cumber glanced back at the maze of alleys and historic chambers. 'It's a closed little world that exists inside those gates, isn't it.'

Loxley agreed. 'It sure is, but it can also be a hugely lucrative one.'

Cumber thought back to the conversation in Buxton's chambers. 'Hopefully we will find out something useful in *The George.*'

'Sounds like a good place for a pub lunch after we've seen Mrs Buxton in Richmond,' Loxley replied.

Cumber could not suppress a grin. 'You know, sir, this job can be a real bind at times.'

They were soon cruising over Battersea Bridge on their way to 21 Pembroke Villas. Cumber had been informed on the police radio that Mrs Buxton had felt sufficiently restored to be able to travel to Bart's Hospital that morning. She had duly identified her husband's body and had returned home soon after, still accompanied by WPC Saunders. It was also definitely confirmed that robbery had not been the motive, as both Buxton's wallet and the contents of his briefcase had been left intact. It was not long before Loxley and Cumber were parked outside a large three-storey Victorian villa facing on to Richmond Green. Cumber whistled softly. 'It looks more like a hotel.'

Loxley was not slow to remind him. 'Well, I did tell you the legal profession could be lucrative.'

They ascended the front steps that led to a bright red door. After Loxley had twice banged the shiny brass knocker, WPC Saunders eventually opened it and showed them into a spacious entrance hall. The stairs to both the upper and lower levels were directly opposite, but the WPC guided them to the left into the empty drawing room.

The WPC explained, 'Mrs Buxton went for a lie down immediately after returning from Bart's with instructions to wake her when you arrived, sir.'

Loxley looked concerned. 'Do you think she will be ready to talk to us?'

'She says she wants to get it over with, sir.'

'She will obviously need some continued support.'

'There is a sister who is on her way up from Cornwall who is going to stay with her, sir.'

Loxley nodded his approval before WPC Saunders left the room to wake Mrs Buxton. While they waited the two men took in their expansive surroundings. The wooden floor was highly polished, while the moulded ceiling cornices gave the room a slightly palatial feel. A gas fire set in a carved marble hearth gave the room some much needed warmth. Loxley glanced out of the sash window which overlooked Richmond Green at the front of the house. He reflected sadly to himself that the gifted young barrister had certainly been cut down in the prime years of his life. The door to the drawing room suddenly opened to reveal Mrs Buxton. Elegant and smartly dressed, she seemed to glide into the room before introducing herself.

Loxley apologised for disturbing her at such a traumatic time, before asking if she was ready to answer a few questions. Obviously holding herself together with great willpower, she agreed to assist in any way in helping to find her late husband's killer. As she sat herself down on the sofa, her red-rimmed eyes clearly reflected to Loxley the painful extent of her grief. He noticed that she was holding a small cardboard box. Loxley began by gently inquiring, 'I take it that it was not unusual for Mr Buxton to be working late at his chambers?'

Her eyes filled with tears as she answered, 'It was more often than not. Rupert loved his work with a passion.'

'When did you last hear from him?'

'He rang me at about 11:30pm to tell me he was just leaving the chambers.'

'Did he always travel home the same way?'

'It was his usual routine to get the District Line at Temple Station.'

Loxley could see that she was finding the whole situation increasingly distressing, but he had to press on. 'I want you to think very carefully, Mrs Buxton. Had your husband recently been aware of anyone or anything that may have suggested a threat to his wellbeing?'

She paused briefly before answering, 'I was talking about this with your lady constable earlier in the day.' Both Loxley and Cumber glanced over at WPC Saunders and she nodded back to them in confirmation. Mrs Buxton continued, 'In the past he would always have the odd threatening letter or occasional angry confrontation in the street after cases; he accepted that it came with the territory.' She faltered slightly before continuing, 'He would keep these letters just in case something should occur, but usually nothing ever did.' She suddenly opened the cardboard box and handed Loxley the envelope lying on top of the pile. 'That note was slipped through our letter box one evening last week.'

Loxley cuffed his hand in a handkerchief before pulling the note from the envelope. In big printed handwriting that was quite close to appearing childlike, it read:

YOU MAY THINK YOU ARE CLEVER BUT EVEN THE GREAT HOUDINI COULD NOT ESCAPE DEATH.

BE AFRAID.

The detectives scrutinised the note intently before Cumber studiously copied the wording into his notebook. Loxley then folded the paper and carefully placed it back into the envelope. 'What was your husband's reaction to reading it?' he asked.

Mrs Buxton appeared to be staring into space as she remembered. 'There was a difference this time. Normally he would file it away like the others and appear untroubled. But this time he mentioned that he had recently felt that he was being stalked, both at work and when travelling home.'

It was DS Cumber who asked the obvious question, 'Did he ever get a good look at the stalker?'

'Over the space of a few days he said he had become increasingly aware of a small stocky man in a black tracksuit top. He had seen him both in the Inner Temple and also on the train. He was also sure he had glimpsed him once as he exited Richmond Tube station.'

'Did he think of calling the police?' Loxley enquired.

Mrs Buxton looked resigned as she answered, 'It was never Rupert's way to be intimidated. He said he was going to confront the stalker at an opportune moment.'

Loxley gestured towards the cardboard box she was still holding. 'May I borrow the rest of the letters for possible evidence?'

She handed the box over. 'Of course. Rupert will have no further need for them now.' The finality of what she said seemed to suddenly overwhelm her with grief, as she lost all composure and sobbed uncontrollably. WPC Saunders moved swiftly across the room in order to comfort her.

The two detectives looked across at each other uncomfortably before Loxley said, 'We will leave you in peace now, Mrs Buxton, you have been most helpful. Sorry to have to disturb you at such a difficult time but I hope you realise that we have to ask these questions.' Mrs Buxton nodded her head in acknowledgement as she continued to sob.

As they retreated to the door, Cumber turned and said, 'Believe me, Mrs Buxton, we will do everything we can to bring your husband's killer to justice.' Just before they left the room Loxley beckoned to WPC Saunders.

Closing the door behind her, the WPC looked troubled as she joined them in the hallway. 'Mentally she is in a bad place, sir, obviously I will stay with her till her sister arrives.'

Loxley agreed, 'Of course.'

As they listened to the sounds of raw grief emanating from behind the closed door, WPC Saunders solemnly added, 'She told me this morning, sir that they had only recently found out that she was pregnant with their first child.'

Loxley could not stop himself from expressing a low sigh of sympathy. They left the house in sombre silence. As Loxley drove away, it occurred to him that even after all his years in the force, there could still be desolate situations that left him with feelings just too deep for words.

It was not until the Audi was cruising back down the Chelsea Embankment, that the silence between the two men was broken by the sound of the police radio. It was DS Parrish. 'Just to keep you informed, sir, I have spoken again with the barrister who found Buxton on the ground.'

Loxley answered, 'Anything to go on?'

'Unfortunately not, sir, he could not add anything to his original statement. He says he was not aware of seeing anyone suspicious.'

Loxley replied, 'Pity' before adding, 'There's a junior partner who worked in Buxton's chambers, a Mr...', Loxley paused whilst Cumber opened his notebook and showed him the appropriate page, 'Simon Ashley. See if you can get anything useful out of him.'

'Yes, sir.'

'Meanwhile we are off to *The George* in the Strand; seems Buxton met someone in there last night. We will meet up at the Yard later tonight for a progress review meeting.' As the radio fell silent, Loxley looked across to Cumber. 'What is it between you and Parrish?'

Cumber replied a little sharply. 'Not much I hope.'

Loxley went on, 'It must be something because there are times when I see you almost visibly tense at the sound of his voice.'

Cumber laughed defensively. 'Let's just say that we don't get on as we should.'

Loxley needed to know more. 'Any particular reason?'

Cumber gazed out of the car window and took some time to answer as they passed the Houses of Parliament. It was not in his nature to bad-mouth a colleague, but he realised that his issues with Parrish would have to be resolved sooner or later. He chose his words carefully, 'I think he sees me more as a rival than a colleague.'

Loxley had always suspected that it might be more a case of professional jealousy rather than personal animosity. As Loxley turned right into the Strand at Trafalgar Square he asked, 'Do you think his attitude towards you could be a problem for the team going forward?'

Cumber thought for a moment before answering, 'I really hope not.'

Loxley could see from his junior officer's expression that he was far from convinced. They drove on in silence before parking the Audi in Arundel Street, just a short walk from *The George*. It was late afternoon and the pub was already full of newspaper hacks, legal clerks and solicitors. Loxley struggled to make himself heard over the hubbub as he ordered two pints of John Smiths Bitter.

Cumber had meanwhile forced his way through the crowds surrounding the food area and ordered two Chicken Kiev and Chips. They managed to find a small table that had just been vacated, still untidily cluttered with empty pint glasses and greasy food plates. Carefully placing the two pints of John Smiths amongst the debris, Loxley remarked, 'So this is where Rupert Buxton liked to counsel his clients.'

'Seems a world away from his comfortable office in the Temple,' Cumber replied. A harassed-looking staff member approached the table and cleared the remains left by the previous customers. Savouring a long swill from his pint glass Cumber asked, 'So do you think that the author of the note is the murderer?'

'It's obviously possible; certainly Buxton was perturbed enough to want to confront the stalker.' Loxley thought back to the wording in the note, 'With his crack about Houdini, he certainly had a nice line in ironic menace.' A waitress suddenly emerged through the crowds carrying the Chicken Kiev. The two men temporarily suspended their speculation and tucked hungrily into their meals. All the time they were eating they overheard snatched snippets of conversation coming from the other customers. Some of it related to the horrific murder of the night before, but there was also some heated discussion regarding the on-going newspaper print strike in Docklands which had been making a big impact on Fleet Street. After swiftly finishing their food Loxley looked across to the bar area. He quickly identified the more relaxed looking landlord amongst the busy staff members.

Loxley turned back to Cumber. 'Figured out yet which one is the landlord?'

Cumber glanced across before replying sarcastically, 'Could it be the man with the florid complexion who seems to be watching everyone else doing the work?'

Loxley smiled. 'Bingo, we will make a detective out of you yet.' They rose from the table and approached the bar. Loxley beckoned over the red-faced man. 'Are you the landlord, sir?'

The genial features of the man creased into an expression of recognition. 'I certainly am, gents, and I think I know who you two are.'

Loxley displayed his name and badge number. 'Can we go somewhere quiet?'

'Of course, I wondered how long it would be before you turned up.' He showed them through to the backroom behind the bar. The room was small and dingy, but they managed to find a couple of bar stools that had been placed there for storage.

Loxley went straight to the point. 'I understand that Rupert Buxton was a regular customer of yours, Mr ...?'

'Ballard, Ted Ballard.' Cumber duly wrote down the name in his notebook. Ballard went on, 'Yes, he was a good customer but he never gave too much away; he was always a bit aloof.'

Loxley proceeded, 'I understand he was in here last night.'

'Yes, he was drinking with another man who I had not seen before.'

Cumber interjected, 'Can you describe him?'

'He was quite distinctive, tall, Crombie coat and a trilby, middle aged.'

While Cumber scribbled his notes Loxley asked, 'Did you notice what time they left?'

The landlord thought for a while before answering. 'Buxton left before the other man, sometime after eight. The man with the hat stayed on for another drink before leaving.'

Loxley enquired further, 'Have any of your staff who were working here last night come up with any observations that might prove useful?'

'I have spoken to them all about the murder as you would expect, but there was nothing added to what I have just told you.'

Cumber thought to ask another question. 'I appreciate that in a pub so close to the courts you must have all types of customers, Mr Ballard, but did anyone drinking in the pub last night strike you as a bit out of the ordinary?'

Ted Ballard thought long and hard before answering, 'As you say, officer, we do get all sorts of characters in here, but there was one young fellow on his own who was drinking heavily and looking a bit hostile. He wore a black tracksuit top.'

Loxley and Cumber tensed slightly and exchanged glances. 'Can you describe his build?' Cumber asked.

The answer from Ballard came back instant and positive. 'Short and thick set. Miserable sod he was, I served him a double scotch.'

'About what time was that?'

'Sometime just after 10 o'clock. I remember because it was just before I changed the barrel on the Carlsburg. He must have left before half-ten because the pub was beginning to empty by then and I am sure I would have noticed him.'

Loxley did his best to contain his optimism as he handed over his contact number. 'Thank you, Mr Ballard, you have been most helpful. Get in touch if you see, hear or think of anything more that could be useful.' The detectives felt a slight spring in their step as they left the pub and walked back along the Strand to the car. Passing the Evening Standard news-stand, they noticed the stark headline which read 'Barrister slaughtered in Temple'. They hurried on, feeling as if they were closing in fast on their prey.

CHAPTER THREE

A FAMILY AFFAIR

At seven-thirty that evening the offices of New Scotland Yard were a hive of activity. There had been a good initial response from the public in providing information. The downside was that after patient investigation, the majority of the data had led to very little that could be deemed as valuable. Still there was an excited buzz as staff moved about busily collating and filing the reports. Chief Superintendent Bill Kemp had arranged for a progress review gathering in the main meeting room for eight p.m. DC Bob Norton, in his role as crime scene co-ordinator, was busy setting up the information boards as Loxley, Cumber and Parrish entered the room. They were eventually joined by Bill Kemp, Dr Tom Conway and DS Steve Harmer. After equipping themselves with pads, pens and coffee, Bill Kemp started proceedings by asking Bob Norton if the SOCOs had come up with anything of value yet. Norton answered, 'Sorry to say, sir, not much to report so far except for a few common cotton fibres.'

'Any joy in identifying them?' Kemp asked.

'Not yet, sir. They are still analysing them, but up to now nothing distinctive.'

'So no fingerprints?' asked Loxley.

Norton shook his head. 'I think we can safely assume that the murderer wore gloves.'

Bill Kemp turned to Dr Tom Conway. 'So are we dealing with a particularly efficient killer here, Tom?'

'I think so. Both the method and the swiftness of the kill look to be highly competent.'

Loxley verbalised what everyone was thinking. 'So you think it was probably a professional hit.'

Dr Conway agreed. 'It looks that way. What I can say with some certainty is that the assailant was probably left-handed and the weapon was sharp and thin like a razor or a scalpel.'

Both Loxley and Kemp looked at DS Harmer.

'Historic cases, Steve, anything to report?' Kemp asked.

'Well there are plenty of possibilities for long term grudges,' Harmer replied. 'Both amongst victims and certain police officers,' he added with a smile towards Loxley.

There was some subdued laughter as Loxley assured everyone that both his wife and the restaurant manager in Broxbourne could validate his alibi.

Bill Kemp enquired, 'Nothing so far to suggest that the IRA were involved in this one, Steve?'

'Nothing that I can see, sir.'

Harmer went on. 'If we concentrate on the victims and the families who were on the wrong end of Buxton's defensive skills over the last year, then we are probably talking about twenty cases.'

James Cumber glanced at Loxley. 'I think we may be able to narrow it down.' There was an interested silence as Cumber got to his feet and approached the information boards. He started writing as he spoke. 'Buxton's wife told us that he was being stalked by a small stocky man in a dark tracksuit. A man matching that description was also seen in *The George* pub in the Strand at the same time as Buxton was drinking in there last night. We also have a threatening letter that was pushed through his letterbox at his home in Richmond. Forensic are now checking it for fingerprints.'

'What was the wording?' Bill Kemp asked.

Cumber consulted his notebook before reproducing the words on the information board for everyone to see.

'Anything that stands out about the note itself?' Kemp asked.

'It was written on an A4 sheet, writing somewhat childish, with the letters D and Y being particularly distinctive.'

DS Parrish suddenly exclaimed loudly, 'Hold on a minute, this rings a bell.' He started shuffling through some notes containing witness information. With a shout of triumph he said, 'Here it is. A newspaper hack called Arthur Thorn has phoned in to say that he saw a suspicious looking character walking briskly up Essex Street as he stood outside *The Edgar Wallace* pub around midnight. He says he was on the short side and wearing a tracksuit top with the hood up.'

Loxley said, 'Get in touch with Mr Thorn so we can question him. By the way, did you get anything useful from the other barrister, Simon Ashley?'

Parrish shook his head. 'Nothing of value, sir. What he did say was that though he admired Buxton, he had always found him a bit of a cold fish who kept a certain amount of distance between himself and his fellow workers in the chambers.'

Loxley suddenly remembered the notes he had taken down relating to the folder left on Buxton's desk at his chambers. Going over to the information board he copied from his notebook the name Charles Patterson, before adding the words: Charged with fraud relating to supposedly fine wines and fake gemstones. He turned to Cumber. 'I reckon this was potentially Buxton's last case, see if we have anything on Patterson.'

It was not long after some further speculative discussion that Superintendent Kemp suddenly broke up the meeting by loudly stating, 'This all sounds very encouraging, let's follow up on all these leads pronto.'

Loxley walked back to his office accompanied by Steve Harmer. Loxley handed him the cardboard box containing the rest of the threatening letters. 'Keep sniffing into the historic cases, Steve, I feel that is where we will get our man.'

Ever enthusiastic for this kind of project, Harmer replied, 'I am on it, sir,' before retreating to his office next door.

Loxley entered his room and sat down behind his desk. Not for the first time it occurred to him how lucky he was that at times like these he could call on dogged professionals like Steve Harmer. He made a quick phone call to Janet telling her not to expect him home much before midnight, before going over the case facts that they had acquired so far. Already it seemed that they were not far away from a possible arrest but something was bothering him. If, as Dr Conway had confirmed, they were dealing with a highly efficient killer, would that same man be foolish enough to parade himself so brazenly as the short stocky man had appeared to do. His thoughtful deliberations were interrupted by Cumber poking his head around the door. 'Is it convenient, sir?'

Loxley beckoned him in. 'What have you got?'

Cumber was holding the threatening note. 'Looks like we have drawn a blank regarding finger-prints. Only the Buxtons' dabs have been detected. I suppose it's not surprising the author was careful not to leave any.'

'Exactly what I was just thinking,' Loxley replied. 'We have a man who has been careful and forensically aware regarding both the note and the actual murder, but on the other hand if the hooded figure is our man he has been amazingly reckless in letting himself be seen in public places.'

After a thoughtful pause Cumber agreed, 'Yes there is certainly an inconsistency if it is the same man. But then we are talking about a vicious killer here, perhaps we are wrong to expect his behaviour to be rational.'

Loxley, deep in thought, answered slowly, 'Indeed.'

Cumber sat down on the seat opposite his boss before declaring brightly, 'On the plus side we do have an interesting development regarding the fraudster Charles Patterson. This is not the first time he has got himself on the wrong side of the law with his little misdemeanours.'

Loxley was all attention. 'Go on.'

Cumber handed his boss a bulky folder as he explained, 'He has built up quite a career as a conman. It is usually aimed at the high-end market of wine and jewellery.'

As Loxley flicked through the various case histories of Mr Patterson his attention was drawn to the section detailing his physical characteristics, dress code and police photo. 'I don't think there is much doubt that we have found Buxton's drinking companion in *The George.*' The image showed a distinguished-looking man in his forties. Sporting a carefully maintained moustache, he was described as 6ft 2in of lean build, smartly dressed with a penchant for wearing gold cufflinks and a trilby hat.

Cumber remarked, 'The landlord at *The George* couldn't have described him any better. This shows his last known address as Paultons Square, Chelsea. I'll get uniform to bring him in right now.'

*

DCI Loxley looked across his desk at the shabby, dishevelled figure of newspaper man Arthur Thorn. He could not only detect the distinct odour of Southern Comfort on his breath, but also a distasteful mix of tobacco and body odour on his damp, unwashed clothing. DS Parrish had taken longer than was expected in bringing Thorn to Scotland Yard, as he had not found him in his newspaper office. He had eventually fished him out of one of the many drinking establishments that were dotted around and about Fleet Street. Loxley was attempting to get an accurate account of his sighting of the suspicious man seen walking rapidly away from the murder scene. 'Now think carefully, Mr Thorn, tell me exactly what you saw.'

The newspaperman stroked his unshaven jaw carefully before answering, 'I had just stepped out of the *Edgar* around midnight. I stood outside for a minute or so as I wanted to clear my head.'

Loxley glanced across at Parrish before surmising, 'So I take it you were a touch the worse for wear?'

Mr Thorn looked defensive as he answered sharply, 'I had sunk a few I don't deny but I know what I saw, you can take my word on that.'

Loxley encouraged him, 'Go on.'

'I suddenly became aware of a stocky hooded figure walking rapidly up Essex Street from the direction of the Embankment. He was on the other side of the road and as he got closer he kept his head down with his hands thrust deeply into his pockets. When he was directly opposite, he stared at me from under his hood. Even though I was feeling a bit tipsy, his hostile expression chilled me to the bone.'

'He looked like he had something to hide?'

Thorn almost shuddered at the memory. 'No doubt about it, he looked like he had been up to no good.'

'What happened next?'

'Because I had felt so intimidated I waited to see which way he would go. He got to the end of Essex Street and turned left into Aldwych. I waited a few minutes before turning right into the Strand. I thought no more of it until I saw the headlines this lunchtime.'

Parrish had a question. 'Do you drink late every evening, Mr Thorn?'

The newspaperman suddenly looked almost childlike. 'I find it helps me cope with the pressures. The Murdoch dispute is not helping, so much uncertainty around Fleet Street.'

Loxley looked at the dismal figure before him and felt moved to suggest, 'Take it from me, Arthur, the answer to your problems is not in the bottom of a glass. That way is a very slippery slope.'

After thanking him for the information, Parrish escorted the slightly distraught figure of Mr Thorn from the building. When Parrish returned Loxley asked him, 'What do you think?'

'It sounds like he saw our man, sir, even though he has obviously got a drink problem.'

Loxley agreed, 'Yes, not one of Fleet Street's finest, though I think his account of events is sound.' The door suddenly opened and a clearly irritated James Cumber escorted a tall smartly dressed gentleman into the room. The contrast from the scruffy, unhygienic newspaperman who had just departed could not have been more marked. Loxley invited the man to sit down before addressing him, 'Mr Patterson, I take it you realise that you were one of the last people to see Rupert Buxton alive?'

Mr Patterson seemed more than put out as he answered, 'Of course I do, this whole episode is bloody inconvenient.

I am sure we could have conducted this interview over the phone rather than me having to be carted halfway across London at this time of night.'

Cumber was quick to respond with aggressive sarcasm. 'Yes what a nuisance it must be for you to help us with our enquiries after losing your brief at such a crucial time. Try telling that sob story to Buxtons's pregnant widow.'

Loxley motioned for Cumber to stay calm as he could see that there had obviously been some previous friction between the two men in the short walk to Loxley's office. Loxley enquired, 'I take it you would eventually have got around to telling us about your little meeting in *The George* just a few hours before Rupert Buxton was found murdered, Mr Patterson?'

'Of course I would have. I am sorry about the whole business but as you probably know I have a fraud charge hanging over me, consequently I instinctively had no great inclination to go running to the police at the drop of a hat. As it is with the loss of Mr Buxton I have lost my best chance of proving my innocence. Do you realise how difficult it is to get a decent defence barrister these days?'

Loxley was unimpressed. 'My heart bleeds for you. Now tell me about last night in *The George.*'

'We were obviously discussing my case and my chances of proving that I am a highly principled purveyor of fine wine and upmarket jewellery.'

Loxley suppressed a grin as he studied the smooth distinguished-looking character that sat opposite him. He certainly gave him full marks for presentation. From his immaculately manicured fingernails down to his highly polished leather brogues, he simply oozed a confident persona that could quite easily come across as plausible if more than a touch arrogant. The level of superior entitlement that conmen like Patterson displayed never ceased to amaze him. He often thought that they seemed every bit as deluded by their own duplicitous patter and falsehoods as the unfortunate victims that they preyed on. Loxley pressed on, 'Tell me about the meeting'

'My solicitor had arranged for me to meet Buxton in *The George* so that he could peruse my case-notes with a view to possibly representing me in court.'

'Did the meeting go well?' Loxley asked.

'It was first class. I was greatly encouraged by some of his observations about the case against me. So much so that we both agreed to work together in order to get my rightful justice.'

Loxley leaned forward and lowered his tone of voice, 'Now I want you to think carefully about last night and tell me of anything that may have a bearing on the murder of Mr Buxton.'

Patterson adopted a thoughtful pose before speaking, 'As I say the meeting went well. The pub was quite busy and Buxton had various brief conversations with other customers in the duration of the evening. He was obviously well known and there were a considerable number of other members of the legal profession present.' There was a brief pause before Patterson went on, 'There was one incident that struck me as a bit odd.'

Both Loxley and Cumber were in perfect unison when saying together, 'Go on.'

'At one stage in the middle of our conversation Buxton excused himself before approaching a slightly unsavoury-looking character at the end of the bar. From the distance from where I was looking the body language suggested a hint of hostility on both sides.'

'How long did the conversation last?' Cumber asked.

'Oh it could only have been a minute. Buxton came back quite unruffled as though nothing had happened and we resumed our meeting.'

'I take it Mr Buxton left the pub first?' Loxley asked.

'Yes, he left a little after eight. Because the meeting had gone so well I felt quite exhilarated and stayed a little longer to buy myself one for the road.'

It was left to Cumber to ask the obvious question, 'Can you describe the unsavoury-looking individual?'

Paterson did not hesitate in his response. 'Oh yes, short and unshaven wearing a dark tracksuit top.'

A satisfied Loxley wrapped up the interview. 'Thank you, Mr Patterson, you have been most helpful. We will get an officer to drive you home.'

Brian Parrish escorted Paterson from the room with Loxley and Cumber left to chew over the information. Cumber looked thoughtful. 'Once again our supposed professional killer would appear more than a touch incautious if not downright brazen.'

'If the man in the tracksuit top is the killer?'

Cumber opined, 'It certainly points to him.'

Loxley had to agree. 'Yes it does, though could he have had a more efficient accomplice?'

'Interesting theory, sir, it might explain it.' After some further discussion they agreed to go home for a few hours as it was close to midnight. It was just as they were about to leave that Parrish, Harmer and Norton, entered the room with a collective look of triumph.

Harmer was the first to speak. 'I think we are on to something, sir.'

'Let's have it, Steve,' Loxley responded.

Harmer did not need much encouraging. 'A Buxton case going back six months involving two big feuding families that live on the Stockwell Lodge Estate. The two families in question are the Tylers and the Raffertys, both well known in the area for some violent misdemeanours through the years. We have several family members on our records, with a few of them locked up as we speak.' Both Loxley and Cumber were well aware of the two families, having had dealings with them on numerous occasions. Harmer went on, 'I don't know if you can remember the occasion when there was a mighty ruck between them ending with Tommy Tyler being stabbed with a screwdriver on the staircase in a block of flats. It was a particularly nasty one with Tyler hospitalised for six weeks after almost croaking.'

Both Loxley and Cumber had some recollection of the incident as Harmer went on, 'Rupert Buxton was asked to defend Jimmy Rafferty who maintained it was self-defence all along. I think you can guess the rest.'

Cumber rose to the challenge. 'Don't tell me, Buxton gets him off the attempted murder charge much to the displeasure of the Tyler tribe.'

Harmer nodded in confirmation. 'After the reduced sentence was announced a near riot later ensued outside the court, with both families having to be forcibly separated.'

Loxley was still not convinced. 'But Buxton has left a trail of pissed off victims, so what makes this one stand out?'

Harmer could hardly restrain his excitement. 'I am glad you asked that question, sir. As I was going through Buxton's historic cases I put this one on my shortlist for investigation. I had already taken a photocopy of the 'Houdini' note, so as a quick exercise I compared the handwriting to all the signatures we have of the Tyler family members.' There was an expectant silence before Harmer continued, 'And this is what I found.' With a theatrical flourish Harmer produced the photocopy of the 'Houdini' note alongside a childish-looking signature which could be just made out to read Danny Tyler. The distinctive letters D and Y in the note were identical to those in the signature. It was pretty obvious to everyone present that the handwriting looked to be of the same hand.

Loxley scrutinised the handwriting more closely. There seemed to be very little doubt that Danny Tyler was the likely author of the note. 'From what I can remember of Danny Tyler he also matches the physical description.'

Obviously enjoying the moment, Harmer answered, '5ft 6in, sir.'

'Does the family still live at the same address in Stockwell?' Loxley asked.

This time Parrish replied, 'He was last known to be living with some of the brothers on the estate and no change as far as we know.'

Loxley was quick to respond. 'I think both you and Cumber should go pick him up straight away. Take an armed response team and a warrant for his arrest. I do not need to remind you that there is a sizable community of West Indian origin in that area, so remember to be sensitive.' Only a year had passed since the Broadwater Farm riot in the autumn of 1985, with Loxley thinking that the last thing they needed right now was a repeat of that tragic scenario. He turned to Bob Norton. 'If you can go and prepare the interview rooms, Bob, meanwhile I will keep the 'Super' updated on this latest development.' He glanced across to Harmer, 'Excellent work, Steve.' Harmer grinned in appreciation at the compliment, his features visibly glowing with satisfaction as he left the room.

*

Cumber popped another Wrigley's spearmint into his mouth as the police driver brought the squad car to a halt in Stockwell Park Road. He was also accompanied in the car by Brian Parrish, but the two of them had shared few words in the tense drive across to South London. Particles of condensation floated in the cool air around the streetlights, as Cumber glanced in the rear view mirror to see a large unmarked police vehicle pull up behind them containing five fully armed police officers. At the best of times the Stockwell Lodge Estate was a miserable environment but in the early hours of a cold, damp November morning, it looked a menacing, desolate place. Cumber could not help feeling dispirited as he looked out at a bleak terrain of peeling walls scrawled with graffiti and a road littered with empty coke cans and torn newspapers. Cumber looked towards the block of flats where the Tyler family were still registered as residents, before saying to no one in particular, 'Somehow I don't think we should expect a good reception.' Parrish still remained broodily silent as they alighted from the car. After being joined by the five armed officers at the entrance to the flats, Cumber felt obliged to make a short speech, 'Expect the unexpected, boys, and we should be all right,' before adding a word of caution: 'I am sure that I don't have to remind you that the firearms really are a last resort.' As speeches go it was hardly 'Churchillian', but it was all he could think to say at the time. They entered the flats and paused on the cold stone staircase in front of a lift door defaced by urban scribble. As was usual in these dimly lit sink estates, a strong smell of urine hung in the air, while what looked like the odd discarded syringe and used condom lay scattered about the stained floor. The Tyler residence was situated on the first floor, so Cumber led the way as they quietly ascended the stairs. Arriving at the door of the flat, he happened to notice that the door was in serious need of a lick of paint. He took a deep breath and rang the bell. The slightly dainty chimes that rang across the dismal, draughty balcony offered a stark contrast to the surroundings. A tense minute passed before the silence was broken by a voice from inside. 'Who is it?'

It was Parrish that responded first. 'It's the police; we want to speak with Danny.'

There was another silent spell before the voice answered again. 'Danny does not live here anymore.'

Cumber decided it was time to up the ante. 'Will you open the door nice and quietly as we do not want to have to break it open?'

The voice came back more agitated. 'What do you want him for?'

'If you let us come in we will tell you,' Parrish replied.

There was a further silent delay before the voice was heard again. 'Just hold on a minute, I'll get me trousers on.' As they waited on the gloomy balcony, it suddenly occurred to Parrish that though it was a first floor flat with a considerable drop, a back window escape could be a possibility. After mentioning this to Cumber, he hurriedly descended the stairs accompanied by one of the armed officers. A few further seconds went by before there was a rattling of locks and the door to the flat was opened by a tallish, frail looking young man wearing a white T-shirt and jeans. With the man confronting them obviously not matching the physical description of Danny Tyler, Cumber and the accompanying officers wasted no time in further small talk as they pushed their way past him to search the flat.

Down at the bottom of the flats Parrish cursed as he banged his shin against a metal railing, before continuing to make his way across the muddy grass at the rear of the building. Roughly making out the correct exit windows for the Tyler flat, he could see that a concrete block of sheds about eight feet below could make the drop possible.

It was then that the armed officer next to him let out a shout, 'Look, there's someone dropping down.'

Parrish could just about make out two figures. One had already dropped to the ground and the other was still standing on top of the shed. Both Parrish and his companion burst into a sprint to give chase. As they neared the shed, one of the men ran off into the maze of concrete passageways. Ordering the armed officer to give chase, Parrish turned his attention to the man who still remained on the roof. 'It would be sensible to hand yourself over quietly, fella, our officers are fully armed.' The figure on the roof seemed at first to have accepted his fate but then suddenly made a leap for freedom. Hitting the muddy grass with a thump, he let out a yell of pain before trying unsuccessfully to hobble away from Parrish. Parrish moved towards the injured man, 'Good effort, fella, but was it worth risking a broken ankle?'

Back at the flat, Cumber had quickly established that there was just one member of the Tyler tribe present. From his feeble appearance, Cumber immediately surmised that he must be the brother Tommy, the original victim of the Raffertys who had almost died. One of the armed officers informed him that all the windows that faced the rear of the flat appeared to be closed. To satisfy himself he systematically entered each of the back rooms in order to examine them. After confirming all three windows were closed he opened one of them to see if Parrish was within shouting distance and noticed a concrete structure some eight foot below. As his eyes grew more accustomed to the dark he could see two figures on the grass below - one of which he was sure was the tall, stout figure of Brian Parrish. It was at that moment he caught sight of a third person furtively sliding down the side of the shed. The figure then ran towards Parrish and knocked him to the ground. Cumber let out a cry of adrenaline-filled outrage, before rushing out of the flat followed by one of the armed officers.

At first a dazed Parrish was not quite sure what had happened. One minute he had been standing over the injured escapee, the next he had felt a stunning blow to the side of his face before hitting the ground heavily. As his scrambled senses began to come back he could feel a heavy weight holding him down. A loud voice was shouting. 'Go, Danny, while you have the chance.' With a mighty effort Parrish tried to push off his assailant, only for another blow to knock him momentarily senseless once more. Again in dazed anger he tried to fight back, but pinned as he was, he was at a distinct disadvantage.

As Cumber ran across the grass at the rear of the flats he could see that Parrish was on the receiving end of a severe beating. At that precise moment it did not matter to him that personal animosity existed between the two of them, he could only feel the almost tribal indignation that one of their own was getting beaten to a pulp. As he closed in, he could see Parrish's assailant raising his arm to administer another heavy blow. Thanks to the intervention of Cumber that blow never arrived at its intended destination. Launching himself in athletic fury, Cumber grappled ferociously with Parrish's attacker, before much-needed assistance arrived in the form of his armed colleague. A dazed and bruised Parrish managed to utter, 'Danny Tyler is the injured one trying to get away.' Cumber glanced up to see their number one suspect limping heavily; struggling to run away in a futile attempt to escape.

*

'So it looks like it could be a family affair then?' Chief Superintendent Bill Kemp was digesting the recent developments of the Buxton case as he sat across his desk from Loxley. When Cumber and Parrish had left to pick up Danny Tyler in Stockwell, Loxley had wasted little time in bringing his 'Super' up to speed, after first ringing home to tell Janet it looked like it was going to be yet another long night. Bill Kemp took a sip of his coffee before asking, 'Do you know much about the family background?'

Loxley likewise took a mouthful of coffee before answering, 'The dad was killed a few years back after being stabbed in a pub brawl, whilst I believe the mum passed away last year.'

'Yes now you come to mention it, I do have a faint recollection of the incident with the dad. Pretty nasty as I remember. How many brothers are there?'

'I think there are six of them in total,' Loxley paused thoughtfully before adding, 'all close in age and all of them pretty much involved in gang and drug crime since their early teens. Two of them are doing a stretch in Pentonville as we speak.'

With a wry smile Bill Kemp commented, 'Sounds more like the wild bunch,' and then asking more seriously, 'Do you think they would be capable of committing this crime?'

'As a group it's possible, but the evidence so far points only to Danny Tyler.' Their musings were suddenly interrupted by the high-toned trill of the telephone. It was Cumber reporting in from his car-phone.

*

Some ten minutes later Cumber replaced the mouthpiece on the car radio and sat back in the car seat after finishing his report to Joe Loxley. As they completed the drive back to New Scotland Yard his mind was still racing with the events of the evening. He had arrested both Danny Tyler and Parrish's attacker, who had eventually been identified as Danny's brother Jimmy. The other brother had managed to escape the clutches of the chasing officer by losing him in the numerous concrete mazes of the estate. Cumber was not unduly worried about that, he was more than happy with his catch. As they had left the estate with the two handcuffed brothers there had been some shouted abuse from a few awakened residents but much to his relief nothing too serious or disruptive. Parrish had been dropped off with one of the officers at the Lambeth Hospital for overnight observation. He had taken a bit of a battering and Cumber reminded himself that it could have been a lot worse had it not been for his personal intervention. When Parrish had finally got to his feet, he had not expected any gratitude and sure enough none had been forthcoming.

Cumber allowed himself a grin as he mumbled under his breath, 'Ungrateful bastard.' After a thorough search of the flat they had taken away some knives and illegal substances for forensic examination, but regrettably he had to inform a disappointed Joe Loxley that there seemed to be no sign of the thin-bladed murder weapon described by the Doc at the murder scene. Suddenly overcome with fatigue, Cumber sank further back in his seat and closed his eyes.

CHAPTER FOUR

A SWIFT RESULT

Joe Loxley sat in his office appreciating a few snatched moments of peace before he had to go down to the interview room to interrogate Danny Tyler. Since Cumber had returned with the Tyler brothers a couple of hours earlier, the investigation area at New Scotland Yard had been teeming with noise and activity. Cumber had given him the passage of events as they had unfolded in Stockwell, including the level of abuse that had been hurled at them from a few local residents when they had departed the estate. As was increasingly the case nowadays, Loxley found himself thinking back to that conversation with some regret. He had been in the force long enough to remember when the police had been regarded by the general public with much more respect and a lot less hostility. It now saddened him to think that those days seemed to be long gone. With hindsight he could now see that the tragic death of the New Zealander Blair Peach at an Anti-Nazi demonstration in Southall back in the Seventies had been a pivotal point in beginning to lose a huge slice of that public trust. This tragedy had occurred at a time when confrontations between the police and rioters at the summer Notting Hill Carnival had become an annual event. Now in 1986, it occurred to Loxley that whether you agreed with Thatcher's policies or not, the ideological politics of her government had not helped to improve things, with the more recent 1984 picket-line battles between the police and the miners still fresh in everyone's memory. Fortifying himself with another mouthful of coffee, Loxley consciously forced his negative thoughts back to the case in hand. Jimmy Tyler was secure in the cell charged with assault on DS Parrish. Cumber had also told him about the frail-looking young man they had left back at the flat, who it was later confirmed had been Tommy, the stab victim in the original brawl with the Raffertys and the possible motive for Buxton's murder.

Loxley rose from his desk. He had deliberately left Danny Tyler to stew in the interview room for no other reason than to get him a little more anxious and annoyed. He figured that in that agitated state, he would be more likely to say something incriminating. As he made his way past Cumber's office window on his way to the interview room, he motioned for his young sidekick to join him.

The interview room was small, bleak and dreary, lit by one high, barred window and a bare bulb sealed by a metal grille. Danny Tyler sat forlornly behind a metal table, secured to the floor by four rusty bolts. Both crime co-ordinator DC Norton and DS Harmer were sat opposite him as they shared a jug of water drunk out of paper cups.

Loxley was keen to get started. 'OK, Steve, you can leave him with us now.'

Harmer rose from his fold-up chair. 'Can I just have a quick word outside, sir?'

Norton got busy setting up the tape recorder as Loxley and Harmer stepped outside the room. Once in the corridor Loxley asked, 'What's up Steve?'

Harmer looked slightly excited as he answered. 'He has hardly said a word all the time he has been in there, but one significant thing I did notice was that he used his left-hand when he poured his water from the jug.' As an afterthought he added, 'He also looks very nervous.'

Loxley replied, 'What, not the usual chip on the shoulder and urban cockiness?'

'Not at all, in fact completely the opposite.'

'What about his injury?'

'Doc said it's a sprained ankle. It's been strapped-up and we have dosed him up on painkillers.'

Loxley instructed. 'Give us fifteen minutes with him and then bring in the Buxton letter and Tyler's signature.'

'Yes, sir.'

As Harmer scurried briskly up the corridor, he was passed by Ken Bailey, the duty solicitor who asked, 'Is Danny Tyler in there?'

Loxley confirmed his enquiry before saying, 'You're a bit behind today, Ken, thought you would have already had him fully briefed.'

Bailey put his eyes to the ceiling. 'It was supposed to be my day off. Can I have a quick word with him in private before we start?'

'Of course.'

As Bailey entered the room, Loxley stood back in the doorway and beckoned for both Cumber and Norton to join him outside. Once he was alone with the prisoner, Bailey briefly instructed Tyler that it would be best for all concerned if he answered the questions simply and truthfully without incriminating himself. Bailey then summoned the three detectives back into the room before retiring to a seat in the corner. Loxley and Cumber sat down at the table directly opposite Danny Tyler, while DC Norton took a less encroaching chair away from the table. Cumber turned on the tape recorder before Loxley stated the time, date and people present. He then gave Tyler his official 'Miranda' caution, with Tyler all the while looking down at his feet as he was informed about the disadvantages of not saying now something he might later rely on in court.

'Ok, Danny.' said Loxley, Why did you run away?'

Danny Tyler looked up from his feet and stared at Loxley anxiously. Loxley was undeterred. 'Why did you run away, Danny?'

'The same reason any of our family runs away from the police.'

'And what would that be?'

'You're happy to fit us up with anything you can't solve.'

'Have you got any particular crime in mind?'

Danny again looked down at his feet.

Loxley pressed on, 'I think you know the crime we are interested in, Danny.'

Danny looked up. 'I didn't do it.'

Cumber took over and went straight to the point. 'Are you talking about the murder of Rupert Buxton, Danny?'

Danny answered agitatedly, 'I dunno anything about it.'

'I think you do.' Cumber responded.

Danny looked down at the floor once more.

Cumber went on, 'We know that you did not appreciate the court verdict regarding the stabbing of your brother Tommy. I think you held Rupert Buxton responsible.'

Danny suddenly raised his voice, 'Why? Wouldn't you? The court case was a joke.'

'Is that why you stalked him, Danny, waiting for your chance to get even?'

'I dunno what you're talking about.'

'Oh I think you do, Danny. I think you and your brothers were after him for a little bit of retribution, only you went just a little bit too far and murdered him.'

Danny shouted loudly, 'You can't pin this one on me, I dunno anything about it.'

Ken Bailey gave Cumber a warning glance.

Loxley took up the reins. 'Where were you between the hours of eleven p.m. and midnight on Monday night?'

Danny rubbed his forehead before answering, 'At home.'

'And I suppose your brothers will confirm that?'

'Course they will, because it's true.'

'You can get a good pint in *The George* outside the law courts can't you, Danny?' said Cumber casually.

Danny sat back in his chair and crossed his arms, his mouth set in a hard line.

'You were seen, Danny, don't deny it, we have good witnesses.'

Danny Tyler remained silent. It was at this point that there was a knock on the door and Steve Harmer entered. Cumber narrated this occurrence on the tape before turning it off while Harmer handed some paperwork to Loxley.

As Harmer went to leave the room, he turned and said, 'Can I borrow James for a moment?'

Cumber quickly went outside and returned a minute later. With everyone seated once more, Cumber reactivated the tape recorder with Loxley giving a running commentary as he carefully placed the 'Houdini' note and Danny's signature on the desk in front of him.

Loxley politely instructed him to scrutinise the two items before saying, 'I think you would agree, Danny that you do not have to be a handwriting expert to see that these two samples could have been written by the same hand.'

There was a long silence before Ken Bailey offered his client some gentle advice. 'At this stage, Danny it would be best for you to tell the truth.'

Cumber added soberly, 'Murder is a serious business, Danny. If you are innocent of the Buxton killing, now is the time to be straight with us.'

Danny looked both agitated and frightened but remained silent. Bailey then made a request. 'Would it be possible for me to have some time alone with Danny?' Loxley agreed to this request and turned off the tape once more.

Once outside the room Loxley, Norton and Cumber made their way to the coffee machine. Cumber turned to Loxley. 'I think he is about to crack.'

Loxley looked thoughtful. 'He is certainly running out of wiggle room. What did Steve Harmer have to say to you when he called you outside?'

'It seems that Danny was shooting his mouth off about Buxton's murder yesterday in the local betting shop as if he knew something. Unfortunately for him, he was loud enough for some public-spirited person to phone in to inform us about it'.

Loxley scratched his chin reflectively. 'Does not mean to say he's the murderer, could be someone putting young Danny in the frame.' Turning to Norton he asked, 'What's your opinion, Bob?' Norton did not hesitate in his reply, 'If he didn't do it I think he certainly knows who did.'

There was a reflective silence as the three men drained their coffee cups before making their way back to the interview room. Much to their irritation, they were kept waiting outside for a further twenty minutes as they heard muttered conversation coming from within the room. Eventually they were all back seated opposite the surly countenance of Danny Tyler with the tape recorder whirring actively once more. Ken Bailey spoke first from his corner seat, 'My client realises the seriousness of the charges against him and as a consequence, he has decided to make a statement of all the facts as he knows them.' Danny swallowed deeply and grunted his consent before Bailey pulled his chair closer and read slowly from an A4 sheet that had been drawn-up between them.

'After the Rafferty court case we felt that we had been badly let down. As far as we were concerned Buxton was completely out of order. While Tommy was fighting for his life in hospital I could not help thinking of ways of getting back at that privileged bastard. It was at this time that Jimmy came up with the idea of a threatening note. It was Jimmy who wrote it and I thought it was clever, what with the Houdini bit. I decided to keep it in the drawer and then pretty much forgot all about it. When Tommy started to recover and came home we spent most of the time looking after him. It was when I began to realise that he was never going to be the man he was before the stabbing that my sense of injustice began to grow again. The final straw was when I heard that Jimmy Rafferty could be out on the streets again within the year. It was then that I felt an overwhelming urge to make Buxton's life as uncomfortable as possible. At first I just sort of followed him around watching his daily routine, I had no plan as such, just a strong feeling that I wanted to intimidate him. It was after I had followed him home on the tube a couple of times, that I suddenly remembered Jimmy's Houdini note and decided to use it to frighten him. I spoke to Jimmy about it and he was ok with the idea though he warned me to be careful not to leave any 'dabs' on the paper. The next day I copied Jimmy's note in big letters being careful to wear gloves. Soon after I went to Buxton's house one evening and posted it through his letterbox. I never knew for sure if he knew I was following him, not until he came up to me in *The George* on Monday evening and threatened to report me to the police. When I heard the next day that he had been murdered, I cannot pretend I was sorry, but I swear to you now I had nothing to do with his murder.'

Loxley, Norton and Cumber had listened intently to Danny's statement. Loxley thought that it certainly explained a lot of the circumstantial evidence against him such as it went. 'How did you feel after your confrontation with Buxton in *The George*?' he asked.

'Not great.'

'I take it you felt bad because your plan to put the frighteners on him had been a total failure?'

'Yeah, you can never win against people like him. So sure of themselves with all their clever talk.'

'What did you do next?'

'Blew the rest of my money on getting pissed.'

'What time did you leave the pub?'

'Not sure, it must have been after ten o clock. I know I was skint.'

'Where did you go?'

'I walked home.'

'Can anyone confirm that?'

'No. That's why I'm sitting here shitting myself, because after walking across Waterloo Bridge I can't remember anything more about the walk home.'

Cumber took over. 'You expect us to believe that. Do you know what I think, Danny? I think that it was always your intention to wait your chance to get Buxton in a dark alley and give him a good hiding, but after he confronted you in the pub you realised that little plan was a non-runner.'

Danny looked alarmed as his voice rose, 'Not true. I wouldn't say that I hadn't thought of it but you're wrong.'

Cumber persisted, 'I think you and maybe one of your brothers decided to go one further and finish him off. Isn't that right, Danny?'

Danny slammed his fist on the table and shouted, 'No.'

Ken Bailey interrupted while giving Cumber another meaningful stare. 'Calm down, Danny, you have a right to remain silent.'

Cumber went on, 'According to some of the fellow punters in your local betting shop yesterday, you seemed quite pleased about the events on Monday night, Danny, almost to the point of boasting about it.'

Danny now had his hands over his face. 'I was bigging myself up as if I knew something about it, everyone knew how we all felt about Rafferty's pathetic sentence. I was being stupid.'

Loxley had heard enough. 'Probably not for the first time. I will advise you to think very hard about your journey home on Monday night, Danny, because as it stands you look to be guilty either way, guilty of slaughtering Buxton or guilty of being unbelievably foolish.' He then concluded the interrogation by saying, 'This interview is suspended at nine fifty-five a.m. DCI Loxley, DC Norton and DS Cumber are leaving the room to accompany the suspect and his legal representative down to the cells.' Turning off the tape recorder they paused for Ken Bailey to hurriedly gather up his papers and briefcase, before vacating the room.

*

'Well we certainly seem to have enough to hold him,' said Chief Superintendent Bill Kemp as he studied the case notes in his office. He was accompanied by Loxley and Norton, both enjoying a KitKat with their cup of tea.

Kemp went on, 'If it is him, I cannot believe he was alone, the killing seems far too efficient.'

Norton said, 'We are calling in the eye-witness Arthur Thorn to see if we can get a positive ID on Danny being the man who passed him in the Temple area just before mid-night.'

Kemp looked at Loxley, 'Does it look right to you, Joe?'

Loxley looked far from convinced. 'I believe Danny Tyler is idiotic enough for his account to be true,' before adding, 'but at the same time we know from his past that he can be a nasty piece of work when the opportunity arises.' Deep in thought Loxley went on, 'More to the point, would he have been too drunk to carry out such an efficient killing, or was he just drunk enough to go over the top after their little altercation in the pub?'

Bill Kemp looked closely at the notes again. 'What about Parrish's attacker, the brother Jimmy?'

Bob Norton answered, 'He is definitely in the frame; after all, according to Danny he was the original author of the 'Houdini' note.'

'Well at present we have him where we want him; we will see what he has to say later,' said Loxley. 'On the minus side his physical description does not match short and stocky like Danny's, nor according to Steve Harmer is he a left-hander like his brother.'

'Who was the one that got away?' asked Kemp.

'We believe it's the brother Tony, should only be a matter of time before we pick him up,' answered Loxley.

The clock on the office wall read half-past eleven as Kemp shuffled the case notes into a neat pile before glancing at Norton and saying, 'We will handle the lunchtime press conference, Joe, while you get home to Janet and get yourself freshened up.'

Loxley looked grateful. 'Thanks, Bill, I'll be back later this afternoon.'

*

Three hours later Loxley was stretched out fast asleep on his sofa, peacefully oblivious to the puzzle of the Buxton murder. After arriving home in good time he had showered before sharing a Lasagne with Janet, washed down with a decent glass of Cabernet Merlot from Tesco. He would normally have had a beer but Janet had persuaded him to try the wine for a change. Too tired to put up much resistance, he had gone with her wishes and had actually quite enjoyed it. They had briefly touched on the murder case before Janet had moved the conversation on to other things, including giving him the good news that their daughter Clare would be coming home from university in time for Christmas. After the meal they had reclined contentedly on the sofa and watched daytime telly. At one stage they saw their friend Bill Kemp telling the world that two men were being held in connection with the murder of Rupert Buxton on the lunchtime news bulletin. It was soon afterwards that Loxley's eyes gave up the ghost and welcome slumber enveloped him. Janet had risen carefully so as not to wake him, before busying herself with some household chores. As she listened to the comforting sound of his heavy breathing reverberating around the lounge, it reminded Janet once again of just how much she appreciated these all too brief moments when they were both at home together.

*

The unshaven, grubby, facial features of Arthur Thorn looked hard and long at Danny Tyler through the one-way glass screen. 'It could be him, but I cannot be one hundred per cent; there is certainly a strong likeness.'

Cumber could not help sounding a little frustrated with the newspaperman. 'But you couldn't swear to it on oath?'

'To be perfectly honest, no,' Thorn replied with a pained expression.

Cumber cursed under his breath. He looked back through the screen at the disconsolate features of Danny Tyler, as he stood forlornly in the identity parade room accompanied by two officers. Turning back to the newspaperman he made a conscious effort to hide his disappointment. 'Ok, Mr Thorn, thanks for finding the time to attend, I will get an officer to show you out.'

Once Thorn had departed Cumber grabbed himself a coffee, before striding briskly along to the office of DS Harmer. As was usually the case, Steve Harmer was hunched over piles of paper in front of his computer data screen.

Cumber poked his head around the door. 'Is it convenient, Steve?'

Harmer answered without looking up. 'Only if you have something worth interrupting me for.'

Cumber looked apologetic. 'Sadly nothing. The newspaperman's identification was not conclusive.'

'That's a blow but I am sure we are on the right track.'

'It has to be the Tyler family, though I don't think Joe Loxley is convinced,' Cumber replied.

Harmer looked surprised. 'Really?'

'Well, for a start Danny Tyler was supposed to be out of his head on booze when he left *The George;* could he have been in any fit condition to execute such a killing?'

Harmer sounded more certain. 'Let's face it, the whole family are a bunch of head-cases, any one of them could have done it.'

'I can't disagree with you there.'

They were interrupted by DC Norton entering the room. 'Ah, James, glad you are still about, they have just brought in Tony Tyler and have parked him in the interview room. Coming?'

Cumber was up like a shot. 'You bet.'

Entering the room and seeing Tony Tyler standing beside a uniformed officer, Cumber was initially a little disappointed to see that he cut a much taller figure than his brother Danny. Cumber and Norton took a couple of chairs and sat down across the table. Cumber gestured for Tyler to sit down, which he did with a sulky slouch. 'So we finally caught up with you, Tony, I must admit I was quite impressed with the way you gave us the slip. You have my compliments on your intimate knowledge of the Stockwell Estate.' Cumber said disarmingly.

If Tony Tyler was pleased with the compliment he did not show it. His face was creased in a sour scowl. 'I hope this isn't going to take too long. I do have a sick brother to look after.'

'I take it you are aware that we are holding both Danny and Jimmy in connection with the Buxton killing?' Cumber asked.

There was a short silence before Tyler answered, 'Of course I am, it's what you lot do, pinning these crimes on people like us. It's why we do a runner when you lot turn up.'

'May I remind you that it is also people like you that stalk barristers and put threatening notes through their letterbox.'

'Look, I know that Danny was playing silly games with that smart-arse brief, but he wouldn't have slashed his throat in a million years.'

Norton had a question. 'Where were you on Monday night?'

'I had a drink locally and went home around midnight.'

'Where were you drinking?'

'*The Crown* in Coldharbour Lane. I have people who were with me and will back me up.'

'How convenient for you,' said Cumber. 'And I suppose you noticed what time your little brother Danny arrived home that evening?'

'As a matter of fact I didn't.'

'Was he home when you got back?'

Tony Tyler did not hesitate with his answer. 'Yes, but he was pretty pissed.'

Cumber leaned forward. 'Danny has told us he walked home because he was skint and he also said he left *The George* sometime after ten. Now if he was in the state that you suggest do you think he could have walked back to Stockwell in that time?'

Tyler shrugged his shoulders. 'The truth is he was so drunk he can't remember getting home that night. But he was definitely back at the flat when I got home.'

'We have a sighting that suggests he was still hanging around the Temple at midnight.'

Tyler replied sharply, 'Rubbish.'

For a full fifteen seconds Cumber looked hard into Tony Tyler's face, looking for signs of deception. Tyler returned his gaze with a steady stare. Cumber finally stood up and announced he had to make a phone call.

*

The phone in Loxley's lounge trilled into life, causing him to wake up and stir languidly on to his side.

Janet, answering the call, recognised the familiar voice of James Cumber. 'Hello, Janet sorry to be a pain, but is Joe there?'

She answered him amicably, 'Oh hi, James, I will just see if I can rouse him, he was unconscious on the sofa the last time I saw him.' She looked across to where a slowly awakening Joe Loxley was having some difficulty in returning to the land of the living. She walked over to him. 'Joe, it's James Cumber for you.' Loxley pulled himself upright and vigorously scratched the back of his head before taking the phone.

'Hello, James, what's up?'

'Just a quick update, sir, we pulled in Tony Tyler and questioned him. He was not happy about us taking him away from his sick brother. His line is much the same as the others. Basically that Danny was playing silly games but he would never have murdered Buxton. Still question marks regarding Danny's journey home though, Tony is insisting that Danny arrived home before midnight on Monday evening, for what it's worth. Also, it looks like we have drawn a blank with our man from Fleet Street, Mr Thorn. Though there was an obvious likeness, he still could not swear to Danny being the same man who he saw outside the *Edgar.*'

'That's a blow.' Loxley hesitated for a second, 'Ok, James, let Tony go home to look after his brother with the instruction for him not to stray too far, we have got the other two under lock and key for the moment. Which reminds me, what's the latest on Parrish?'

'The last I heard the hospital is letting him go home this evening.'

'He should be grateful to you from what I heard.'

Cumber gave a discernible chuckle. 'I don't expect too much from that quarter, sir.'

Loxley replied a little sharply, 'Well I do, James, and when the appropriate moment comes I will tell him so.'

A slightly embarrassed Cumber mumbled his thanks before Loxley went on, 'Get yourself home now, James, I think we have gone as far as we can today. Give yourself a leisurely morning tomorrow; remember you still have the house robberies in Bethnal Green to crack.'

Before Cumber could begin to utter a response Loxley had rung off. Suddenly feeling weary he returned to the interview room to inform Tony Tyler that for the moment he was free to go.

Tyler rose from the table and once more looked Cumber in the eye. 'Believe me you are wrong on this one, I know what it looks like but Danny and Jimmy are not your men.'

Cumber replied more assuredly than he was actually feeling, 'We will be the judge of that.'

When Tony Tyler had left the room with the uniformed officer, Norton let out a deep breath. 'It's got to be them.'

Cumber replied, 'I hear what you are saying, Bob, and I cannot disagree, but I am feeling increasingly uneasy that the pieces are not quite fitting.' The two men slowly gathered their case-notes before vacating the room. Some fifteen minutes later Cumber's shiny, red XR3I was pulling out of New Scotland Yard's underground car park and heading home to Shoreditch.

CHAPTER FIVE

TO CATCH A THIEF

James Cumber sleepily stretched his arm out of the bed, clumsily knocking his alarm clock onto the floor as he tried to silence its insistent bleeping. Turning over onto his back and managing to open both eyes, he allowed the clock to bleep a few more times before reaching down and switching it off. Not surprisingly after almost three days without sleep, he had slept deep and well. Standing up on his tiptoes he indulged himself with a good stretch, before going to the small kitchenette area to prepare himself some tea and toast. He remembered when the morning tea and toast had always been Tina's job. He realised that it was always when he thought of the little things that he missed her the most. It had been just over a year ago when she had first moved in excitedly to share his new one bedroom flat in Kingsland Road. But now in what seemed the blink of an eye it was all over and she was gone. There was no doubt that the split had hit him hard. As he poured his tea he pondered why it always seemed to be the case that the relationships he valued most seemed to be the most difficult to hold onto? He had never had any trouble when it came to attracting female attention, but it seemed to be a recurring pattern that the liaisons he took most seriously always ended miserably. Tina had undoubtedly resented the hours he spent at New Scotland Yard, but he had always made sure that he had put in the extra effort to compensate when they had been together. Perhaps that was the problem - he had been trying too hard. Now if only he could find someone like Janet Loxley; now there was a proper wife for a detective. How he envied Joe Loxley's settled home life. But then he reminded himself that in life it all seemed to be about swings and roundabouts. Though Loxley never said too much about it, he had gathered enough in conversation that as a child, Loxley had not experienced anything like the secure family life that he had been fortunate enough to enjoy.

The toaster popped up two slices as he turned on the television in the living room for some breakfast telly. The news was still full of the Buxton murder and the two arrested men. As he buttered the toast his thoughts began to turn again to the Tyler brothers. After a good night's sleep he was feeling more confident that they had to be involved. On the drive home the night before he had not felt so sure but he had been tired, allowing negative thoughts to cloud his judgement. Now in the cold light of day and weighing it up objectively, he felt more optimistic that they were on the right track. It was not too long before his thoughts returned to Tina. Sitting in the living room looking around him, he found that even the basic modern furniture units that surrounded him evoked bitter-sweet memories of her. Purchased from MFI as a flat-pack, he fondly remembered the laughs that he and Tina had enjoyed on the weekend they had put it all together. Letting out a heavy sigh, he finished his toast before allowing himself the luxury of a leisurely shower. An hour later he was lounging in front of the television dressed in just his boxer shorts, watching a news item revealing that the successful Aberdeen manager Alex Ferguson had been appointed at Manchester United. His thoughts on this sporting development were interrupted by the telephone. 'Good morning, James, trust you slept well.' It was Joe Loxley.

'Like a proverbial log, sir.'

'Good, sounds like you are going to need the energy. We have had another report of a burglary in Bethnal Green, Number Six Baxendale Street. The house was occupied by a widow who goes by the name of Turtle. It looks exactly the same pattern as the others, forced entry at the back of the house in the late afternoon with no fingerprints.'

Cumber felt his usual surge of adrenalin as he moved into detective mode. He wrote down the name and address and noticed that it was only a few doors away from his lifelong friend Bobby Collins. 'If it's OK with you, sir, I would like to get on with the house to house today. I have the suspect list with me.'

'That's what I was going to suggest. Seeing you are already in that neck of the woods, I will get Bethnal Green station to send over a couple of uniform to pick you up.'

'Cheers, sir.'

Loxley was just about to ring off when he added, 'By the way we have another possible sighting of the murderer in the Buxton case. A young city worker has phoned in saying that when he was trying to hail a taxi on the embankment just after eleven o' clock on Monday night, he noticed a figure with his hood up hanging about on the other side of the road. He says he was looking through the railings at the entrance of Temple Gardens; could be useful.'

'We could certainly do with a breakthrough; a bit of conclusive evidence would be a good start.'

Loxley agreed, 'Though the brothers are a nasty bunch, there are still too many grey areas for my liking. I'll talk with you later.'

Cumber replaced the phone before hurrying into his bedroom to get dressed.

*

An hour later Cumber was in the passenger seat of a Metropolitan Police-owned Rover SDI V8, accompanied by two uniformed officers. As they passed Shoreditch Church and drove southward up Shoreditch High Street before taking a left into Bethnal Green Road, Cumber brought the constables up to speed on their prospective duties. After taking a left into Barnet Grove, they found a suitable spot to park the car. They left the vehicle, and braving the chill wind, they walked towards a small network of streets characterised by rows of small old-fashioned terrace houses. Cumber took a moment to gaze at the unaltered streets where he used to play as a child;

countless nostalgic memories of his childhood came flooding back. Making a conscious effort to snap out of his misty reminiscence, he handed out a sheet of paper to each officer. 'If you two take Wellington Row, Durant Street, Quilter Street and Elwin Street, I will deal with Baxendale Street and Wimbolt Street. Remember we want to know where these people were between four and six yesterday afternoon and get every alibi verified. We will meet back at the car. Any questions?'

One of the officers responded, 'No that's clear enough, sir.'

The officers briefly glanced at the sheets once more, before turning on their heels and setting off to their allocated areas. Cumber looked down at his list. Yesterday's burglary was only a couple of doors away from Bobby's house. He pulled his coat collar up high around his neck and headed towards Baxendale Street. It seemed a good place to start.

*

'So you don't think you can identify him one hundred per cent?' asked Loxley. He was standing alongside DC Norton and a smartly-suited young man with fashionably gelled hair.

Taking another look through the two-way screen at Danny Tyler the young man looked uncertain. 'It could be the same bloke. It's just that the dude I saw wore his hood up. I did not get the full profile.'

Norton pressed him further, 'But in terms of his height, build and what you saw of his face it could be him?'

There was just a brief pause before the young man answered, 'Definitely.'

Loxley wrapped it up. 'Thank you, Mr Lyons, we may want to contact you again.'

While Norton showed the young man off the premises, Loxley strolled thoughtfully back to his office. After visiting the coffee machine he entered his room and sat down. What had initially promised to be an open and shut result was now proving more than a little difficult. All the brothers had been aware that Danny had been intimidating Buxton, and Jimmy had been quite open about the fact that he was the original author of the 'Houdini' note. Though Loxley knew that Jimmy Tyler needed little reason to batter a copper and run away, his excuse that he knew that Danny would figure highly on the suspect list for Buxton's murder because of the threatening note rang true. Added to that there was Danny's confrontation with Buxton in *The George* on the night of the murder, plus the two possible sightings of Danny near the murder site, his left-handedness and the fact that there was no one who could verify his walk home at the time he stated. Not surprisingly there had been no sign of anything like the murder weapon found at the Tyler flat, for if guilty, they would have had ample time to dispose of it.

Loxley's line of thought was interrupted by Bob Norton popping his head around the door. 'What did you think of our 'Yuppie' eyewitness?'

'Very smart young lad, an Essex boy made good and proud of it, but I'm pretty sure his partial identification would not be enough on its own.'

Norton pulled a face. 'You are still not convinced are you, sir?'

'We definitely need some concrete evidence. I'm hoping that Danny will have a sudden return of memory regarding his journey home, now he's had time to stew over his situation.' Loxley decided. 'Let's get him and the duty solicitor back in the room.'

*

A few hundred yards west of New Scotland Yard, Timothy Galton, Right Honourable member for the constituency of Uxbridge, was busily going through his papers in his office in Westminster. As was normally the case, it had been a hectic morning and he was now preparing to leave for a meeting at his local surgery. He had occasionally glanced up at the small television screen he had mounted on his wall as it gave regular news bulletins. The reporter was currently giving an update on the progress of the investigations into the murder of his old fellow graduate Rupert Buxton. They had been at Oxford together and had enjoyed both academic and sporting success in their time there. Though over the last ten years they had lost touch as they cultivated their very different careers, the brutal murder of his old friend had still come as a great shock. The latest bulletin was confirming that two men were being held in connection with the killing. Galton rose from his desk, gathered his papers and turned off the television. The air was crisp and cool as he left the Houses of Parliament and hailed a black cab in Parliament Square. As he was entering the taxi he became vaguely aware of a familiar figure in his peripheral vision. It had only been the merest glimpse in the crowds of people and he could not be sure. Feeling a little anxious, he turned around to look through the rear window as the taxi pulled away. Apart from the usual mix of tourists and people going about their business there was now no sign of the person he thought he had recognised. In that moment he very much hoped he had been mistaken.

*

James Cumber paused outside the door of No 6 Baxendale Street. It had been a long afternoon. From his own original list of nineteen, he had effectively eliminated ten of the names. Many of those names had been out at work at the time of the burglary, but after a few quick phone calls their alibis had been verified by their employers. A couple more with no previous criminality had been eliminated purely because of Cumber's instinctive nose for a villain, including his old mate Bobby Collins. That left nine who were still in the frame. Some had said they were home alone at the time of the previous afternoon's burglary, others had only their relations to confirm their whereabouts - not always convincing in Cumber's experience. He had now returned to the house in Baxendale Street where the crime had been committed the previous day. Though the burglary had been investigated by a uniformed officer the previous evening, he thought it would be a good opportunity to take a look at the scene of the crime himself.

As he looked at the door, he remembered that back in the Sixties the house had been occupied by an old fellow called Tom, who ran a grocery stall in Petticoat Lane. Mrs Turtle was obviously a more recent resident of No 6 Baxendale. He took hold of the large ornate, brass knocker that decorated the navy blue front door and gave it two loud thumps. After a wait of about thirty seconds, the door was cautiously opened by a small woman whom he judged to be in her mid-seventies. Looking through the narrow gap that the door chain allowed she asked loudly, 'What do you want?'

Showing his police ID card, Cumber replied, 'Afternoon, Mrs Turtle, I am sorry to disturb you, but would it be possible for me to ask a few more questions regarding your unfortunate break-in yesterday afternoon?'

'Have you caught the thieving bastard?'

'No, but I am sure it will only be a matter of time, Mrs Turtle.'

She hesitated for a few seconds before releasing the door chain and allowing Cumber to enter. As she led him through her narrow hall, Cumber detected a strong aroma of kippers and onions. After entering the lounge, he seated himself on the end of a hard couch heavily upholstered in green velvet.

Mrs Turtle lowered herself into an armchair draped in white lace. 'I'm not quite sure what else you want to know,' she said. 'I told the young policeman everything yesterday.'

'I just want to go over a few facts, Mrs Turtle. I understand that you were out yesterday afternoon.'

'Yes, I always go out on a Wednesday afternoon to see my sister in Columbia Road. We do a bit of shopping and I go back with her to have a cup of tea.'

'What time did you return?'

'About half-six, I am never later than that.'

'When did you realise that you had been burgled?'

'Almost right away. I went into the kitchen at the back and felt a cold draft. Then I saw some glass on the floor and the small window was smashed.'

'Can you remind me what was taken?'

'All the change that I put in my glass jars lined up in the kitchen and my late husband's loyalty watch.' Just managing to keep her emotions in check she went on, 'I remember that watch being my Bert's pride and joy, the day he was awarded it by the railway he could not keep the smile off his face. Genuinely gold plated it was and etched with his initials A T.'

Cumber felt sufficiently moved to say, 'We will do our best to recover it for you, Mrs Turtle. Can you remember how much money you had stored in the jars?'

'As I told your officer yesterday it is hard to say, definitely over twenty pound maybe thirty; it makes my blood boil to think of it, the brass cheek. Everyone's talking about it, I think this is the tenth break-in around these parts in the last month, people are afraid to go out and leave their houses empty.'

Cumber knew it was in fact more than ten, but he saw no point in either angering or worrying the lady further. He looked at her troubled face and felt a genuine wave of sympathy. 'I am really sorry that you have had to endure this experience, Mrs Turtle, I promise there will be no effort spared in catching whoever it is.'

Mrs Turtle stared intently at Cumber as if seeing him for the first time. 'You are a kind one. You must be about the same age as my son Keith. I don't see much of him nowadays, he lives somewhere up north.'

Disarmed by this information, Cumber thought it best to give an appropriate reflective pause before he asked, 'Can I have a look at the broken window now, Mrs Turtle?'

She rose from her chair surprisingly briskly. 'Of course you can, dearie.'

They went further down the narrow dimly lit passageway before emerging into the scullery at the back of the house. The smashed window had been temporarily blocked with some loosely attached cardboard. Cumber immediately noted that the window chosen for entry would have been one of the more difficult to squeeze through. He opened the door that led out to the back of the house. Standing in the small backyard that passed for a garden, he could see that the burglar had again exhibited extremely nimble climbing skills to reach the targeted entry point.

Mrs Turtle stood watching him as he crouched down to look at the floor, before asking, 'You'll have a cup of tea, won't you?'

Cumber wanted to decline, but after looking at her hopeful expression did not have the heart to refuse, 'That would be nice.'

Her features visibly cheered up as she turned and headed for the kitchen. Cumber soon found himself seated back in the front room sipping from a bone china cup commemorating the 1977 Jubilee celebrations. As they enjoyed a strong-leafed cup of tea, he briefly entertained the elderly lady with tales of his childhood growing up in the area. Eventually leaving Mrs Turtle, he decided on the spur of the moment to pay a quick visit to his old house in nearby Shipton Street. His parents would not be expecting him and he always liked to surprise them. After receiving his customary warm welcome and the usual maternal fuss from his mum, he forced down another cup of tea before he was allowed to leave the house and make the short walk back to Barnet Grove.

Finally reuniting with the two police officers sitting patiently in the car, he apologised for keeping them waiting before comparing notes on their list of suspects. They concluded that they had reduced the original total suspect list to twenty-five. Having viewed the mode of entry in Mrs Turtle's burglary, Cumber could see that there was now another justification for elimination - namely physical size. It was obvious that it would have been extremely difficult for someone of even average build to have wriggled his way through that poky, cramped window frame. The remaining suspects would need to be assessed on physical capability in addition to their alibis. Driving away from Barnet Grove en route for New Scotland Yard, Cumber touched base with DCI Loxley on the car radio phone.

*

Loxley had just returned to his office feeling a little frustrated after another unsatisfactory interview with Danny Tyler, when he heard the familiar voice of his junior partner. 'Hello, James, hope you've had a more encouraging day than me so far.'

'You don't sound too happy, sir.'

'Just had a second interview with Danny Tyler, tried all the old interrogation tricks like empathy and understanding but still no further forward.'

'He still doesn't remember anything more after leaving the pub on Monday night?'

'Not a flicker, if he is as innocent as he claims then he is not making it any easier for himself. How was your day?'

'Made some progress, now got the list down to twenty-five.'

'Sounds like you are getting there. How many of those names have previous misdemeanours?'

'I make it about a dozen, though having seen the mode of entry on yesterday's burglary I think I might have to adjust the parameters downwards in terms of age.'

'Do what you have to do but I would concentrate on the dirty dozen first.'

'Will do, sir.'

Loxley changed the subject. 'We are going to have a progress-review meeting tonight with the 'Super', see what the next steps are regarding the Buxton case. Almost as an afterthought Loxley added, 'You can have the night off, I will see you in the morning.'

Finding it hard to keep the disappointment from his voice Cumber replied, 'Do I have to, sir?'

'That's an order, now have a good evening.'

Cumber felt a sinking feeling as he heard the line cut off. He never liked being out of the loop; as he always wanted to be at the hub of the action. Even worse it gave him extra solitary time to brood on his break-up with Tina. He let out a deep breath and instructed the driver to divert to Kingsland Road, Shoreditch, before leaning back in his seat and trying to clear his mind.

*

Putting the phone down Loxley felt that a bit more rest would certainly not do Cumber any harm, but if he was honest he also had an ulterior motive for his charitable action. Parrish would be present at the progress meeting that evening after being given medical clearance to return to his duties. Loxley felt that it would be a good opportunity to inform him of Cumber's impending promotion, whilst at the same time gauging whether his reaction would be a positive one.

Bob Norton entered the office. 'Meeting is scheduled for six, sir, just going to prepare the room.'

Loxley responded, 'Thanks, Bob see you there.' As the door closed he turned his attention back to the Buxton murder-notes placed on the desk in front of him. Everything in front of him pointed to the Tylers being involved in the murder. He just wished he could rid himself of the feeling that it just didn't feel right.

One hour later the boardroom in Scotland Yard was once again occupied by all members of the murder team with the exception of Cumber. At the head of a table cluttered with coffee cups, note-pads and discarded biscuit wrappers, was Bill Kemp, accompanied by Loxley, Harmer, Parrish and Dr Tom Conway. Crime scene co-ordinator Bob Norton was once again standing up in front of an information board.

'OK,' said Kemp, looking at the faces turned towards him, 'Let's confirm what we've got to secure these arrests.'

Norton pointed to his board with a ruler before beginning to highlight the crucial points. 'MOTIVE, With the Buxton court case in which the Tylers felt hard done by there is no doubt about that. OPPORTUNITY, Danny Tyler has not only admitted that he held a grudge and had been stalking Buxton, but he also admits to posting the 'Houdini' threatening note through Buxton's letterbox. Which brings us to the whereabouts of Danny Tyler at the time of the murder? Significantly it cannot be proven where he was between eleven and twelve on Monday evening. What we do know, because he has admitted to the fact, is that he had an altercation with Buxton in *The George* after he was confronted by him on the night of the murder. The landlord of the pub estimates he left the premises sometime after ten, whilst confirming that he drank a significant amount of whiskey. Tyler says he had to walk home after drinking all his money away and apart from crossing Waterloo Bridge, cannot remember anything about the journey home. Conveniently, but perhaps not surprisingly, both Jimmy and Tony Tyler have said that Danny arrived home before midnight. We have two possible sightings of the murderer, just before and just after the murder. Both descriptions bear a very strong resemblance to Danny Tyler but are not conclusive. Finally the Doc thinks the killer was left-handed. Danny Tyler is left-handed.' Norton put down his ruler and joined the others around the table.

Bill Kemp remained quietly thoughtful while he scrutinised the detail before turning to Dr Conway, 'In your opinion, Tom, could a man full of whisky execute such a clinical kill?'

Dr Conway answered in measured tones, 'It's difficult to be certain but it's not impossible. It all depends on the alcohol tolerance of the individual and the expertise of the killer.'

Kemp turned to Loxley and asked more in hope than expectation, 'No sign of the murder weapon I suppose, Joe?'

'Not a sign as yet, but of course the family would have had plenty of time to dispose of it.'

Kemp went on, 'I certainly think there is enough here to hold them; what do you think, Joe?'

Loxley looked slightly pensive. 'I agree with you, there is certainly enough circumstantial evidence, but there also remains considerable room for doubt. The two eyewitness descriptions are very close but not conclusive, plus does Danny Tyler have the level of expertise suggested by the Doc? Of course after the altercation in the pub, Tyler could have had an expert, left-handed accomplice to do the deed. The fact is at this stage we just don't know.'

The analysis was left hanging in the air for a few moments before Bill Kemp made a decision. 'I suggest we carry on building the case and see if one of the family let their guard slip under the pressure.' He looked around the table. 'Agreed?' Norton, Harmer and Parrish agreed almost immediately. It was only Loxley that hesitated for the briefest of moments before giving his approval.

As they rose from the table Loxley looked across to Parrish. 'Can you stay behind for a minute, Brian?'

Parrish, still aching and moving rather stiffly sat back down. 'Yes, sir.' His rugged features still bore the signs of the heavy beating he had received from Tommy Tyler.

With only the two of them left in the room Loxley asked, 'Good to see you back, hope the bruises are less painful?'

'I'm getting better, sir.'

'I'm glad to hear it, for it looks like we are going to need a fully fit team building this case.'

'Yes, sir.'

'I have got DS Cumber presently working on the Bethnal Green burglaries so we are going to need every man fit and able. I heard that James saved you from a further battering.' Loxley studied Parrish's expression closely for his reaction.

'Did he? I think I was a little too out of it to notice at the time.'

Loxley mentally noted the somewhat grudging response, 'Which reminds me, Cumber is up for a promotion to DI; I think he is going to get it.'

Loxley detected a slight flicker of disappointment in Parrish's facial expression. 'Do you think he is ready for it, sir?'

Loxley went straight to the point, 'I do, but more importantly, do you?'

'It's never easy to tell.'

'Actually for me it's not that difficult. I think he will make an excellent DI. If for any reason you have a problem and are not happy with the situation I want you to tell me right now.'

Parrish shifted uncomfortably in his seat before shrugging his shoulders and asking, 'Why would I have a problem?'

'Because it's written all over your face, Brian, I don't have to be a detective to notice that. If you really feel you can't work with him as your superior then tell me now and I will arrange a transfer. I cannot afford to have any festering resentment in my team.'

There was a pensive silence before Parrish responded, 'I won't deny that I also wanted that promotion, but now it's done I will always work for the good of the team, that's all I can say, sir.'

'That's the reply I was waiting for, Brian, now let's get out there and get this Buxton case nailed.' The two men rose from the table as one and left the room.

*

Cumber felt restless. Though it was a rare luxury to have some spare time on his hands in the middle of the week, his mind was still preoccupied with both the Buxton murder case and the Bethnal Green burglaries. He had tried to relax by watching some television, but the guests on Terry Wogan's early evening chat show had failed to entertain him. Thinking that food might be the answer, he went to his fridge. The sparseness of the food provision again reminded him painfully of how different it had been when Tina had shared the flat. Then there had always seemed to be been an abundance of foodstuff to choose from, but now he gazed gloomily on some cheese, a half-carton of milk, a few eggs and a half-full tomato sauce bottle. Finally settling for a cheese sandwich and a can of Foster's lager, he first went to his tape deck and slipped in a cassette of U2'S album *Unforgettable Fire* before seating himself in front of the window overlooking the traffic in Kingsland Road. As he sat there chomping on his sandwich and listening to Bono belting out the lyrics of *In the Name of Love* he at last felt himself beginning to relax.

By the time he had drained the contents of his second can of Fosters he was feeling a lot more tranquil, but still could not quite rid himself of the feeling that he should be doing something. He suddenly thought of Bobby Collins and decided to give him a ring.

An hour later he was standing at the bar of the *Birdcage* pub in Columbia Road sharing a pint with his old mate. Considering it was a Thursday evening the Victorian pub was enjoying a lively patronage. As was frequently the case, Bobby Collins was being his usual cheerful, entertaining self. They swilled their pints enthusiastically, as Cumber told Collins about his encounter with Mrs Turtle from earlier in the day.

Bobby expressed his admiration for the old dear, 'Oh yeah, she's a good old sort, full of spirit.'

'Yes I did pick up on that.' said Cumber, thinking back to her steely determination not to be intimidated.

'Have you got any idea who the burglar is yet?'

'We have some names but nothing concrete.' Cumber guided his friend away from the crowded bar area before asking, 'Got any interesting conversations to report?'

'There are always rumours, but I wouldn't repeat any of them to you because that's all they are.'

'So you don't think any of them are worth a light?'

'No, but if I do hear anything that sounds a bit more solid you will be the first to know, my friend.'

'Glad to hear it.'

They both swallowed deeply from their glasses before making their way back to the bar. As they stood waiting to be served, Cumber managed to catch the eye of the pub landlord Harry Lawson. Loud of voice and ruddy of complexion, he was a typical cockney, but nevertheless was an avid fan of Manchester United football club.

'Two pints of Carling please, Harry.'

The landlord moved smoothly onto the pumps. 'Well, boys, what do you think about our new manager, Alex Ferguson?'

Bobby Collins could not resist a dig. 'Far too Scottish, he won't last a season.'

'Oh really, I seem to remember that Spurs wanted him for manager a couple of years ago when Burkinshaw left.'

Collins was unfazed. 'Now we know better. We are quite happy with 'Pleaty' thank-you very much.'

As the landlord handed over the pints he grinned and winked. 'You are welcome to 'Pleaty', time will be the judge if we have the better man.'

Collins had to have the last word. 'I do think it's about time you supported a London team like a proper cockney.'

The landlord smiled back mockingly before handing Cumber his change and moving up the bar to serve someone else.

Bobby Collins turned back to Cumber. 'Oh that reminds me put this in your diary. I have two tickets for the Coventry game on Saturday the 15th.'

'Count me in on that one.' said Cumber, pencilling the date carefully into his note book. As he looked up his attention was caught by the sight of a large well-built man with a mop of dark curly hair standing across the bar. He seemed to be holding court in front of a small crowd of men who appeared to be hanging on to his every word. It was someone with whom Cumber was very familiar. Terry Philpot was one nasty piece of work with a penchant for violence. He had been in and out of prison all his life for various crimes, with the usual common denominator being his appetite for cold-hearted brutality.

Suddenly becoming aware of Cumber's presence, Philpot looked across and grinned genially in recognition, before raising his glass and mouthing the word, 'Cheers.'

Noticing the exchange, Bobby Collins was quick to enquire, 'Looks like you two know each other. Is he a wrong-un?'

'Just a bit. It's unusual to see him in this territory, Hoxton is his usual manor.'

'I've seen him around the place quite a lot in recent weeks. He always seems to have a crowd around him, laughing at his jokes.'

'That's because they are all frightened of him. Believe me he's not funny.' replied Cumber.

They moved away from the bar, and with the rest of the evening being spent in pleasant alcoholic reminiscence, any further thoughts of Terry Philpot were put firmly to the back of Cumber's mind.

CHAPTER SIX

DISPATCH IN WESTMINSTER

'I will keep digging, sir, just in case we have missed something,' said DS Harmer. He handed back the cardboard box with the threatening letters and retreated from Loxley's office. Loxley placed the box in his in-tray and wearily rubbed his eyes. It was a Saturday afternoon and it had been over a week since they had arrested the Tyler brothers. Frustratingly they had made no further progress in finding the crucial evidence that could prove that they were the killers. The brothers had stuck firmly to their stories with no sign of either of them deviating from their original statements. In an attempt to gather some further crucial evidence, the case had featured on the popular television programme 'Crimewatch' with Superintendent Kemp playing a prominent role in his interview with the presenter Nick Ross. This had initially stimulated a number of promising phone calls, but as was so often the case, when this new source of information had been subjected to closer scrutiny it had proved disappointing.

Loxley leaned back in his chair and stretched his long legs. He felt that the building seemed quieter than usual for a Saturday, with far fewer phones ringing and less opening and closing of doors. It could be like that sometimes and he was grateful. The only highlight of his day so far was an invite to dinner that evening from the 'Super' and his wife. It was a get together that was long overdue and he had wasted no time in ringing Janet with the news. She had been very pleased with the invitation and they were both looking forward to it. His mind wandered for a second as he thought of James Cumber enjoying a day off at White Hart Lane. He looked at his watch and worked out that there were about fifteen minutes left to play. Hopefully Spurs already had the game won. Forcing himself to get back to the investigation, he chewed on the end of his pen as he replayed the tapes of the recent interviews. Each time he listened to them the more convinced he became that the brothers' stories could be genuine. With them both sitting alone in their cells not a million miles away, it was not a feeling that made him feel very comfortable.

He took a sip of his Diet Coke and put on his reading glasses, then reread the witness statements one more time. The time drifted by and he was about halfway through when he was interrupted by the phone, and the excited voice of Cumber. 'Do you know the score, sir?'

Loxley guessed from the boisterous background noise that Cumber was calling from a pub phone somewhere within the local environs of White Hart Lane. 'Please tell me they won, I could do with some good news,'

'Just about, they scraped it 1-0. What would we do without Clive Allen?'

Loxley felt his spirits lift momentarily. 'Don't tell me he has hit the onion bag again. He can do no wrong this season. Well that's another three points, onward and upward.'

Curbing his own excitement and lowering his voice Cumber changed the subject. 'I take it we are no further forward on the Buxton case?'

Loxley put his doubts to one side and did his best to sound upbeat. 'Nothing yet, but we will keep pushing. Something has to give.' Loxley suddenly remembered some more unwelcome news that had come to his attention that morning. 'Sorry to put a downer on the Spurs victory, James, but there was another burglary in Bethnal Green yesterday afternoon.'

Cumber could not help letting out an expletive. 'Shit'. He had spent the whole of the last week going through the alibis of his suspect list and was still no nearer to getting a result.

'How many people still left on your list?' Loxley asked.

'We had got it down to three and they all knew they were being watched. I can't believe that it is any of them.'

'Whoever the cheeky blighter is, you have to admire their nerve.'

Cumber was unimpressed. 'Excuse me if I don't share your opinion, sir, the way I am feeling at the moment the word admire does not begin to cover it.'

'You are excused, which reminds me I am about to head home.'

'Have a good night, sir.'

'I intend to. It's not every day that the 'Super' offers to take us out to dinner.'

Before Cumber could think of a suitably humorous reply, Loxley had ended the call.

*

Bill Kemp lounged back contentedly on his leather-backed sofa whilst swirling a glass of Napoleon Aigle Rouge Cognac in his hand. He was feeling satisfyingly mellow as he watched the tall figure of his old colleague Joe Loxley crouched over the snooker table. He had just played a superb safety shot and he was enjoying himself as he observed Loxley struggling to get an angle on his cue. They were in his spacious five-bedroomed detached house in Brook Rise, Chigwell, having returned from the *'Olde Kings Head'* in the High Street. The food in the upstairs restaurant had been up to its usual standard and Kemp felt comfortably sated. With his two children having long flown the nest, he had converted one of the bedrooms into a games room complete with drinks bar and full-sized snooker table. It was a game that he and Joe had played on countless occasions back in the Seventies when they had worked together so closely. The evening in the pub had been a great success and soon after getting home they had left Janet and Ann talking in the lounge in order to resume their old rivalry on the green baize. Now in the games room there was an audible sigh of frustration from Loxley as his attempted safety shot left an opening. Bill Kemp rose eagerly from his chair to approach the table. Their game had come down to four balls and he needed the lot. 'You have left me a tricky one there, Joe.'

'Not tricky enough,' replied Loxley ruefully.

Kemp crouched over the table, his face a picture of concentration. His arm came back smoothly before efficiently potting the brown at the end of the table. He had left himself a difficult blue but he was on a roll as he proceeded to clinically sink it. Loxley could only look on in admiration as his chief then followed up by nailing a tricky pink, leaving a straightforward looking solitary black. As Kemp confidently chalked the top of his cue in preparation to deliver the winning shot he turned to Loxley. 'By the way, young Cumber's promotion has come through.'

Loxley was pleased to hear it. Not only was it good news for Cumber, but also at that moment it came as a welcome diversion from the game. 'Excellent news, he will be well chuffed.'

As Kemp leaned over the table he said, 'I will tell him officially on Monday.'

Whether it was the brief conversation on police matters that had broken his concentration or his own complacency, Kemp unaccountably twitched as he played his expected winning shot, leaving the crucial black a tantalising inch from the pocket. He stared disbelievingly at the table before exclaiming with some feeling, 'Bugger.'

Loxley struggled to keep the grin from his face as he moved towards the table and then slowly and deliberately potted the black.

Kemp threw his cue stick down in exasperation. 'Now there was a time when you were eager for promotion that you would have deliberately missed that shot just to let me win.'

Loxley allowed himself a grin. 'Times change, I guess.'

Kemp sat back down on his sofa. Picking up his cognac and sighing heavily he agreed, 'They certainly do, Joe, they most certainly do.'

Loxley picked up his drink and sat down next to him. There was a comfortable silence before Kemp spoke once more.

'I have enjoyed tonight, Joe, just like the old days.'

Loxley smiled his agreement.

Kemp went on, 'Mind you, the dinner was not the only reason I invited you here tonight.'

Loxley was curious. 'Wasn't it?'

'Keep it under your hat but I am thinking of taking the pension next year.'

Loxley was more than surprised. 'Retiring?'

'I am about ready for it, Joe, you have to know when to leave the stage.'

Loxley's immediate emotion was one of sadness, they had been through so much. 'I would not try to dissuade you, Bill, you know your feelings more than anyone.'

'It's been a good career but let's be honest, Joe, it's a losing battle. Crime never goes away; in fact the streets today are less safe than when I started thirty years ago. It's disappointing.'

Loxley replied thoughtfully, 'In a free society you can't stop crimes like violence, prostitution, robbery and drugs. They are always going to be there. We can only do our level best to clear up the mess that's left behind. To your immense credit, Bill, you have always done that.'

Kemp looked grateful for the compliment and did his best to sound more optimistic. 'You're right, Joe, it's the little victories that make it worthwhile. Hopefully we will get one this week with the Tyler brothers.'

Loxley answered more revealingly than he would have liked, 'Hopefully.'

'Come on, Joe, out with it. I have known you far too long to not know when something is troubling you.'

Loxley took another sip of his drink before replying, 'When we first got the link with the brothers I was pretty much certain, but the longer the case has gone on the more doubts I have that it was them.'

Kemp sat bolt upright on the sofa. 'Why?'

Loxley replied immediately, 'The method of the killing and the Tylers do not match up, it doesn't feel right.'

Kemp sounded perturbed, 'I can't say I like what you are saying, Joe. I really hope your renowned intuitive skills are wrong on this one.'

Loxley emptied his glass of Cognac with one last swig. 'So do I,' he replied.

Any chance of further discussion on the case was suddenly interrupted when Janet popped her head around the door. 'There's a pot of coffee on the go if you two are interested.'

Bill Kemp, grateful for the intervention, promptly rose from the sofa. 'Good idea, we are just about done here.' They walked through to a large, well-furnished lounge. Ann Kemp looked up cheerfully as they entered, her face made ruddy by the comforting heat of the room. As she carefully poured the coffee, the soulful voice of Paul Young emanated softly from the music centre in the background. Loxley settled himself next to Janet on the sofa.

Ann was obviously pleased with how the evening had gone. 'It's been so nice to see you this evening, really good to catch up with you both. Just like old times.'

After glancing pointedly at Loxley, Janet added, 'Yes, it's good to get these two away from Scotland Yard occasionally.'

Kemp replied, 'As I have always told Ann, she will soon get fed up with me when I am under her feet all day.'

'Oh, I am sure I would find you plenty of things to do,' Ann responded forcefully.

Kemp pulled an expression of mock horror. 'Help.'

The rest of the evening passed in pleasant and relaxed conversation lasting into the early hours, with both men being careful to obey their wives' instructions by not indulging in any more talk about the Buxton murder.

*

Cumber emptied the last remnants of his crisp packet into his mouth. It was Sunday night and he was lounging on his sofa distractedly watching the first episode of a television series called *The Singing Detective*. It had been a lazy weekend but he had spent most of the day thinking about the Bethnal Green burglaries. When Loxley had told him there had been another break-in, he had felt instantly deflated. With it being highly unlikely that any of the three names left on his list could have been the perpetrator, he felt he was very much back to square one. As was always the case when he was away from New Scotland Yard, he felt restless and eager to get back to the centre of things. The latest burglary had taken place in Quilter Street, still well within the area covered in their house to house searches. The intruder had again demonstrated a considerable amount of agility, combined with the ability to squeeze through the tightest of spaces. Cumber had originally set the age parameter at fifteen to thirty on his original list, which had seemed reasonable at the time. But if the theory still held that the burglar was living locally, it was becoming blindingly obvious that he would have to rethink those age restrictions.

Deep in thought, he was halfway through his can of Carling, when the phone rang. It was Bobby Collins.

'Evening, Jimmy. What are you up to?'

'Not a lot. Watching something on the telly about a detective, I can't make it out to be honest.'

'Fancy a beer?'

Cumber glanced at the beer can he was holding. 'I've have already got one thanks.'

'I mean in the pub.'

Cumber hesitated for a brief moment. 'Tempting, but I have to get up sharp tomorrow. I suppose you have heard that there was another burglary, in Quilter Street?'

'Nearly everyone in the area was talking about it this morning; the locals are getting agitated. It was quite a lot of cash by all accounts, stashed away in food boxes under the stairs. It breaks your heart. I know old Tompkins pretty well, he drinks regularly in the *Beehive*.'

Cumber felt concerned. 'If I don't nail this case soon I won't be able to show my face in my own manor.'

'That reminds me, I know what I wanted to tell you. You remember that geezer we saw drinking in the *Beehive* that evening. The one you recognised?'

Cumber remembered. 'Terry Philpot?'

'That's him. Well I found out this morning that he has moved in with Mrs Batley in Wimbolt Street. You remember the Batleys at Number 14?'

'Yes a cheerful and friendly young couple, always ready to enjoy a laugh. 'What happened to Mr Batley?'

'They split up about a year ago.'

'Sorry to hear that. Don't they have a couple of kids?'

'Jamie and Kim.'

'Believe me, villains like Philpot living in the area is not great news for the locals,' said Cumber, thinking of his own parents in particular, before adding, 'as I said before he is one nasty piece of work.'

'So you said. Could he be your burglar?'

'No chance, he is too big and ugly to climb through those windows. All the same it would be much appreciated if you keep your ears to the ground, Bobby. Trouble tends to follow him about.'

Collins answered with a hint of sarcasm, 'Will do, sir. Will I get any financial reward for this unofficial police work?'

Cumber chuckled. 'There could be a pint in it for you.'

'Thanks a bunch.'

Having travelled together the previous day to see Spurs at White Hart Lane, the conversation then drifted on to football, with both of them enjoying a brief appraisal of the game before the phone call ended. Cumber lounged back on his sofa and once more turned his attention to the television and the dubious pleasures of *The Singing Detective.*

*

PC Jack Larkins pulled up the collar of his heavy-duty police jacket and exhaled a puff of warm breath into the cold night air. He was glad he had remembered to put his thermals on. Someone had mentioned that it was going to be a 'Brass Monkey' evening and they had not been wrong. Normally he would have been enjoying the solitude of the pavement beat with the occasional interaction with the public, but on a night like this even he could see the attraction of a warm patrol car. At that moment he would even have been prepared to put up with the juvenile banter he usually endured whilst confined in a patrol car with some of his younger colleagues. He looked at his watch and gave a slight grunt of satisfaction. His beat was coming to an end and he could now make his way back to Canon Row police station. The environs of Westminster had been quieter than usual, even for a Monday evening. Now apart from the occasional worker hurriedly making their way home and the distant hum of late night traffic on the Westminster Bridge, London appeared to be moving peacefully towards slumber. It was just coming up to midnight as he turned left into Marsham Street and headed east. With any luck his wife Marjorie would have kept the promise she had made earlier that morning and prepared him his favourite steak and kidney pudding. He calculated that he would be back at his Kennington home within the hour with the pudding hopefully on the simmer.

As the echoing chimes of Big Ben struck twelve, he turned right into Page Street in order to take the shortcut through St John's Gardens. He had passed this way some ten minutes before and all had been quiet. As he entered the gated entrance at the western end of the gardens, he could just make out the dark inert shape of someone lying prostrate on the path some twenty yards ahead of him. It would not be an unusual occurrence for drunken vagrants to be found obstructing the garden pathways late at night so Larkins was not too perturbed. It was only when he drew nearer and noticed that it was a man lying face up with an arm outstretched towards a small attaché case positioned a few feet away on the path that he felt his pulse begin to quicken.

*

DS Harmer logged out of his computer screen and rubbed his eyes. He had spent the whole day trawling once again through the historic court cases of Rupert Buxton. Though he still felt sure in his own mind that the Tylers were behind the murder, he felt increasingly frustrated that they had not found the compelling piece of evidence that would eliminate any doubt. The clock on the wall of his office informed him it was past midnight and his tired body was telling him it was time to go home. New Scotland Yard was soothingly quiet, with just the odd distant footstep and raised voice outside his office reminding him that he was not the only sad individual left working in the building. Apart from his own fruitless efforts in the Buxton case it had otherwise been an interesting day. Young James Cumber had been informed of his promotion that morning, meaning there had been plenty of celebration cakes on offer accompanied by a general jollity that would not normally have existed on a miserable Monday. Harmer had not been the least surprised by Cumber's elevation, thinking him well worthy of the step-up. He himself had never pushed for career advancement, being perfectly happy in his chosen comfort zone.

After making a phone call to his long suffering wife - she would never go to bed until he arrived home - he rose stiffly from his desk and slipped his coat on. As he opened the door of his office to leave, he was surprised to be confronted by DC Norton looking stunned and lost in thought. Instantly alerted by Norton's troubled expression Harmer inquired, 'What's up?'

'There has been another throat slashing, this time in St John's Gardens.'

*

Loxley's face was grim as he stared down at the handsome features of Timothy Galton, the now deceased Conservative MP for Uxbridge, lying motionless on the ground. After Harmer had rung him at his home to inform him of the murder, he had wasted no time in calling Bill Kemp. The conversation had been uncomfortable, with Loxley being fully aware that his Chief would now have to handle the embarrassing fallout at the inevitable press conference that would follow. The scene he was now surveying in St John's Gardens was uncannily similar to the Buxton murder, even down to the positioning of the body and the blood flow from the victim's neck. It had not taken long to establish the identity of the victim, for not only was Galton one of Thatcher's young lions and a rising star at Westminster, he was also a well-known face due to him being an accomplished television performer. As Loxley watched the SOCOs carry out their sombre examination under the strategically placed floodlights, he was joined by his newly promoted sidekick James Cumber with a welcome coffee.

Loxley took a warming sip before saying, 'Well DI Cumber, you have certainly timed your promotion perfectly. This case is turning into a real humdinger and no mistake.'

Cumber allowed himself a rueful smile. 'Has the Doc confirmed that the murder was done by the same hand?'

'Ninety nine per cent. Unfortunately it appears that we have a very professional serial killer on our hands.'

Cumber shook his head. 'It looked like the Tyler families involvement was a sure thing, right down to the Danny Tyler description.'

'As of this moment all bets are off. We will have to release the Tyler brothers immediately.'

Over in the far corner of the gardens Norton and Parrish had just finished questioning PC Larkins and were returning to the murder site. Loxley beckoned them over. 'Anything useful?'

Parrish grimaced. 'Nothing much, sir, PC Larkins says he had walked through the gardens about ten minutes earlier, and found the body on his return trip. Says he did not hear or see anything.'

Loxley could not help letting out a grunt of exasperation. 'Surely someone must have seen something.'

Cumber suggested, 'Hopefully we'll get something useful when we establish Galton's movements.'

Loxley asked, 'Next of kin been informed?'

Parrish answered, 'Galton was unmarried, sir, lived around the corner in Page Street. He was obviously making his way home. Believe his parents live somewhere in Surrey.'

'Make sure we get them informed as soon as we can. I think it will be a good idea to set up an incident room in Canon Row. It's closer to parliament and we need to get as much information about Galton's lifestyle and movements as possible.'

Crime co-ordinator Bob Norton responded, 'I will get that organised, sir.'

Loxley signalled his appreciation before taking one last gulp of his rapidly cooling coffee. The SOCOs still had some way to go with their examination and an ambulance crew were already lurking nearby waiting to take Galton's body away to St Thomas's Hospital. It was now four o'clock in the morning.

Loxley announced, 'We'll discuss the investigation strategy back at the Yard in a few hours. Make sure the area is taped-off, the murder tent is in place and the information request boards are out before morning. Meanwhile I'll get back to the Yard and report to the 'Super'. I can't say I am looking forward to it.'

Loxley's mind was racing as he walked back to his car in nearby Horseferry Road. Making a conscious effort to focus his thinking he made a quick phone call to New Scotland Yard. Only seconds later he heard himself giving the official instruction to formalise the release papers for the Tyler brothers.

CHAPTER SEVEN

A COLLEGIATE CONNECTION

Superintendent Bill Kemp looked grim as he sat down alongside Joe Loxley at the boardroom table. Knowing he had to face a challenging and embarrassing press conference in front of the television cameras that afternoon, combined with the knowledge that there was still a highly efficient serial killer on the loose had put him in a foul mood. News of a body being found in Westminster had first been reported on the early morning news, but when the identity of the high profile victim was revealed a couple of hours later the news spread across the country like wildfire. The crowded boardroom was filled once again with members of the murder investigation team, with many of the support staff having to stand due to lack of seating. DC Bob Norton was again the focal point of the meeting as he stood in front of his information board.

There was more than a hint of nervous tension as the room fell silent and all eyes fixed on a serious-looking Bill Kemp. There was a detectably long pause as the

Superintendent gathered his thoughts before starting the proceedings. 'I hope I don't need to tell you how important this case now is. Not only because we appear to have a maniac on the streets who is very likely to kill again, but also in view of the widely publicised wrongful arrest of the Tyler brothers and the high public profile of the latest victim our very own credibility is now at stake.' There was some uncomfortable fidgeting and grunted agreement around the room before Kemp went on, 'I urge every one of us here to be calm and methodical in our investigation of this case. We will need to apply ourselves one hundred per cent correctly if we are to nail this bastard.'

This statement was greeted with some more subdued murmuring. Bill Kemp then turned to Dr Tom Conway, 'Right, Tom, give us the benefit of your expertise.'

The doctor stood up. 'The execution of the crime was an exact replica of the Buxton murder. Left-handed from behind, blood spatter suggesting right to left, victim then lowered backwards to the ground.'

'Putting aside for one moment the extra detail that the murder was again perpetrated on a Monday evening, do you think it was definitely the same man?' asked Kemp.

Dr Conway did not hesitate. 'Same left-handed killer, same weapon, it has to be.'

Kemp looked up at Norton. 'What have you got, Bob?'

Bob Norton cleared his throat. 'Unlike with the Buxton murder, we so far have no eye-witness reports of a short stocky hooded man. In fact at this stage we have no reported sighting of anybody. PC Larkins saw nothing suspicious when he passed through the gardens at about

11.45pm, but on his way back ten minutes later he finds Galton lying dead. The SOCOs have already discovered some footprints behind a bush that was adjacent to the path where Galton was lying, seems pretty obvious that's where the killer waited in hiding. Forensic have so far established from the prints that the assailant was wearing trainers, plus they have discovered more clothing fibres that are identical to those found at the Buxton murder. As yet we do not have a full account of Galton's movements throughout the day. But what we have established is that he had been working late in the House of Commons as he often did and that he was on his way home to his flat in Page Street. As far as we know he lived alone in the flat. Regarding the extra significance of the murder again taking place on a Monday night it's still far too early to say.'

Loxley interrupted at this point and turned to Bill Kemp. 'Fortunately we managed to track down Galton's parents in Weybridge and inform them just in time before the morning news bulletins revealed his name.'

Norton went on, 'On a much more encouraging note we have found some interesting connections between the two victims.'

Bill Kemp looked intrigued. 'Go on.'

'Both of them were 32 years old and they graduated from St Benedict's College in Oxford at the same time in 1976.' There was a significant silence in the room as the assembled detectives absorbed the implications of Norton's words.

It was James Cumber who was first to ask the obvious question, 'Do we have any evidence that Buxton and Galton have kept in touch through the years?'

'At this early stage we have nothing to suggest that they did, though of course it is entirely possible,' Norton answered.

'Worth having another chat with Mrs Buxton, at some stage, she might know if they kept in contact,' Loxley suggested.

Cumber scribbled a note on his pad. 'We'll get that arranged.'

Loxley was looking thoughtful. 'In view of what's happened with the Tylers it would be wise not to underestimate the possibility of coincidence, but there is no doubt of the potential importance of this link. It could well prove fruitful to explore this connection at St Benedict's College. I think this could well be a job for you, Steve.'

Steve Harmer had managed to grab some much needed shut eye in one of the station rooms in the early hours and was now back to his eager self. 'I'll make a start on compiling a list of all the St Benedict's graduates of 1976.'

Loxley approved. 'Good man. I also think that we should pay the college a visit at some stage and do a bit of historic digging. Hopefully we may find something crucial will crawl out of the woodwork.'

Bill Kemp had been listening intently. 'No matter how small or seemingly immaterial, it's definitely worth the effort in following it up; meanwhile go over all Galton's television appearances and public statements, see if he is likely to have made any enemies.'

Loxley turned to Norton. 'If you can take care of the incident room at Canon Row with Parrish, DI Cumber and I will conduct the investigation on the ground in Westminster.'

Brian Parrish, who still seemed to be adjusting to the new pecking order regarding Cumber, muttered a slightly subdued compliance.

'What's the present situation with the Tylers?' Bill Kemp asked.

'They have both been released. Jimmy is out on bail pending charges of assaulting a policeman in the execution of his duty,' Loxley answered.

Kemp let out a grunt of exasperation. 'I still cannot fathom the short and stocky sightings on the Embankment and at *The Edgar* .'

Cumber suggested, 'I think it could still have been Danny Tyler who was seen, sir. He probably thought it best to deny he was in the area because he was in enough trouble already.'

'Then again,' added Loxley, 'he could be telling the truth when he said he was so out of his head when he left the pub and couldn't remember anything.'

Bill Kemp did not sound totally convinced, 'It would still not surprise me if it transpires further down the line that the Tylers have played some part in this debacle. Continue to keep an eye on them.' He stood up, clapped his hands and addressed the whole room. 'When DS Harmer compiles his list of graduates from the class of 76

I want you all over them like a rash. Hopefully we'll find our killer in that list; let's go get him.'

There was a scraping of chairs and an excited buzz in the air as the murder team exited the room. Bill Kemp stood back and motioned for Loxley to stay behind.

Closing the door behind the departing crowd, Kemp turned to Loxley. 'Unfortunately, Joe, it looks like the doubts you expressed on Saturday night are well founded after all. The media treatment in the next few hours is going to be a tough gig. I don't mind saying I am not looking forward to the televised press conference this afternoon, not to mention seeing the newspaper headlines tomorrow morning.'

Loxley could see that his old partner had taken the unwelcome turn of events very personally. 'Don't take it all on your shoulders, Bill, we're all in this together. You know more than any one that circumstances can conspire against you, no matter how professional your approach.'

Kemp sighed deeply. 'This certainly feels like one of those times.'

'Do you want me alongside you at the press conference this afternoon?'

Kemp was decisive in his answer. 'I appreciate the gesture, Joe, but that won't be necessary. There is only one place I want you and that's out there tracking down this nutcase.'

*

Loxley glanced at his wristwatch. He and Cumber were five minutes early for their appointment with Galton's

Private Secretary Bernard Tompkins, at the Houses of Parliament. They were standing outside the St Stephen's entrance of the Westminster Palace, with the busy afternoon traffic providing a noisy backdrop to their usual good natured-banter. At the appointed time they were greeted by a small neatly dressed man who Loxley judged to be in his early forties. He shook both their hands, before politely instructing Loxley and Cumber to follow him through the entrance and up a long staircase. At the top of the stairs they turned into a main hall flanked by some marble statues of notable political figures who had served Britain with distinction in the past. They then walked down a mural-lined corridor before climbing a few more steps and entering a dimly lit room with a creaky door.

Bernard Tompkins looked apologetic. 'I am sorry, gentlemen, but this is the only room available at present for a private conversation.'

Loxley raised his hand. 'No need to apologise, Mr Tompkins, this will do nicely.'

The room was furnished with three green leather chairs decorated with brass studs, the walls being covered by coarse-grained oak panelling and heavy flock paper. The daylight outside was struggling to filter through the mullioned windows. Once they were all seated Loxley felt free to proceed with his enquiries and Cumber produced his notebook and pen.

'Thanks once again, Mr Tompkins, for agreeing to see us at such short notice. I appreciate you must be very shocked.'

Tompkin's pink face clouded over. 'Totally stunned, it all seems very surreal.'

'I am sure it does, Mr Tompkins. In your own time, is it possible for you to give me details of Mr Galton's routine yesterday?'

Tompkins produced a small leather-bound diary from his pocket. 'That's fairly easy. He arrived at his office around ten o'clock in the morning and worked there on his boxes until lunchtime. He had lunch in the Goring Dining Room with Nigel Faversham before retiring to the Commons Tea Room. I met him there for an update on his schedule for the coming week. He then returned to his office to work on some constituency matters until five o'clock. I had another quick conversation with him in the Commons Library before I left him at around six-thirty in the evening.'

'Would that be regarded as a normal day for Mr Galton regarding his routine?'

'Pretty much, he was very focused on his parliamentary work. He often worked long hours and was very industrious.'

'Were there other people in the library when you left him?'

'Oh yes, several.'

'Can you give me any names?'

Tompkins brow creased in thought. 'I certainly remember that Tim Blake and John Nugent were present.'

Cumber looked up from his notepad. 'Would it be possible for us to speak to either of them today?'

'I will certainly try to pin them down for you.'

Loxley went on, 'Obviously I have to ask whether you had noticed anything in Mr Galton's behaviour recently that suggested he was worried about anything.'

'Nothing obvious, as I've said he always seemed totally consumed with his work. At the present time he was particularly passionate about community projects in Uxbridge. A redevelopment of the old shopping centre with more recreational space was very much on his present agenda.'

'I understand that he had been recently promoted to a Cabinet post.'

'That is correct. He was Minister for Administrative Affairs.'

'Could you describe to me in brief terms what that job entails?'

'It is basically a roving brief to investigate and control administrative inefficiency and overspending throughout the system.'

Loxley changed tack. 'Had you ever heard him refer to the recent Rupert Buxton murder?'

'No not personally, but I had heard from others that Mr Galton had mentioned at the time of the murder that they had both attended the same college in Oxford.'

'Did Mr Galton have a particular trusted chum at Westminster who could possibly have some more intimate information for us?'

Tompkins allowed himself a slight smile for the first time. 'As you may have heard, inspector, politics can be a dirty game, with trusted chums in particular being in short supply, but I would say Nigel Faversham would come closest to that description.'

As Cumber scribbled the name, Loxley wrapped up the interview, 'Thank you for your time, Mr Tompkins. If it could be possible to talk to Mr Blake or Mr Nugent that would be very helpful.'

Tompkins rose from his chair. 'Certainly, I will see if I can track them down. Would you like any tea or coffee, gentlemen?'

Cumber was the quickest to reply, 'That would be nice.'

'I will get it arranged.'

When Tompkins left the room, the two inspectors took the opportunity to get up from their chairs and stretch their legs. They walked over to the dusty mullioned window that looked down on to the shadowed courtyards and alleys that existed within the historic confines of the palace grounds.

Cumber was the first to speak. 'These murders are certainly taking us into the hidden corners of the establishment. Before this case I honestly had no idea how enclosed and quaint these institutions actually were.'

'Call it education, James, you never stop learning,' Loxley said, smiling.

Cumber looked genuinely fascinated as he gazed out of the window. 'It is certainly an eye-opener.'

It was not long before there was a knock at the door and a kindly-looking tea lady entered the room pushing a trolley. Instantly cheered by this welcome sight, the two men soon found themselves being treated to tea and biscuits. Loxley instinctively dunked his biscuit in his tea. 'You just can't beat a cuppa straight from the urn, beats all that machine crap every time.' Cumber, his mouth full of biscuit, could only nod in contented agreement.

Ten minutes later they were interviewing the Honourable Member for South Thanet, John Nugent. Dapper of appearance and brisk in manner, the MP appeared to be quite thrilled that he had been called to assist in the murder enquiry. When asked by Loxley if he had seen Galton leave the library, his eyes widened with barely concealed excitement. 'Most definitely, he left about nine o'clock.'

'Did he mention if he was going straight home?' Loxley asked.

'Normally he would wind down at the end of the day with a drink or two in the Commons Bar before going home, but last night he told us he was meeting up with Nigel Faversham across the road on College Green.'

Cumber turned to Bernard Tompkins. 'Is Mr Faversham around today?'

'No, I believe he was very shaken by the news and could not face coming in.'

'Do you know where we can get in touch with him?'

'I believe he has a parliamentary flat in Royal Street off the Lambeth Palace Road; I can get you his address and phone number.'

Cumber scribbled the initial information down in his notebook. 'That would be very helpful.'

*

Forty minutes later Loxley and Cumber were introducing themselves to Mr Faversham on the security intercom of his luxury flat overlooking the River Thames. After some early hesitation and nervousness on the part of Mr Faversham, the two detectives had finally managed to convince him that it would really be in his best interest to let them come up to the flat. After finally being admitted, they were confronted by a tall hunched figure with a mop of dishevelled hair. Faversham was still in his dressing gown. Loxley thought that though he could only have been in his late thirties his appearance at that moment made him look a good ten years older. Mumbling an apology for his undressed state, he awkwardly motioned for them to take a seat. Loxley glanced around the large lounge area. The décor was minimalist in the extreme, with the white tiled floor and blank walls accentuating the feeling of emptiness. The only furniture on display was the black leather three-piece, a glass coffee table and a Panasonic TV which was turned on full volume and emitting an echo in the sparse surroundings.

Requesting that Faversham turn the volume down on the TV, Loxley took a seat opposite the MP. He decided to open his questioning in a gentle mode. 'I have heard that Mr Galton was a good friend of yours, so I can appreciate this tragedy must be a great shock to you.'

Faversham put his head in his hands and spoke to the floor. 'I just cannot believe it. When I left him last night he was so full of ideas about what he wanted to achieve in politics; he never stopped planning for the future.' His voice tailed off suddenly, as if suddenly hit with the stark realisation that now there would never be a future for his friend.

'In your own time, Mr Faversham, can you tell us your movements after you left the House of Commons last night?'

Faversham visibly struggled to retain his composure. 'I had lunch with Timothy yesterday and we arranged to meet on the College Green at nine o'clock in the evening. We were discussing how to make some potential savings in government expenditure and we had identified some fruitful areas. We would often arrange to meet in the evening as it was not always suitable to discuss department budgets in the day with other colleagues around. Last night we ended up in *The Marquis of Granby* pub in Romney Street. This would normally be our routine as it was conveniently situated on the route home to his flat in Page Street.'

'About what time did you leave the pub last night?'

'Earlier than usual as it happens. At about ten-thirty, Tim suddenly remembered some papers he had left in his office which were to do with redevelopment in his local constituency. He had to go back and get them because he had planned to go straight to his Uxbridge surgery this morning. We walked back together and the last time I saw him he was entering the parliament building. I must confess that being so close to such a calamity has totally unnerved me; I feel quite ill thinking about it.' He looked towards Loxley as if for some reassurance. 'Could I be in danger?'

Loxley did his best to comfort him. 'Highly unlikely, Mr Faversham, it seems pretty obvious that Mr Galton was the target.'

Cumber gently asked, 'Just out of interest, Mr Faversham, would you mind telling us where you were educated?'

The MP seemed momentarily thrown by Cumber's question. 'Oh er Cambridge, Magdelene College. Why?'

Cumber did his best to sound soothing, 'Just a line of enquiry that's all, Mr Faversham?'

A look of realisation suddenly passed across Faversham's face. 'Oh, you are thinking about the Oxford College connection between the previous victim and Tim.'

'It could be a coincidence,' Loxley said, 'but on the other hand it could be highly significant. Did Mr Galton talk much about the Buxton murder?'

'He did mention that Mr Buxton was one of his old chums at Oxford. I don't remember him saying much, but he certainly was not oblivious to the investigation and I remember him being pleased when the police arrested the two suspects.'

Loxley was curious. 'You say pleased, would you say there was also an element of relief?'

'Possibly. Looking back there is no doubt that there was a general lightening of his mood.'

'He had made no mention of any further acquaintance with Buxton since those Oxford days?'

'No, I can be definite about that because I can remember him specifically mentioning how he had lost touch with Buxton and many others from his time at

Oxford. He suggested it was down to his obsessive dedication to a political career.'

As they rose to make their departure, Loxley's attention was diverted back to the television. A news bulletin had been echoing in the background and was unsurprisingly full of the murder. The newshounds had a great story to cover. Not only had there been the brutal sudden death of a high profile politician with the very real possibility of more murders to come, but also the obvious enjoyment of the police embarrassment with the wrongful arrest of the Tyler brothers. The images on the screen suddenly switched to the police press conference at Canon Row. For Loxley it made for uncomfortable viewing, as he watched his old friend Bill Kemp doing his best to explain away the unfortunate turn of events.

*

Chief Superintendent Bill Kemp leaned back against the wall and savoured the last stick of his KitKat. The press conference that he had endured had been one of the most awkward he could ever remember and he was glad it was behind him. He was now standing in the special incident room that had been hurriedly set up in Canon Row. The room was filled with frenzied activity, with a busy Brian Parrish ensuring there were extra phone lines while also assigning the appropriate roles to the recruited civilian staff. Bill Kemp looked on approvingly as the impressive quantities of human resource were eventually seated into various groups of receivers, statement readers and action allocators.

Slowly recovering his composure after his ordeal at the hands of the press, Kemp was approached by Bob Norton who handed him a cup of tea. In his capacity as crime co-ordinator Norton had sat beside Bill Kemp at the press conference and had been well aware of his chief's discomfort. 'This is personal now, Bob,' said Kemp. 'I don't want to ever feel that feeble again.'

'We'll get him, sir, I have no doubt about that.'

'The sooner the bloody better.'

'We have a good team on the case, sir, we just need a bit of luck that's all.'

Kemp was unimpressed. 'You have been in this game long enough to know that you make your own luck, Bob. In this particular case we simply can't afford the luxury of being unlucky again, we would simply be a laughing stock.'

With a final instruction to Norton to keep him posted, Kemp drained his cup and left the room to return to New Scotland Yard.

*

Loxley and Cumber stood on the small east-facing balcony of Timothy Galton's flat. Looking down on the very spot where the body was discovered in St John's Gardens, Loxley did not find it difficult to imagine a nocturnal knife-wielding stalker lurking furtively in the bushes below. Looking out across the Westminster rooftops, the balcony afforded a great view of Big Ben with the meandering River Thames flowing timelessly beyond. On the more distant horizon, the imposing towers of the

Barbican complex and the City of London dominated the fading winter skyline. They had headed straight for the flat after leaving Nigel Faversham. Letting themselves in with the keys obtained from Galton's attaché case found at the murder scene, they had both been immediately drawn to the glass door that led out to the balcony.

As they admired the panoramic view, Cumber was the first to speak, 'It makes me feel a bit spooked to think that our murderer is still out there somewhere.'

Loxley had mixed feelings. 'I know what you mean but I hope for our sakes that he is still out there. I would hate to think that he has skipped the country.' Suddenly shivering in the cold air Loxley said, 'Let's go back inside and have a snoop around, see if we can get an angle on Galton.'

Loxley took a look around the living room while Cumber entered the bedroom area. The flat was well furnished, Loxley thought, giving him a good idea of Galton's blue-chip lifestyle. The furniture looked solid and expensive, with a large stereo system displaying an impressive rack of long-playing albums. A lot of Pink Floyd and Genesis, Loxley noticed, but there were also some classical pieces by Verdi and Beethoven. Beside the TV stood a bookcase stacked with videos. Loxley was immediately struck by how many of these were of a sporting nature, with athletics and rugby union being particularly well represented. Not surprisingly there were some heavy duty books too, covering subjects as diverse as philosophy, sociology, sports psychology and politics. Thick rugs cushioned the shiny wood flooring, whilst a couple of abstract prints adorned the walls. Loxley gave these a cursory glance before moving through to the kitchen.

Cumber meanwhile was casting an eye over the decently sized bedroom. Large enough to accommodate a king-sized double bed, there was also a rowing machine on the floor alongside. On the bedside table there was a shaded lamp and a large notebook. Cumber picked it up and looked inside. The pages were full of sketches and development plans, presumably, Cumber thought, for his constituency of Uxbridge. Putting down the notebook, Cumber went over to a large wardrobe and opened it. It was stuffed full of clothes and shoes. Cumber noted appreciatively that the suits were expensive, with bold labels displaying Armani, Lauren and Klein. After whistling softly under his breath he caught sight of a framed photograph on the dressing table. It was of a young Galton fully gowned on his graduation day in Oxford. Cumber surmised that the two older people standing either side of him were his proud parents.

Back in the kitchen Loxley was contemplating the contents of the fridge. There were what looked like the remains of a Chinese takeaway, some milk, eggs, and a bottle of salad cream. On the floor there was a wine rack full of good quality reds. A cutting edge espresso machine completed the picture.

Loxley walked through to the bedroom. 'Mr Galton certainly knew a bit of quality when he saw it.'

Cumber shouted from the bathroom, 'Wait till you take a look at the suits in the wardrobe.'

Loxley picked up the photo. 'Anything significant in his toiletries?'

Cumber was looking in the bathroom cabinet. 'No, the usual, shampoo, toothpaste, painkillers, razor, shaving cream and hair products.'

Loxley returned the photo to the dresser and opened the wardrobe. 'No prescription drugs?'

'Nothing at all, it looks like he was as fit as a fiddle.'

Mentally acknowledging Cumber's point about Galton's expensive suits, Loxley closed the wardrobe, picked up the notebook and walked back in the living room. As Cumber joined him Loxley was browsing the notebook contents.

Loxley finally closed the book and commented, 'I notice there has been no mention of a girlfriend?'

'He must have had them, rich good looking fella like him. He probably had several.'

A thought occurred to Loxley. 'Don't think there was a bit more to his relationship with Faversham?'

Picking up on the inference Cumber asked, 'Think it's relevant?'

Loxley shrugged his shoulders. 'Probably not.' His attention was suddenly drawn to a small section of newspaper sticking out from under the leather cushion on the settee. Loxley lifted the cushion and glanced at the paper. It was a backdated copy of the *Daily Mail* with the headlines covering the murder of Rupert Buxton. 'He was obviously sufficiently interested in the Buxton case to want to keep an old newspaper.'

Looking over Loxley's shoulder at the front page headlines Cumber said, 'I don't suppose it would be too surprising if he took an interest in the slaughter of his old Oxford acquaintance.'

As Loxley opened the paper to scan the inside pages an A5 sheet dropped to the floor. Cumber reached first to pick it up. Written on one side was what appeared to be a small shopping list. The items listed were a French loaf, Brie, onions, tomatoes, bleach and toilet duck. At the bottom of the page added almost as an afterthought there was a question mark and the word varnish with a capital V.

Cumber showed it to Loxley. 'Significant?'

Loxley gave the shopping list a quick scrutiny. 'Only if the murderer proves to be an employee at Waitrose.'

Cumber smiled and placed the A5 sheet on the coffee table.

After briefly glancing through the two page feature on the murder, Loxley replaced the newspaper under the cushion before asking Cumber, 'Fancy a trip to Oxford in the morning?'

Cumber was not slow to answer. 'You bet.' They took one more glance around the flat, before locking up and making their way back to New Scotland Yard.

*

'How are you getting on, Steve?' Bill Kemp asked hopefully, as he entered the office of Steve Harmer at New Scotland Yard. Kemp had wasted no time after his return from Canon Row in seeking out the DS he affectionately called 'Bloodhound'.

Harmer was in his familiar pose hunched over his computer screen. Looking up he answered, 'If we can safely assume that the murderer is not a woman, sir, we are left with a list of about 150 male graduates from the 1976 batch.'

Kemp grimaced. 'Obviously we are going to need assistance from every police force in the land tracking that lot down; I bet they have scattered far and wide. I take it you are starting with anyone who resides in London and the surrounding areas before moving further afield.'

'Yes, sir. Hopefully it should not be too much trouble assembling the occupations and residences, but it is obviously going to take a fair amount of manpower checking them out.'

Kemp looked determined. 'We have been given the resources, let me know if you want any assistance on this one, Steve; we need to do whatever it takes.'

Though Harmer prided his self on his solitary doggedness, even he recognised he would need assistance in this particular case, where speed was of the essence. 'It would certainly be helpful if there is any extra resource made available to me, sir.'

'Consider it done.'

Just before he left the room Kemp added as an afterthought, 'Steve, I think it would be a good idea to make sure that each and every one of the St Benedict's old boys signs an interview sheet after they are contacted, with a further instruction to the officers involved to note any left-handers.'

Harmer took hold of a notepad. 'I will see to it, sir.'

*

Loxley's Audi 5000CS swung smoothly off the M40 at Junction 8 heading for Oxford. Accompanied by Cumber, Loxley was not exactly sure what he was expecting to achieve with his visit to the college, but as always, he felt he worked better when getting an idea of the lifestyle and life experience of the murder victims. The news on the car radio had been full of the London murders, constantly reminding him of the pressure they were under to get a result. As Loxley drove through the High Street he was surprised to experience a brief pang of nostalgia. Back in his early days as a rookie constable in the Sixties, he had been stationed at Oxford for a couple of months. He remembered how, as a young impressionable man, he had admired the wealth of wonderfully sculptured buildings and enjoyed the unique collegiate atmosphere. Cumber, who was seeing Oxford for the first time, had dozed fitfully throughout the journey, but was now gazing interestedly out of the car window. They passed the Carfax Tower before turning right into New Inn Hall Street, before eventually parking in the Gloucester Street car park. Both men were keen to vacate the Audi, relieved to be able to stretch their limbs in the cold, clear morning air.

Cumber pulled up his coat collar and rubbed his hands. 'Can we get a coffee?'

'You read my thoughts,' Loxley answered.

After finding a convenient breakfast café in Cornmarket, they sat down at a table near the window that looked out onto the street. They were soon tucking into some hot buttered toast and a pot of coffee, welcoming the temporary diversion from their duties.

Cumber took a sip of his coffee and glanced out of the window. 'Interesting place, Oxford.'

'I thought you would like it. Wait till you see the set-up at the college that will really open your eyes.'

'What time are they expecting us?'

Loxley looked at his watch. 'In about fifteen minutes.' Seeing Cumber's slightly anxious expression, Loxley quickly reassured him, 'It's all right, it's only a short walk away.'

They were soon making their way along Ship Street towards the college, which was situated in Turl Street. Gazing at the abundant number of unattended parked bikes, Cumber could not help enquiring, 'Is cycle crime ever an issue here?'

Loxley laughed. 'This is Oxford, James, not Hackney. The people here like to think that this is the centre of civilisation.'

Arriving at the gates of the college, they entered a grand turreted entrance and introduced themselves to rather gruff elderly gent seated in the Porters' Lodge. The man, who Loxley assumed to be the porter, took some time in scanning his appointment notes before finally finding their names and asking them to follow him to the Rector's Lodgings. They were led through an archway which opened out on to an immaculately manicured quadrangle dominated by a towering structure that Loxley guessed to be some sort of chapel. Skirting the quadrangle they passed through the impressive cloisters, their footsteps echoing beneath them on the paved stone. They eventually came to a halt outside an attractive Georgian-style building where honey yellow Cotswold stone was intermittently glimpsed through the ivy clinging to the walls. The porter led them to the middle door of three and rang a large bell hanging on the outside.

The door was promptly opened by a large, bearded man who introduced himself as Tim Wilson Hurst, the resident Rector, and then said in a loud, booming voice, 'Please come right in, gentlemen.'

The front door opened directly onto a surprisingly small crowded living space which Loxley noticed had an odour that combined musty books with the unmistakable fragrance of furniture polish. Politely refusing the Rector's offer of tea and biscuits, Loxley and Cumber seated themselves down low on a soft cushioned divan. As the Rector poured his own tea, Loxley took in his surroundings. Bookshelves crammed with tomes of academia rose up on two sides, with the standard writing desk and drawers positioned in front of a window overlooking the quad. A narrow staircase rose up at the back of the room, adjacent to a very small kitchen area.

'You like my abode, Inspector?' the Rector asked earnestly.

Loxley smiled politely. 'It's very cosy.'

The Rector laughed loudly. 'It suits me, Inspector, I like everything within touching distance. I see it very much as my second home.' After taking a sip of his tea the Rector adopted a more serious tone, 'I realise that it is rather unfortunate circumstances that have brought you here, gentlemen. I do hope I can be of assistance.'

Not totally sure of his line of enquiry, Loxley thought it best to begin on a courteous note. 'I appreciate you finding the time to talk to us, sir, but as I hope you understand, the brutal murder of two old St Benedict's boys who graduated in the same year simply cannot be ignored.'

'Oh, I understand perfectly, Inspector; it does seem a worrying coincidence in regard to the potential future reputation of St Benedict's.'

'I would hope, sir, that when we do finally solve the case it will not end up reflecting too badly on the college.'

'Whatever the fallout is, Inspector, we will just have to deal with the reality of the outcome.'

'I am sure that would be the best approach, sir. Would you mind telling me how long you have held your present position?'

'Four years. I took over from the legendary James Wilberforce who had been here ten years.' The Rector laughed loudly at the memory. 'He was a difficult act to follow I can tell you.'

'So I take it that he was the Rector back in 1976?'

'He was. Sadly the great man passed away two years ago.'

'Sorry to hear that, he was obviously greatly respected.'

The Rector's eyes twinkled. 'A St Benedict's legend, Inspector, in both life and death.'

Loxley decided to cut to the chase. 'Is there anyone here amongst your existing masters who would have links back to 1976?'

The Rector thought for a second before suddenly rising from his chair and selecting a large book from one of the shelves. Returning to his seat he said, 'It has to be our History Fellow, Francis Lightfoot. He is our resident celebrity author, you know.'

He placed the book on the small table between them. He encouraged both Loxley and Cumber to look at the title, which read *The Complete History of St Benedict's in the Turl.* The Rector went on enthusiastically, 'It is a great read, I fully recommend it. Francis has been at the college for the best part of twenty five years and as you can see,' he said grinning and pointing again at the heavy volume placed on the table, 'his knowledge of St Benedict's history is encyclopaedic.'

Loxley had to agree. 'Would it be convenient for us to have a word with him?'

The Rector looked at his watch. 'Let's see, he should be just coming up to his mid-morning break.' He rose from his seat once more and picked up the telephone. After a brief conversation in which he explained the situation to the person at the other end of the line, the Rector replaced the receiver and cheerily confirmed that Mr Lightfoot was on his way.

It was only a matter of minutes before the history master was ringing the outside bell. After some swift introductions, Mr Lightfoot sat down opposite Loxley and Cumber. He was a small man, smartly dressed in a leather-elbowed check jacket and sharply creased trousers. Loxley judged him to be in his mid-fifties.

The Rector, who had remained standing, said with his now familiar jocularity, 'I have already informed the two officers that you are our resident celebrity author, Francis.'

Lightfoot looked slightly embarrassed. 'Hardly celebrity status I can assure you.'

Loxley motioned to the book that was still placed on the table. 'Well, either way it looks a very impressive body of work, Mr Lightfoot.'

The master, still looking a tad uncomfortable with the attention, did his best to sound modest. 'Thank you. It kept me busy over the holidays.'

Loxley got down to business. 'I understand that you were a master here back in 1976 when Rupert Buxton and Timothy Galton were undergraduates.'

'That is correct.'

'I would certainly appreciate if you can cast your mind back and give us any personal memories of them, anything that might be helpful to us, any insight into the type of people they were. I realise that after ten years, it could prove difficult.'

'As it happens I do remember them quite clearly, mainly because they were such outstanding individuals.'

Loxley leant forward encouragingly.

The master focused his eyes towards the floor as he recalled, 'The two of them were often together. They were both outstanding sportsmen and highly intelligent scholars, much admired by their peers and proudly valued by the college.'

Cumber encouraged him to go further, 'Do you remember anything of a more personal nature that could possibly be of value to the investigation?'

Lightfoot thought for a few seconds. 'Of course with this type of good-looking and talented individual there is often a discernible arrogance underneath the charm. I can certainly remember both of them being extremely popular with the ladies, with Galton in particular being keen to take advantage of this appeal.'

Loxley asked thoughtfully, 'So are you suggesting, Mr Lightfoot, that along with the admiration and prestige there was always the risk of a certain degree of envy and jealousy?'

'Most definitely, with human nature being what it is.'

Loxley pressed on. 'Mr Lightfoot, I realise this is a long shot but can you remember anything in particular relating to Galton and Buxton that would have suggested anyone harbouring a long time grudge?'

The history master paused for a few seconds as he looked in the distance, as if recalling something that might be relevant, before dismissively answering, 'Oh no, nothing even remotely so serious as to lead to their slaughter some ten years later.'

Loxley managed to keep the disappointment from his face. 'Shame; still if anything occurs to you, Mr Lightfoot, no matter how small, please do not hesitate to give us a call.'

Driving back to London, Loxley felt the visit had been worthwhile. Though they had not gained anything tangible in terms of leads, he still somehow had a gut feeling that they had moved a shade closer to tracking down the murderer. The people at the college had been very accommodating, even to the point where they had been offered a brief tour of the college before they left. He glanced across at Cumber. 'So, James what do you think?'

'I thought the whole set-up was very impressive; the Rector was a character. I don't remember any of my teachers being like that in Bethnal Green.'

'That's why he is in Oxford; they only have the best.'

'Lightfoot was interesting, too. Was it my imagination or did I detect he was talking from some personal recollection when he mentioned the competitive nature of the college?'

'Yes, I picked up on that. Difficult to say for sure if it was something that related directly to our two murder victims. I would hate to think he was holding something back that could be crucial. Most probably unrelated to the case, more likely he had a personal memory that he did not want to share publicly. We all have them.'

'I guess so,' said Cumber with a sidelong glance towards Loxley. 'Anyway, going from what Lightfoot did tell us, it seems we were wrong to question Galton's sexual preferences.'

Loxley agreed. 'It would certainly appear so. It seems our Uxbridge MP was a bit of a ram with the ladies.'

Cumber laughed. 'Still the bottom line is we are no further forward regarding suspects and motive.'

Loxley adopted a slightly sarcastic tone. 'True, after all what have we got? We have two handsome young graduates who are successful with the opposite sex. Both of them from wealthy families who also happened to be high-achieving academics and sporting champions to boot. What's there not to like?'

Enjoying the sarcasm but picking up the wider point, Cumber replied, 'Well, I suppose when you put it like that, they may not have been everyone's cup of tea.'

Loxley allowed himself a chuckle. 'Exactly.' He put his foot down on the accelerator. 'Let's get back and see how Steve Harmer is progressing with the class of 76.'

CHAPTER EIGHT

A CASE SOLVED

'Found anything useful yet, Brian?' asked Bob Norton hopefully, looking across at Parrish from behind a table piled high with sheets of paper. Parrish, who was busy processing the large volume of information placed before him, managed a negative shake of his head before ploughing on. The attendance at the special Incident room in Canon Row throughout the day had been disappointingly patchy, consisting mainly of a few well-meaning members of the public, and a fair amount of Westminster politicians. Norton thought that even allowing for the fact that politicians were notoriously eager to give their opinions or views, the high profile publicity and close proximity of the murder site had seemed to heighten this inherent instinct even further. Most of the politicians had been keen to give Timothy Galton a positive character reference, though interestingly there had been a few that suggested his well-guarded private life could be a bit racy. As was usually the case, it had been dealing with the information gleaned from the large amount of telephone calls that had taken up most of the time in the incident room. Norton's watch told him it was fast approaching early evening. Apart from the two rows of civilians on the telephone banks, the room had emptied considerably from earlier in the day and Norton began to appreciate the comparative peace and quiet. He wondered how DCI Loxley and Cumber had fared in Oxford. Though he was an optimist by nature, even he was realistic enough not to expect them to return with the case miraculously solved. Nonetheless, he was still hopeful that their digging in Oxford would reveal evidence that would give them something tangible to work on.

As he glanced up from his desk he became aware of a tall, smartly dressed man lurking uncertainly in the doorway. Norton felt obliged to help him out. 'Can I help you, sir?'

The man appeared to make a conscious effort to compose himself before entering the room. 'Good evening, my name is Nigel Faversham, I am looking for Inspector Loxley.'

Norton was familiar with the politician's name, having been kept fully informed regarding Loxley's visit to Faversham's flat the day before. 'Good evening, Mr Faversham, I am sorry but DCI Loxley is in Oxford today. Can I help?'

Faversham sat down hesitantly in the chair opposite. Norton noticed that his face looked tired and drawn, with his manner showing none of the certainty and confidence usually displayed by an active MP. 'Are you feeling ok, sir, can I get you a coffee?'

Faversham turned down the offer politely before going on to say, 'I am not sure whether this is important but it keeps going over in my mind.'

Norton leaned forward. 'Go on, Mr Faversham.'

'It was one evening in late September on Westminster Bridge. Timothy and I had just left the 'Commons' and we were on our way over to County Hall for a general meeting relating to London education funding. We were in conversation when I distinctly heard a voice shout the name 'Tim'. The voice came from somewhere on the other side of the bridge, but Timothy appeared not to hear it. His name was then shouted several times and where at first the voice had sounded friendly, it became increasingly more agitated as Timothy continued to ignore it. I took a quick glance in the direction of the voice and could just about make out a figure in the gloom. It was a man and he appeared to be a little the worse for wear.'

Norton was writing the statement down. 'Drunk?'

'It appeared so. I looked across at Timothy and asked him jokingly if the man was a friend of his, but he appeared not to see the joke and gave me a look that suggested it would be best not to enquire further. You see, Timothy was a fiercely ambitious politician and liked to keep his private life very low profile.'

Norton looked up from his notes. 'From what you knew of Mr Galton, did he have anything serious in particular he may have wished to hide?'

'No more than any other young men I am sure who are single and red-blooded. But he did have a weakness for the young model girls that frequent the West End clubs and on more than one occasion I was called upon to cover his tracks on these clandestine adventures.'

'In what way did you cover him?'

'By keeping his nocturnal escapades secret, heading off inquisitive newshounds, appealing to people's better nature, that sort of thing.'

'Would any of it been scandalous enough to have done his career lasting damage?'

'To be honest I don't know, but rightly or wrongly, he certainly thought there was that possibility. What I do know is that he could be ferociously protective of anything he saw as a threat to his political ambitions.'

'So we have an over-familiar and aggressive drunk on Westminster Bridge who Galton is choosing to ignore; anything else to add?'

'In view of what has now happened, what followed makes it more sinister.'

Norton signalled his encouragement, as Faversham seemed to falter and become more agitated as he remembered. 'As I say, the drunken man's manner became much more hostile. I could not hear everything he said but the gist of it was that Timothy would come to regret his pig ignorance in not acknowledging him. He then started to stumble after us, all the time shouting increasingly menacing threats. At one stage he was almost hit by a bus as he tried to stagger across the road towards us.'

'When you say menacing threats, do you mean to Galton's life?'

'Very much so and in a voice that sounded alarmingly sincere in its intent.'

'What happened then?'

'To my surprise Timothy began to break into a trot. I could not keep up with him and by the time I reached the top of the steps that led down to County Hall, Timothy was already entering the building. I did sneak another look back across the bridge before I descended, but I could no longer see the man.'

'And you don't think you could describe him?'

'Not really, apart from the fact that he was obviously drunk or drugged.'

'Once you were inside County Hall, did Mr Galton regain his composure?'

'Don't forget I knew him very well and though he was still outwardly smooth and composed, I could see that he had been shaken up a little by the encounter. So much so that when the time came to leave County Hall, he uncommonly ordered a mini-cab and invited a few people back to his flat for a nightcap. I got the distinct impression he did not want to leave the building alone.'

'And you never mentioned the incident to him again?'

Faversham shook his head. 'No, never. To be honest there would have been no point. I could see from his disposition that the whole episode was strictly off-limits.'

Norton finished his notes before thanking Faversham for his time and personally showing him to the door. Faversham's story was certainly interesting, but did it have any relevance to the two murders?

*

'Is it too much to hope that you have stumbled on something to crack this case while we have been away, Steve?' asked Loxley hopefully, as he and Cumber entered Harmer's office.

As per usual Steve Harmer was busily hunched over his computer. He looked up from his screen. 'Not yet, sir. I wish I could tell you something positive but so far nothing significant. What I can say is that the list of occupations are certainly impressive, anything from BBC executives and legal wizards to GPs in Harley Street and computer gurus in the City of London. Not to mention some eminent surgeons and esteemed academics.'

'The surgeons could be interesting in view of the suspected murder weapon,' Cumber remarked.

'I suppose it would be asking too much for you to have found some 'Demon Barbers' amongst the list, Steve?' joked Loxley.

Harmer smiled. 'Not yet, sir. I take it your visit to Oxford failed to turn anything up?'

Loxley pulled a face. 'Nothing much, though it certainly gave us a good insight into the culture and the character of the victims.' He surveyed the impressive array of helpers in the room. 'Good to see that you have been given some extra resources, Steve?'

'Can't complain, sir, no sooner had I requested some extra bodies and it was done.'

Loxley nodded his approval before turning to Cumber. 'I am just going to update the 'Super', see you later for a coffee in the canteen.'

Cumber patted his belly. 'Which reminds me, my stomach feels like my throat's been cut. Can I get you guys anything?' he asked, looking at the team of helpers.

Harmer gestured towards the numerous empty plastic Lucozade bottles littered on his desk. 'Another one of those would be nice thanks, James, I mean, sir.' He still had some difficulty remembering Cumber's promotion.

Cumber ignored the slip-up and looked incredulously at the vast array of empty bottles. 'You must have the bladder of a camel.'

Harmer grinned sheepishly, for his love of Lucozade was legendary, he felt it kept up his levels of concentration.

Noting down Harmer's further request of coffees all round for his team, both Loxley and Cumber left the room together.

*

'How was the Super?' Cumber asked, removing the saucer he had placed on top of Loxley's coffee cup in order to keep it warm. Loxley had just returned to the canteen from Bill Kemp's office where he had been giving him an account of their Oxford visit.

'I think troubled and gloomy would be how I would describe him.' Loxley sipped his coffee before taking a bite from a ham and tomato roll.

Cumber had already finished his quiche and was now munching a chocolate Penguin biscuit. 'Not surprising, those press conferences must have been tough.'

Loxley thought back to the conversation a few days earlier at Kemp's house. He had no doubt that the stress of recent events had probably reinforced his decision to retire. 'Yes, there is no question they have left a mark on him.'

It was not long before they were joined at the table by Bob Norton, who had just returned from his duties at Canon Row. Loxley gave him an update of their inquiries at St Benedict's and asked him if anything useful had materialised in the Special Incident Room. After a brief discussion about the time it took processing the amount of well-intentioned information that invariably proved to be useless, they touched on the vanity of politicians and what seemed to be their almost childlike need for attention. Norton then related to them the curious story told by Nigel Faversham. Both Loxley and Cumber listened carefully, intrigued by the possible relevance to the case.

'And he could not give you a good description?' Loxley asked.

'Unfortunately I think at the time he was too intimidated to take a good look.'

'That's a shame; certainly Galton's reaction to the incident could be significant.'

Cumber agreed. 'Yes, it is interesting that Galton felt the need to run away.'

'Is Faversham reliable?' Loxley asked. 'He seems very highly-strung, he could be keeping something back. After all, you say he was quite open in admitting that he used to cover up Galton's nocturnal adventures.'

Norton answered, 'It's difficult to be certain but it looks as if he was telling the truth about Galton and Buxton not keeping in touch after they graduated. DS Parrish got in touch with Mrs Buxton and she had no recollection of either of them ever meeting Galton.'

Loxley drained his coffee, and rose from the table. 'I suggest that patience is the key while we wait for Steve Harmer and his team to complete their work. In the meantime we should all try to get some sleep; it's been a long forty-eight hours.'

*

They all looked tired, Loxley thought, as the murder team gathered once again in the New Scotland Yard boardroom on Friday morning. He had managed to get home and see Janet on Wednesday night after returning from Oxford and again on the following evening, but sleep had not come easily to him. Even with Janet's soothing presence he had found his mind racing like a Formula One car. His overtired mental capacities had conjured up theories, motives and solutions, in ever increasing variation as he stirred restlessly in his bed.

Detective Superintendent Kemp sat stony-faced as he poured himself a glass of water. 'So we are not much further forward.'

'No, sir.' answered Bob Norton. 'On the positive side Steve Harmer and his team have now identified and tracked down all the addresses of the St Benedict's class of 76.'

Loxley took over. 'All of them are now being contacted with a view to being interviewed starting with the southern-based addresses.'

Kemp looked around the room. 'Anything else?'

'There is this peculiar incident on Westminster Bridge which Nigel Faversham related,' answered Norton. 'The downside is we have no way of knowing whether it has anything to do with the case.'

Kemp consulted his notes laid out on the table in front of him. 'Oh yes, the abusive man on the bridge. What do you think, Joe?'

Loxley looked thoughtful. 'It's not so much that Galton was abused; that must happen to politicians all the time. It's Galton's reaction to it that makes it interesting.'

Cumber agreed, 'If it happened as Faversham described, then Galton showed real fear. That has to be significant.'

Kemp nodded. 'I agree. That's what it makes it so dammed annoying that we cannot get a description.'

Cumber gave his opinion, 'Unfortunately Faversham seems to have the nervous disposition of a man who spooks easily. He was probably more frightened than Galton.'

'It certainly does not do us any favours, that's for sure,' said Kemp as he took another sip of water. 'I think in view of the Monday night pattern with the first two murders, it would be wise to swamp the streets with uniform and squad cars this coming Monday. We cannot afford another slaughter on the street while we appear to be clueless and doing nothing. Typically, now that the government have lost one of their own it has decided to open its coffers and give us unlimited funds on the budget. We should make full use of it.'

Loxley adopted a wry expression. 'Just shows that they can always find more money when it suits them, sir. A large police presence should ensure that our murderer keeps a low profile, but if he is bold enough to venture out we should be better placed to catch him.' He turned to Norton. 'I will leave you to get that operation fully mobilised, Bob, along with DS Parrish.'

Loxley glanced across at Parrish. He could tell from Parrish's slightly preoccupied manner that he was still coming to terms with Cumber's promotion. Loxley made a mental note that it might be a good idea to get the two of them working together on a joint project as soon as possible. The meeting broke up soon afterwards accompanied by the usual sound of scraping chairs and murmured conversation.

*

'We are making good progress with the southern-based graduates, sir.' said Steve Harmer, gratefully accepting Loxley's offer of yet another bottle of Lucozade. It was Friday evening and Loxley had wandered into Harmer's office to get an update. After tracking down the addresses and professions of the graduates and contact being established, Harmer was now interacting with the numerous police patrols who were interviewing the St Benedict's old boys when and where it was convenient.

Loxley asked more in hope than expectation, 'I don't suppose you have unearthed any left-handers so far that look particularly promising?'

'Not just yet, there are a few names that are out of the country on vacation or business; the good news is they are all scheduled to return in the next week or so.' Harmer crossed off a couple more names on his list. 'I think we are almost ready to spread the net wider.'

'Well, we have all the regional police across the country ready and waiting for the call when you are ready, Steve.'

They were abruptly interrupted by Bob Norton, followed into the room almost immediately by James Cumber. In an excited voice Norton declared, 'I think we may have found our man, sir.'

Both Loxley and Harmer felt a surge of adrenaline as they asked in unison, 'Who?'

Norton sounded breathless. 'Thames River police have identified a body they fished out of the Thames late last night just off Chelsea Bridge. He had some credit cards in his jacket pocket so they got his name pretty quickly. It was only after they did some digging today that they found out something very interesting.' Bob Norton could not help enjoying the expectant expressions on the faces of his fellow officers. 'They discovered that he was educated at Oxford at the same time as Buxton and Galton.'

'I take it that we are talking about a suspected suicide?' Loxley asked.

'Definitely death by drowning they say, been in the water since sometime on Tuesday.' Norton moved forward and handed Loxley a sheet of paper. With Steve Harmer peering over his shoulder Loxley scanned its contents. It read as follows.

NAME. Christopher Hitchens, PROFESSION. School-Teacher. AGE, 33. EDUCATED. Beddows College, Oxford. MARITAL STATUS. Divorced.

Cumber observed, 'Pity it's not the same college, but Beddows is in Brasenose Lane which is just around the corner from St Benedict's.'

Loxley handed the sheet back to Norton. 'It's close enough to be interesting. I want you to find out everything we can about this man, right down to his preferred aftershave if possible. It's an encouraging line of enquiry that's for sure. I will go along and give the 'Super' an update.'

*

Bobby Collins thrust his hands deep into his pockets as he walked swiftly along Columbia Road. Though the night was cold and misty with a light rain giving the pavements a liquid shine, his spirits could not be dampened as it was Friday evening and the start of the weekend. He had been pressured to work late at the printing firm in Great Eastern Street, but had not put up too much of a protest as the overtime pay came in useful. As he neared the end of the road, he became aware of some angry voices echoing on the evening breeze. Noticing that the raised voices were coming from the narrow alley on his left that opened onto Horatio Street, he glanced in the direction of the altercation. What he saw stopped him dead in his tracks.

He had immediately identified the large figure of Terry Philpot as the aggressor, but it was when he saw the small, sobbing figure of Jamie Batley wriggling in his grasp that he felt a great surge of indignation. Keeping himself flat to the wall in the dimly lit alley, Bobby eavesdropped on the argument. It seemed that the crux of the quarrel was that young Jamie was defiantly refusing to do something that an increasingly aggressive Philpot was demanding. Ignoring the dribble of cold rainwater falling on the back of his neck from the guttering above, Bobby edged closer. As the boy sobbed it was difficult to make out exactly what he was saying, but Bobby thought he heard the word 'gaffs'.

Without warning Philpot suddenly raised his hand and struck the boy heavily across the face. Instinctively an outraged Bobby Collins emerged from his hiding place and shouted, 'You can stop that straight away, you bullying bastard.'

Initially taken aback by the unexpected interruption to his brutality, Philpot paused briefly. 'Why don't you piss off and mind your own business.'

Though Philpot was the much bigger man, Bobby was fuelled by rage and stood his ground. 'Let go of the boy.'

'Make me.'

Losing all control, Bobby lunged at the big hulk in front of him. As he struggled to get both his hands around the neck of a surprised Philpot, the young boy managed to wriggle free and within an instant had disappeared into the evening mist. Having caused enough of a distraction to enable the youngster to escape the callous assaults of

Philpot, Bobby now hung on grimly as the overwhelming power of the bigger man began to get the upper hand. His felt his grip on Philpot's neck start to loosen as a series of powerful punches to his body began to have their desired effect. Eventually falling to the ground under the sheer fury of the assault, he realised he was now at Philpot's mercy. The last thing Bobby remembered was curling up into a tight ball for protection, as the big man relentlessly put the boot in.

*

There was an atmosphere of relaxed optimism in the offices of New Scotland Yard on the Saturday morning; The man who had been fished out of the Thames had given everyone connected to the case a timely boost to morale. Not wanting to miss any conclusive developments James Cumber had decided to stay overnight at New Scotland Yard, grabbing some sleep when he could and taking advantage of the shower facilities. Of course there was still a lot of work to be done in establishing a connection to the murders, but the general consensus around the place seemed to be that it could only be a matter of time.

Steve Harmer popped his head around the door. 'Anything definite on the Thames suicide, sir?'

Cumber was still finding it strange to be addressed so officially; he supposed he would get used to his new status in time. 'Not yet, Steve. But we should be hearing something soon. Bob Norton and his team have been working through the night and there's a briefing going on with DCI Loxley as we speak.'

'I have been told from on high to hold fire on the remainder of the 1976 graduates so there must be some grounds for optimism.' said Harmer, entering the room.

'That's got to be a good sign.'

They were interrupted by the sound of Cumber's phone ringing. Cumber picked up the receiver and hardly had the chance to ask who was calling, before he found himself listening to the tentative voice of what sounded like an elderly lady at the other end of the line.

'Hello, is that young Jimmy Cumber?'

Cumber thought immediately that there was something about the voice that sounded familiar. 'Yes it is.'

'It's Ethel Collins, Bobby's mum.'

Cumber answered in recognition, 'Of course it is.' Why should his friend's mum be ringing him at the station? 'What can I do for you, Mrs Collins?'

'It's about my Bobby. He was badly beaten up last night and is in the Mile End hospital.'

'Christ, where did this happen?'

'Columbia Road, when he was coming home late from work last night.'

Cumber took a little time to digest the information. Bobby was not normally one to get himself involved in violent conflict and would usually go out of his way to avoid any aggravation. 'Was he mugged?'

It was at this point that Mrs Collins sounded a bit tearful. 'That's the problem, Jimmy, he won't tell me how it happened. But he did say that he wants to talk to you about something very important.'

Cumber looked at his watch. 'Don't worry, Mrs Collins, I will pay him a visit as soon as I can.'

Cumber thoughtfully replaced the receiver.

Harmer, who had been listening to the call, asked him, 'Problem?'

'Don't know exactly. Seems my old mate has taken a beating and has ended up in the Mile End Hospital. His mum says he's got something important to tell me.'

'Better get along to him then.'

Cumber was torn by indecision. Part of him wanted to stay to hear the results of Bob Norton's investigations into the suicide suspect but Harmer's advice made up his mind. Putting on his coat Cumber said, 'Yes, Steve, you're right. If anybody asks, I have just popped out for some important business, shouldn't take too long.'

*

'So you are telling me that Hitchens was up to his neck in gambling debts,' said Loxley. He was sitting in his office with Bob Norton and Brian Parrish.

'Not so much up to his neck,' answered Norton, 'more a case of hung, drawn and quartered. From all our enquiries it seems to have cost him his marriage, his job and ultimately his life.'

'So we have established that he had more than enough reasons to throw himself off Chelsea Bridge. Unfortunately it hardly qualifies him to be our murderer.'

Norton went on, 'He was dismissed from his job at Redlands Tutorial College in Sutton under suspicious circumstances. Something to do with funds going missing earlier in the year. No charges were brought but his contract was terminated without references.'

Loxley turned to DS Parrish. 'I understand you spoke to his ex-wife this morning, Brian.'

'That's right, sir, they split up over two years ago. She confirmed that his gambling habit was totally out of control and was the major reason for the divorce.'

Loxley looked deflated. 'Regrettably it does not sound like our man. As regards his betting I take it we are not talking about a small speculation on the nags in a Mecca betting shop here?'

Norton replied, 'God no, he was a regular customer at the Ritz Casino in Piccadilly, with Blackjack being his particular favourite.'

Loxley found it hard to keep the disappointment from his voice. 'Well done lads, sounds like you have done some productive digging, but if we cannot find any links between Hitchens and our two victims by this afternoon, give Steve Harmer permission to resume his graduate enquiries.'

'I take it we should carry on with our blanket operation strategy for Monday night, sir?' asked Norton.

'I think we have no choice, Bob. In the meantime I will update the 'Super' and try to let him down gently.'

*

Cumber had a protracted search around the surrounding streets, before he finally managed to park his XR3I at the back of the Mile End Hospital in Bradwell Street. The morning was bright, chilly and cheerful, reflected in the smiling faces of the people going about their daily business. It reminded Cumber that, traditionally, Saturday mornings in the East End were always a busy and happy time. It was a chance for people to leave the house to socialise and spend some money after a long working week. Cumber entered the hospital and joined the queue at the reception desk. As he drew nearer to the attractive female receptionist, he realised with a faint nostalgic flutter that it was Susan Frampton. They had first known each other in primary school and he had had a crush on her that had lasted well into his teenage years. In those times he felt, like many of the other boys at the time, that he never had the remotest of chances with her. As he recalled, even in her early teens she had been pretty much off-limits anyway as she had a steady boyfriend. Tommy Stock was the lucky man if he remembered correctly. Not surprisingly at the time he was one of the most envied schoolboys in the area.

As he approached the desk she looked up and a faint look of recognition flashed across her striking features. 'It's Jimmy Cumber, isn't it?'

Extremely flattered that she still remembered him he managed to utter a greeting, 'Hello, Susan, long time no see.'

Flirtatiously tossing back her mane of thick black hair and flashing her large brown eyes she asked him, 'How are you keeping?'

'I'm pretty good.' Though Cumber could not help thinking to himself not half as good as she looked.

'Are you still working in the police force?'

Cumber smiled. 'Why, is it that obvious?'

She laughed. 'It's just that certain look.'

'That puts paid to my planned future career as an undercover cop.' he joked. 'How long have you worked here?'

'About a year.' She pulled a face, 'It's ok, it pays the bills.'

Cumber could not resist asking, 'Are you still with Tommy?'

A momentary look of pained recollection clouded her attractive features. 'Not any more. We split about a year ago.'

Cumber could see that the memory of the break-up was still raw. 'I am sorry to hear that.'

Looking directly into his eyes and composing herself she asked, 'What can I do for you?'

Cumber had briefly forgotten about the point of his visit. 'Oh, can you tell me what ward Bobby Collins is in?'

'That's another name I recognise from the past,' she commented, as she studied her computer screen and established that it was the Wellington Ward on the second floor.

'Thanks, Susan, it's been nice to see you again.' Cumber said.

She smiled. 'Perhaps we can meet up sometime when you are free.'

Struggling to disguise his delighted surprise, he answered, 'I would like that.'

She quickly wrote down her phone number on a note pad and handed it to him. Cumber left the reception and skipped up the two flights of stairs that led to the ward. Since Tina had left the flat he had not had either the inclination or the interest in getting himself involved with anyone else. He was not even sure why Susan had so easily rekindled a little of his romantic interest, but it certainly felt good that for once he was not lamenting the loss of Tina. Any lightening of spirit in Cumber however, was to be quickly diluted by the pitiful sight of his friend laid out in the hospital bed. With both his head and his upper body heavily bandaged, Bobby Collins had obviously taken a brutal beating.

Doing his best to disguise his anger and distress at the sight of his friend, Cumber pulled up a chair at the side of the bed. 'Well, I don't think there is much chance of you being fit for the next Spurs game.'

Collins did his best to offer a smile. The huge swelling on his face made him almost unrecognisable.

Cumber had not been prepared for this. Feeling almost physically sick with outrage he asked, 'Who did this to you, Bobby?'

Through bloated lips Bobby whispered, 'It was Philpott. He done a good job. The doctor just told me he cracked three of my ribs.'

Cumber could not suppress his reaction. 'Bastard, I had a hunch he might have had something to do with it.'

'I caught him bullying young Jamie Batley so I went in to help.'

Cumber felt his fists clenching. 'That was brave of you, Bobby. Were there any witnesses?'

'Not that I know of. It would be my word against his.'

'Don't you worry yourself, I will make sure we will get him for something.'

'I think I know what that something might be.'

Cumber looked interested. 'Go on.'

'I think it was Philpot that was forcing young Jamie to do the burglaries, that's what they were arguing about. As Jamie was crying, I am sure I heard him say 'No Gaffs, no more Gaffs'. That was just before Philpott struck him.'

Cumber knew from growing up in the area that the word 'Gaffs' was a well-used slang word for houses. Unable to contain his excitement he slapped his hand down heavily on the small drinks trolley beside him. 'Of course, it all fits.'

Rising quickly from the bench and giving Collins a comforting pat on the shoulder, Cumber said, 'Good work, Bobby, don't worry we will nail him.' Within fifteen minutes of leaving the hospital, Cumber was ringing New Scotland Yard from his parents' house in Shipton Street.

*

Loxley sat at his desk going through the known facts regarding the life of Christopher Hitchens. He was still faintly hoping that he would stumble upon some tenuous link to Buxton and Galton, but apart from the Oxford connection it was looking increasingly unlikely with every hour that passed. At this stage of the murder investigation the last thing they had needed was yet another unhelpful coincidence but that is exactly what it appeared to be. He had not long returned from one more uncomfortable meeting with the 'Super'. Thinking back to the encounter it occurred to him that he could not remember a time when he had seen his old mentor looking so downhearted and disgruntled. His thoughts were interrupted by the telephone.

'Hello, sir, it's James.'

'What's up?'

'I have just been to see Bobby Collins in the Mile End Hospital; poor sod has taken a beating from Terry Philpott, left him with three cracked ribs.'

Loxley thought back to the happy go lucky character he had met at the Spurs training ground a few months previous. 'I am sorry to hear that, James, give him my best wishes.'

'The good news is I think he has solved the burglary case. It looks like Terry Philpott has been up to his filthy tricks once again. Only this time he has been forcing a twelve year boy to do his dirty work for him.'

'Are you sure?'

Cumber sounded almost breathless, 'As sure as can be. I am around the corner from Wimbolt Street where he is living, but I'll need some back-up and a meat wagon.'

Loxley knew that Philpott could be a dangerous man. From past experience he knew the levels of brutality to which he could stoop. 'I will send a couple of uniform to assist you in a police van.' A sudden afterthought occurred to Loxley, 'Plus DS Parrish.'

Cumber fell briefly silent, consciously subduing his first instinct to protest. But the hesitation was only fleeting, for at that moment Cumber was grateful for any assistance on offer, 'Thanks, sir.'

Some thirty minutes later, Cumber, Parrish and the two uniformed officers were standing at the eastern end of Wimbolt Street. Cumber had wasted no time in bringing Parrish and the two constables up to speed. He was now instructing the uniformed officers to take up positions at the rear of the house, while he and Parrish approached the front door of No 14.

After giving the brass knocker two firm thuds, there was a noticeable delay before the door was finally opened. Cumber first had trouble recognising the world-weary figure of Mrs Batley. Looking much older than he remembered her, he also noticed what appeared to be some purple bruising on one side of her face.

'Hello, Mrs Batley,' said Cumber, flashing his badge, 'Can we come inside and talk?' She made a weak attempt to resist. 'Well, it's not very convenient.'

Cumber gently pressured her, 'It shouldn't take too long, Mrs Batley.'

With a tired look of resignation she nodded her head and they followed her into the house. As she led them into the front parlour she said over her shoulder, 'I'd heard that you worked in the force, young Jimmy, it's good to see a boy from these parts do well.'

Not sure whether she was being sarcastic, Cumber answered, 'I did wonder if you would recognise me.'

'I never forget a face, especially a handsome one like yours.'

'Thanks for the compliment; I will try not to let it go to my head.' joked Cumber. As he looked around the room he thought it very much mirrored the persona of Mrs

Batley. It looked tired, cluttered and untidy, devoid of both expectation and optimism of anything better.

Cumber got straight to the point, 'We are looking for Terry Philpott.'

Mrs Batley had her answer ready, 'He's not been here for a while, last time I saw him must have been a good week ago.'

Cumber half expected such an answer so he wasted no time in asking, 'You don't mind my partner taking a look upstairs?'

'If I did would it stop you?'

'No, but these things are always easier if we have your consent, Mrs Batley.' answered Cumber honestly.

As Parrish went upstairs Cumber pointed to her bruised face. 'That bruise looks nasty, Mrs Batley, mind telling me how you come by it?'

She instinctively put her hand to her face and said somewhat defensively, 'I fell down the stairs.'

'That was a bit careless. What if I said I didn't believe you?'

'That is your choice, young Jimmy.'

Cumber pressed on, 'Yes, we all have to make choices. Why would you choose to protect a man that does that to you, Mrs Batley?'

Before she could answer they heard voices upstairs. Cumber asked, 'Who else is in the house?'

Mrs Batley replied, 'Jamie and Kim,' before turning her head up to the ceiling and shouting, 'Don't you go frightening them.'

'I would like to speak to Jamie if that is all right with you.'

Again she said resignedly, 'Would it change anything if I said it wasn't?'

Cumber did his best to sound compassionate. 'Probably not, but one way to change your life for the better is to tell me where Philpott is.'

Parrish appeared in the doorway with the two children. Kim appeared timid and nervous as she quickly run to her mother's side, whilst Jamie stood in front of the window, a determinedly defiant expression on his face. Cumber didn't need to go too close to see the marks of abuse on his face.

'Hello young Jamie, looks like you have been in the wars.'

The boy shifted uncomfortably but remained silent.

Remembering his conversation in the hospital with Bobby, Cumber decided to up the ante. 'Did Philpott do that to you, Jamie? He is not a very nice man, is he Jamie? He likes getting you to do things that are not right, doesn't he? Things like breaking into empty houses and thieving.'

Jamie's face began to crumple as he fought against his emotions.

Cumber pressed home his advantage by pointing to Mrs Batley, 'Is that how you want to see your mum, Jamie, to be beaten up by that animal Philpott just when he feels like it?'

The boy finally disintegrated under the treatment and ran to his mum in angry tears. Looking at the three of them huddled together frightened and desolate, Cumber could feel his own sense of outrage beginning to rise. Looking at Mrs Batley directly, Cumber said, 'Why would you let such a man into your house? You deserve so much better than that.'

As she drew her two children closer to her she spoke as if the answer was obvious, 'Simple, he said he would look after us.'

For a brief moment Cumber felt his anger tinged with pity, before turning his attention back to the boy. 'It would be much better for you, Jamie, if you can return any of the stolen property.'

Mrs Batley urged her son to answer, 'Do as the policeman says, Jamie, tell him everything.'

He looked at his mum for a good few seconds before turning towards Cumber. 'He took all the money and cigarettes for himself and he used a 'Fence' to get rid of the videos and jewellery. I do have some bits left upstairs in my bedroom.'

Did you ever see this 'Fence'?'

The boy shook his head. 'No.'

It was the answer Cumber expected, Phillpot would have been careful with his contacts. Cumber suggested, 'Shall we take a look upstairs, Jamie?'

Cumber and Parish followed the boy upstairs to his bedroom. It was not a cheerful place. The room was damp and smelly, with the condensation causing the wallpaper to peel on the areas near the ceiling. Cumber noticed that for a boy's bedroom there were very few toys on display; an old battered 'Simon' computer game lay on the shelf, a Rubiks Cube on the floor, a few action figures from

Masters of the Universe. That was about it. Jamie led them over to a large cardboard box in the corner. It was mostly filled with old videos and cassette tapes. Cumber also noticed a pair of tattered gloves which he assumed had been worn in the burglaries. He looked at the boy. 'Is that it?'

Jamie thought for a moment before retrieving something from a drawer in the dresser. 'There's this, I was going to give it back to Mrs Turtle, I was trying to think of a way of doing it.' Cumber found himself holding Mr Turtle's old retirement watch with his etched initials on the back.

Cumber did his best to reassure the boy, 'This will go in your favour, Jamie, I will see to it personally.'

They were abruptly interrupted by a loud commotion that seemed to be coming from the rear of the house.

'Is that Philpott?' Cumber shouted.

Jamie almost screamed the answer, 'He was hiding in the backyard.'

Cumber and Parrish thundered down the stairs and ran through the small kitchen area to the backdoor. They soon realised that the noise was coming from beyond the wall that skirted the end of the yard. After exiting the front door and running frantically round to the back of the house, they were confronted by the sight of the two constables desperately trying to keep Philpott pinned to the floor. As Cumber approached the scene he could not help thinking of the bruising on Mrs Batley's face, the bullying of young Jamie and the sight of his lifelong friend lying in Mile End Hospital with three cracked ribs. Seeing Philpott struggling underneath the constables, he couldn't resist thudding his boot into the big man's torso. It felt good. So good he wanted to do it again and again. As he kicked him once more and was about to deliver another he suddenly felt himself being restrained from behind. It was Brian Parrish. 'What are you doing, James? Do you really want to ruin your career for this piece of shit? You are on the up, don't wreck it now.'

As Cumber stood there slowly coming to his senses, he realised that a red mist had temporarily taken hold of him. Forcing himself to take deep breaths, it didn't take long for him to see the sense in Parrish's words. Freeing himself from Parrish's grip he made a conscious effort to compose himself before saying, 'I make you right, Brian, thanks.'

Parrish replied with a slight smile, 'Count that as one I owed you.' Turning back towards Philpott, who was still cursing and swearing under the weight of the two constables, he added, 'Now let's get this big lump sorted.'

Cumber felt his tension easing as he laughed. In that moment, for the first time since he had known Parrish, he could see there was the possibility that the two of them could now go forward and work together for the good of the force.

After slipping on the handcuffs they managed to get a dazed and scowling Philpott up on his feet. He looked at Cumber in recognition. 'I have your card marked, son, don't you worry about that.'

Cumber stared back at him defiantly, 'I hope you heard that, lads, threatening a police officer with menace; that should be good for a few more years in the slammer.'

Philpott glowered back fiercely at Cumber, but chose to say no more. Cumber felt nothing but disgust and contempt for the big handcuffed man standing in front of him. 'Get him out of my sight.'

As Philpott was led out of the alley towards the police van, a small crowd had gathered to witness the drama. Cumber chose to stay behind after Parrish drove the van away in order to assure the Batley family that Jamie's case would be looked on sympathetically. When it was time to leave the house, Cumber turned to Mrs Batley and said accusingly, 'I suppose it was you that told him we were upstairs so he could do a runner?' Mrs Batley nodded slowly. In his time in the force Cumber had never understood why an abused woman would so often stay loyal to their partner, yet it was a scenario that he came up against time and time again. He tried to get the answer. 'Why try to help him. I don't understand?'

Mrs Batley looked resignedly at him. 'Beggars can't be choosers, young Jimmy; I'm not getting any younger.'

Cumber slowly shook his head. 'Believe me you can do so much better, Mrs Batley.'

As he made the short walk back to his parents' house to collect his car, he was aware that the pessimistic resignation of Mrs Batley had left him feeling slightly depressed. It had been his original intention to drive straight home, but he was unable to resist the temporary comfort that his old family home offered. Once inside the house where they had lived for so many years, his mum's cheerful welcome soon raised his spirits. Putting down the woman's magazine she was reading, she said, 'Oh, we are seeing a lot of you today. Did you sort out the little problem?'

Cumber had not been too specific about the cause for his visit when he had dropped in earlier that day, having deliberately kept it vague. 'Yes, it is all sorted.'

Though his mum could make an educated guess that the reason he was around probably had something to do with the recent spate of burglaries in the area, she had learned through the years not to pry too much into her son's police work. 'Good. Staying for a cup of tea?'

'I could murder one.' Cumber walked through to the small sitting room where his Dad was sitting in his usual chair in front of the television. He was wearing his thick-rimmed reading glasses as he checked his pools coupon against the Saturday afternoon football results on Grandstand. He glanced up from his pools coupon. 'Got two score draws so far, Jimmy, only six to go.'

Cumber laughed. 'Ever the optimist, Dad. How did Spurs get on?'

'Won 4-2,' he replied, without looking up from his coupon.

Cumber punched the air in celebration; he wondered whether Bobby Collins had heard the result yet. That would be a tonic for the poor sod, thought Cumber. He made a mental note to pay his old mate another visit in the hospital at some stage to tell him of Philpott's arrest.

As his mum entered the room with a cup of tea, his Dad threw the coupon down in exasperation. 'Two score draws short, how unlucky is that?'

His mum winked at him in conspiracy before saying, 'Never mind, pet, I suppose I can wait another week for that world cruise you promised me.'

His Dad removed his glasses and leaned back in his loose-covered armchair with a look of resignation, before seeking consolation in his Rizla cigarette papers and tobacco tin.

Cumber thought that his parents, like many of that generation who had experienced the war years, were often sustained by a stoic sense of humour. Sitting down heavily in an armchair, Cumber looked around the room that was so familiar. It could be called cosy rather than spacious, with the furniture leaning more towards comfort than elegance. Once they had exhausted the usual chat relating to individual members of the wider family and local gossip, he became aware of an empty gnawing sensation in the pit of his stomach, reminding him that he had not eaten anything since early that morning. He gratefully accepted his mum's attractive offer of some bacon and eggs, and after doing full justice to her cooking, he excused himself from the table to make a phone call in the hallway.

There was a slight underlying gloominess in Loxley's voice when he answered the phone. 'Hello, sir, it's James.'

'Hello, James, I have just been talking to Brian Parrish, he says your mission was a success.'

'Yes, hopefully Philpott will be off our streets for some time to come. He is one nasty piece of shit. Bit worried about the young boy, though, I hope we can make sure he is protected from the courts.'

Loxley reassured him, 'The boy is a minor, James. As long as he has no previous there should not be a problem.'

'I certainly hope so, that family have been through enough already.'

'Did you find DS Parrish useful?'

Cumber briefly thought back to his loss of control and Parrish's well timed intervention. 'Very much so, sir.'

Loxley liked the answer. 'Good, well at least we have one case solved.'

'From your tone I am taking it that the Thames suicide was a false dawn?'

'You take it correctly. The man's personal life was one big disaster. He was an inveterate gambler with a mountain of debt. Apart from Oxford we could find no further connection between him and the two victims. It's back to the class of 76 I'm afraid.'

'I take it that Steve Harmer is chomping at the bit to resume his investigations.'

'His team are back on the case as we speak.'

'I was wondering, sir, if there was any chance I could take tomorrow morning off to see Bobby in the hospital?'

Loxley answered immediately. 'Of course. In fact, I can do better than that. As a recognition of both you and Bobby's part in cracking the Bethnal Green burglaries you can have the rest of the weekend off. Obviously if there are any developments in the London murder case we will want you in straight away. Otherwise I will see you bright and early on Monday morning. It promises to be a busy day.'

About to issue his usual protest an image of Susan Frampton came into Cumber's mind and he found himself answering, 'If you are sure you can manage without me, sir, that would be great.'

'Positive. Enjoy the weekend.'

Again caught a little bit by surprise by his emerging feelings for Susan, Cumber slowly replaced the phone. Before driving back to his Shoreditch flat, Cumber stopped by at Mrs Turtle's house to hand back her husband's watch. Seeing the look of joy on her face when he handed it over reminded him once again of why he found the often challenging and difficult career of a police detective so richly rewarding.

*

Marcus Varney made sure he could not be seen as he peeped furtively through a gap in the curtain. Initially he had not been too worried when he had heard the chime of the doorbell, but now he felt his pulse quicken considerably at the sight of a uniformed police officer standing on the doorstep. Varney held his breath as the constable remained at the door for what seemed an eternity, before he finally slipped something through the letterbox and turned away. After waiting for another minute, Varney rushed to the door and picked up a letter. He saw it was addressed to his friend, Francis Barnaby; he allowed himself a small sigh of relief before ripping it open.

CHAPTER NINE

SLAUGHTER IN THE SQUARE MILE

It was Monday evening and there was an unmistakable feeling of tension inside the offices of New Scotland Yard. The dark winter streets of London had been flooded with police squad cars and uniformed beat coppers, stretching from Bishopsgate in the east to Chelsea in the west. The Metropolitan police were taking no chances. They simply could not afford another high profile killing while the investigation was still at such a critical stage. If the murderer was still out there planning another Monday night slaying, then they were doing everything in their power to deter him. Chief Superintendent Bill Kemp was pacing the floor of the control room, mentally willing the clock forward to Tuesday morning, whilst all the time dreading a call would come through at any moment to report a third victim. On one side of the room Bob Norton and his assistants were working in close co-operation with a row of seated telephone operators. These operators were the main point of contact with the massive police operation that was taking place on the streets.

Joe Loxley entered the room carrying a tray of coffee from the canteen. 'Thought you could do with a proper cup of coffee, sir.' Loxley always made a point of addressing his old colleague correctly within earshot of subordinate officers.

Kemp looked at him gratefully. 'Thanks, Joe. I have been drinking gallons of the machine stuff, I must be as high as a kite.'

Loxley looked towards the row of heads adorned with earphones that were diligently taking calls. 'Well, if our man is going to have the nerve to strike again we will probably be hearing something in the next hour or so.'

Kemp looked up at the clock on the wall for the umpteenth time. It was approaching eleven o'clock. He felt he needed some positive reassurance. 'We are definitely sure that all the graduates who lived and worked in the South Eastern area of the country have been seen.'

'Absolutely', Loxley answered. 'Every single one of them have produced alibis as to their whereabouts on the night of the murders,' but then he added a caveat. 'That is all except four who are abroad either on holiday or business.' He anticipated the next question forming on Kemp's lips and added quickly, 'They are all expected to be back in the country next week.'

Kemp took a deep swig of his coffee. 'Oh, that tastes good.' After a thoughtful pause he went on, 'The ironic thing about the class of 76 is that if our theory is correct, then in all likelihood any possible future victims in that list could be in there with the murderer.'

'That is why it has been a bit tricky when talking to these people,' Loxley answered. 'After first establishing their innocence, we have had to achieve the delicate balance of telling them to be vigilant without alarming them unduly.'

Kemp rubbed his chin reflectively. 'I suppose some of them would be more easily spooked than others. Have you got a list of the four that are returning to the country next week?'

Loxley pulled a sheet of paper from the inside pocket of his jacket and handed it to Kemp.

Scanning the list with a keen eye, Kemp observed, 'All high fliers as you would expect, an esteemed physicist, a top executive at a pharmaceutical firm, an eminent surgeon at Bart's Hospital and a Harley Street GP.'

'Yes,' Loxley agreed. 'They are all a good advertisement for an Oxford education.'

Kemp held the paper up. 'Mind if I keep this?'

'No problem, Steve Harmer has plenty of copies.'

Bob Norton broke away from the group of operators to pour himself a coffee. 'Nothing much happening, Bob?' Kemp asked him.

'Apart from a few disruptive drunks on the streets it has been an exceptionally quiet night so far.'

'Not the quiet before the storm, I hope,' Kemp replied. 'I want this next hour to go as peacefully as an afternoon siesta.'

'Nothing from Cumber or Parrish, Bob?' Loxley asked. The two young detectives had each been keen to join in with the patrols, rather than fret ineffectually back at New Scotland Yard.

Norton shook his head. 'Not a dicky-bird from either of them, sir.'

Kemp crossed his fingers. 'Let's hope it stays that way.'

*

At the southern end of Southwark Bridge, Cumber got out of the squad car and walked towards the late night hot dog stall. There was a cold breeze whistling up the Thames but it felt good to give his legs a stretch. It had been a strange evening. The police operation had been exciting, but not because of anything actually happening, more in anticipation of what might happen. He ordered three hot dogs, walked back to the car, and handed two of them to the police officers sitting inside. 'There you go, that's the best offer you two are going to get tonight.' As they seized on the foodstuff hungrily, Cumber took a bite of his own hot dog, and walked a little way towards the centre of the bridge. Cumber appreciated the peace and quiet of the eerily empty streets. There was something about the Thames late at night that never failed to fascinate him. Its forbidding inky blackness and the gentle gurgling swirl of its currents somehow vividly evoked the fact that it had always been there - flowing timelessly through the centuries. Lost in reverie his thoughts turned to the Batleys and Bobby Collins. He had managed to fit in a visit to the hospital on the Sunday afternoon to inform Bobby of the successful arrest of Philpott. His friend had offered to testify in court in order to ensure that justice was done, but Cumber had firmly assured him that it would not be necessary. He knew the type of people that Philpott was involved with and there was no way he would have risked exposing his old mate to further danger. He thought back to the arrest of Philpot and his own loss of control. With hindsight he realised that he had allowed the case to get far too close to him and become personal. It was not professional and he really did owe Brian Parrish big time for surprisingly stepping in and saving him from himself.

Almost imperceptibly his thoughts drifted to Susan Frampton. On his visit to Bobby he had hoped to see her at the hospital but disappointingly she had not been on duty behind the reception desk. When he returned home he had wasted little time in phoning her home number and without hesitation she had agreed to see him that evening. They had dined at the *Venus Steak House* in Bethnal Green Road and enjoyed a pleasant evening together. The conversation had been light with occasional nostalgic anecdotes about old schoolteachers and fellow classmates. Looking back he realised that on a personal level they had both been very careful to avoid any mention of their recent painful break-ups. Afterwards he had driven her home and kissed her goodbye at the door. Though he felt a strong attraction for her, he had made a conscious decision to take it slowly. In view of his recent painful experience with Tina, the last thing he needed right now was to make a fool of himself over yet another woman. The distant chime of Big Ben striking 1 o'clock brought him back gently into the moment. Suddenly feeling colder in the strengthening breeze, he pulled the lapels of his coat around his neck and quickly walked back to the car.

*

Qantas Flight QF120 took off from Singapore Changi Airport and quickly reached an altitude of 10,000 feet before banking gently and setting its nose in a northerly direction. As the aeroplane continued to gain height, Francis Barnaby sat in his seat by the window gazing thoughtfully out at the fleecy white clouds. His holiday in Perth, Australia, had been everything he had wished for. The break from his stressful job as a surgeon in Bart's Hospital had been well overdue. He could not remember the last time he had felt so relaxed. He had stayed at his Uncle Bill's holiday apartment overlooking the Swan River Estuary. Thinking of the great time he had enjoyed, it now seemed ridiculous that he had been turning down his uncle's invitation to go visit him for what had seemed like years. In that time he had never seemed able to find a suitable time to leave his job behind for a few weeks. Also if he was being honest with himself, he had never felt comfortable at the thought of leaving his London house empty for such a lengthy period. That was why it had been such a stroke of luck to have bumped into his old university friend Marcus Varney in his local pub. The two of them had been as thick as thieves back in their wild Varsity days and they had still been talking about those old times in Oxford when the barman had rung the bell for last orders. Though he had not seen him for the best part of ten years, he knew that Marcus - or 'Varnish' as he had affectionately called him at Oxford - had gone into the armed forces, having heard and read all about his heroic exploits in the Falklands War some four years earlier. He remembered being a little surprised when Marcus had told him that he had now left the forces and was pursuing a career in advertising. After the pub closed he had invited Marcus back to his house for a coffee and they had continued their conversation long into the early hours. At one point he told Marcus of his uncle's generous invitation to visit him in Australia for a month and of his own reluctance to leave the house empty in that time. He also mentioned that he had thought about renting it out but it needed to be someone he could trust. It was then that Marcus informed him that though based in York, his job often brought him to London for weeks at a time. It had seemed to be the perfect solution. It was almost worth the thumping hangover he had woken up with the next morning. The whole drunken episode had brought back memories of the last days in their time at Oxford. In that period, Marcus had been in danger of letting his drinking get seriously out of control. Going by his experience in the pub that evening, it seemed his old friend was still more than capable of sinking a considerable amount of alcohol.

Barnaby took another sip of water before settling back in the airplane seat and resting his eyes. Try as he might he could never seem to sleep on an aeroplane. The constant drone of the engine and the occasional realisation that he was 30,000 feet up in the air combined to ruin any chance of meaningful slumber. He chose instead to visualise and relive the routine of his days back in Perth. His Uncle Bill had emigrated some twenty years before; armed with some capital to invest, he had made it big in the mineral industry. The holiday apartment had reflected that success, with its prime location being on the banks of the Swan River. Francis had pretty much been given the run of the place, with his uncle making only an occasional visit to check how his nephew was getting on. This had suited Francis. With all the demands and stress of Bart's Hospital, a bit of splendid isolation had been just what the doctor ordered. He had found Perth to be a large, clean, modern city, with the added bonus that it was invariably bathed in brilliant sunshine with a vivid blue sky. Each idyllic day had melted seamlessly into the next as he spent most of his time either strolling in Kings Park or sipping a cool beer at a riverside cafe overlooking the river. His only reading material had been a selection of hugely enjoyable Tom Sharpe paperbacks, which he had borrowed from a friend. Leaning back comfortably in his seat, there was a brief whimsical moment when a part of him wished he could have extended his stay in Australia. Deciding to put these fanciful thoughts to one side, he slipped on the earphones and chose a Roxy Music selection. He closed his eyes as the melodious intro of *More Than This* filled his personal airwaves.

*

Loxley dropped two slices of bread into the toaster and took another sip of his coffee. Though it was just before seven-thirty on the Tuesday morning, he felt encouragingly fresh and awake. He had eventually got home in the early hours feeling both exhausted and relieved that the Monday evening had passed without incident. The house had been dark and empty as Janet was away visiting her parents. Once in bed nature had mercifully kicked in and he had managed to get a few hours of desperately needed sleep. He had been most grateful, for since the second murder in Westminster he had struggled to get any rest at all. In all that time he had found his mind constantly turning over the possibilities and circumstances of the murders, replaying over and over again what he had seen at the crime scenes. He had tried to draw on his own personal experience of similar cases he might have dealt with in the past. He would normally do this in order to help him establish the likely behavioural and personality traits of the unknown perpetrator. Unfortunately, the brazen manner and ruthless efficiency of the killings in this case had made them unique in his experience. Now thinking with a clearer head, he tried logically to put together what he knew so far. There was no doubt that the murders had been planned meticulously, with both victims appearing to be selected and stalked. The crime scenes had been left neat and orderly, even down to the careful laying down of the victim. The fact that there were no clues left at the scene meant the murderer took special care to escape detection - in short a man who was intelligent, controlled and organised. This would normally point to a professional killer but Loxley was not convinced. The modus-operandi bothered him. In his experience, slashing throats was not the most-favoured method of dispatch for a contract killer.

Loxley's thoughts were interrupted by the bread popping out of the toaster. As was always the case when Janet was away on one of her visits to Bournemouth, the house felt far too barren and quiet. Loxley turned on his small transistor radio before buttering his toast and picking up the *Daily Mail* from the doormat. He did not have to search too thoroughly to find an article referring to the murders. This one was about the Oxford connection and the supposedly hidden culture of decadence that lay underneath its civilised façade. Loxley smiled to himself. It was rubbish of course, but you could always rely on some dedicated newshound to find another angle to a good story. Loxley turned to the sports pages which were still full of the Mike Tyson demolition of Trevor Berbick in a heavyweight title fight in Las Vegas over the weekend. He put the newspaper down and turned up the radio to hear the harmonious voices of Peter Gabriel and Kate Bush singing *Don't Give Up*.

He found his thoughts turning back once more to the case. Even though disappointingly they had not found any potential suspect amongst the graduates living in the south of the country, he consoled himself with the thought that it did not mean that their man was not among the names that remained. In these days of motorways to every part of the country and fast reliable cars, the ability to move quickly from one end of the country to the other was now much easier than it had ever been in his memory. Draining the remainder of his coffee, he turned off the transistor, put on his thermal jacket and headed for the door. He felt the next

24 hours were going to be every bit as demanding as in the previous days; he was up for the challenge.

*

Simon Llewelyn strode purposefully into the new cutting edge dealing room of DJZ Capital. As he took his seat at the trading desk, he was greeted with the usual loud banter and friendly abuse from his fellow traders. Ever since the advent of 'Big Bang' a month earlier, it had been like this, stimulating and exciting, with everyday bringing a different challenge. The Thatcher government's de-regulation of the City of London had opened the flood gates to overseas competition and investment, banishing forever the old insular gentlemen's club that had mysteriously existed in the square mile for so long. Along with this liberation came the opportunity for young ambitious men with energy and quick-wittedness to flourish, where even a lack of education needn't be an obstacle. As Llewelyn glanced around at his youthful work colleagues on the dealing desk, he realised he was very much in the minority in having an Oxbridge education. Already in his early thirties, he was also very aware that in terms of age he was already looked on by the others as one of the senior citizens. He rebooted his trading screen and it slowly twinkled into life, arranging itself in attractive orderly columns of blue and red. As he studied his listed securities and overnight position, he realised he had been more than a little fortunate in going home with a small profit from the night before. The previous day's electronic trading had been particularly volatile, fast paced and unpredictable, the sort of day where you often made seat-of-the-pants decisions for no other reason than that it just felt right.

How lucky had he been that day when his cousin Nigel had suggested he should have an interview at a stock-jobbing company where he knew one of the senior partners. This suggestion had come about after a particularly upsetting discussion with his parents about the alarming lack of direction in his life. He remembered the job interview process being ridiculously easy, especially when he had mentioned that he possessed a modicum of computer skills. That was just what the company had wanted to hear, as it was widely anticipated in the City that there would very soon be a move away from the face-to-face dealing towards more on-screen trading. He also vaguely recalled at the time of the interview there being some mention that the planned de-regulation of the city would probably lead to a series of amalgamations between Stock Exchange companies and banks in order to compete with the competition from foreign companies. What he could not have foreseen was the impact this wave of mergers and acquisitions would have on city salaries. Within the year he had been more than pleasantly surprised to find his original starting salary of £25,000 a year swiftly quadrupling to six figures. Not that the money was ever overly important to him or even his main motivation, as unlike most of his colleagues on the desk, he had been fortunate in having prosperous parents. What had been much more valuable to him was finding a place where he felt he fitted in and could be himself. For as long as he could remember he had always felt a bit of an outsider within his social status, uncomfortable with the established order and rebellious in what was expected of him. As a result he had failed to stay the course as a law student after leaving Oxford with mediocre grades. Now with the benefit of a more mature hindsight, he realised that throughout his twenties he had been a 24 carat waster, spending most of his time travelling around Europe and shamefully sponging off his disappointed parents. The most demoralising realisation in that time was that though he had been allowed to pretty much do what he had wanted, it had still not come close to making him feel remotely happy or content.

Now sitting on the trading desk at DJZ Capital, he felt that he was in a place where he belonged. For the first time in his life he felt fulfilled and comfortable in his own skin. This happy state had been largely due to the fact that he had made the rather pleasing discovery that he possessed a natural flair for electronic trading. Totally unexpectedly he had finally found something in which he could excel. He looked across at his colleagues and not for the first time felt a modicum of affection. It occurred to him that many of his colleagues would have been equally at home as bookies on a racecourse or working on a market stall in Petticoat Lane. He found their uncomplicated approach to life infectious and their lack of pretension refreshing. They in turn had appeared to appreciate his eccentric individualism and obvious lack of arrogance born of privilege. Like a close-knit family there were occasions when arguments and disagreements would erupt, and there were times when some of them could be far too egotistical and aggressive - especially after a few too many glasses of Bollinger. Nonetheless despite these eruptions, the slate would invariably be wiped clean the next day with no grudges held and all upsets forgotten. Above all, the single most overriding factor that bonded them all so closely was the shared realisation that they had all found themselves to be in the right place at what appeared to be the right time. Llewelyn felt the usual surge of adrenaline when the lights on his trading phone flashed – it was a chance to make some profit.

*

Qantas flight QF120 slowly dropped altitude as it flew over the channel. Francis Barnaby opened his eyes and rubbed them vigorously. As was usually the case on the rare occasions he had previously endured long haul flights, he had totally failed to get any sleep. The sleepless flight had left him with the feeling of being slightly detached from what was going on around him - as if being enclosed in a room confined by glass windows. He glanced out of the plane to catch a glimpse of the chalky cliffs of Dover glaring a brilliant white in the bright winter sunshine. At least he did not have to report to Bart's Hospital for a couple of days. He had rung his secretary on the day before he left Perth in order to confirm his return date. She had been at pains to reassure him that the hospital had not imploded in his absence, but he had been puzzled when she mentioned that someone from New Scotland Yard had phoned asking of his whereabouts. When she had asked the officer the reason for the call he had replied it was just a line of enquiry and nothing to worry about. However, the officer did make a point of leaving a number for him to ring when he returned from Australia. He had duly written it down on the back of a Foster's beer mat as his secretary read it out over the phone. Alarmed it might be something to do with the house he had rung his home number after the call but could get no immediate reply from Marcus. Much to his relief he did finally manage to get through to him some hours later. After explaining the reason for his call, Marcus had soon put his mind at rest as he assured him that all was under control and there was nothing to worry about. As he gazed out over the green fields of southern England the light flashed on instructing him to fasten his seat belt. He comforted himself with the thought that he would soon be arriving home and falling gratefully into his bed.

*

Simon Llewelyn felt a ball of rolled up paper bounce off his head followed swiftly by a question. 'Hey Simone, fancy some lunch?' Llewelyn chose to ignore the deliberate feminisation of his name. He had got used to it by now, especially from Steve Laker. He particularly liked Steve. The two of them had quickly formed a warm friendship despite their completely different upbringing. Steve Laker in common parlance was as common as muck, but he was also open, friendly, genuine and as sharp as a tack.

Llewelyn covered the mouthpiece of his phone. 'Where do you fancy?'

'I think it's got to be the *Arby.*' Laker was referring to the *Arbitrage,* a popular watering hole situated in Throgmorton Avenue.

'Sounds good to me.'

One of the other traders on the desk could not resist a teasing comment. 'Mind you two don't get arrested and get carted off in a meat wagon.'

Llewelyn could only grin resignedly as the remark provoked a loud burst of good-natured jeering from those assembled on the dealing desk. The trader was making a reference to the interview he had been requested to give to the police the previous week. He managed to respond when the taunting died down. 'If that happens I will make sure that I put you in the frame by naming you all as my accomplices.'

He had been more than a little surprised to receive a phone call from the police relating to the recent London murders. He had not bumped into either Rupert Buxton or Timothy Galton since the Seventies, though he was obviously well aware of Galton's high profile career as a politician. Informing the police of this fact, they had seemed satisfied with his answer. He had obviously been curious that two of his old St Benedict's colleagues had met such tragic untimely ends, but he had in no way up to that point attributed the murders to the university connection. He surmised that the two men had moved in worlds that were completely different from his, so he had vaguely assumed that they had got immersed in some dark murky waters and found themselves out of their depth. When the police had asked him where he had been on the night of the Galton murder it had been easily verified by Catherine's parents, as they were all having dinner that evening at his Barbican flat. It had been a special dinner because it was the night that he and Catherine had announced their engagement. Llewelyn reminded himself that Catherine was another good reason to thank his cousin Nigel. She had already been working at DJZ as an analyst when he had joined the company and they had started dating almost immediately.

The interview with the police had ended friendly enough with the interrogating officer getting him to sign an interview sheet and requesting he should get in contact if anything should occur to him relating to the case. Llewelyn was snapped out of his thoughts as another ball of paper bounced off his head. He looked up just in time to see the back of Steve Laker retreating out of the trading floor.

Looking back over his shoulder Laker shouted, 'Last one at the *Arby* has to buy the final two drinks.' Simon Llewelyn rose from his chair and shook his head with a wry smile. He had never imagined that work could be so much fun.

*

Joe Loxley could not remember the last time he had been able to sit at his desk for such a long uninterrupted period without distractions. He had his small transistor radio tuned in to Radio 1 and was listening to a selection of topical chart tunes as he foraged through the pile of paperwork relating to the 'London Murders' as they were now known. He was once again looking through the remaining names and occupations on the class of 76 file that had yet to be eliminated. By using a combination of his instincts and experience, he was trying to prioritise some of the more likely suspects in an attempt to fast track the investigation. Humming along with *Thorn in my Side* by the Eurythmics he scanned the handful of names he had written in his notebook after going through the list. Included were a few farmers, some military men, even a manager of a fitness centre. After giving it some additional thought, he tore the page out of his notebook before leaving his office to see Steve Harmer.

*

By the time the taxi turned left off High Holborn into Red Lion Street, Francis Barnaby could barely keep his eyes open. The journey from Heathrow had been mercifully free of heavy traffic and the taxi driver had considerately kept his conversation down to a minimum. Barnaby showed his gratitude by offering the driver a generous tip after being dropped off outside his house in Bedford Row. As the satisfied cabbie drove off Barnaby turned towards his house, pleased to see it was still standing. A Georgian house with its front door framed by two rather grand pillars, he always felt a reassuring wave of affection whenever he returned to it. He had already noticed that his black Land Rover was absent from its normal parking place at the front of the house. This did not alarm him unduly as he had given permission for Marcus to keep it running while he was away. Stepping into the main hall he was gratified to see that the house had been kept meticulously tidy. Good old 'Varnish' he thought to himself, just what you would expect from an ex-military man. There was no doubt that Marcus's stint in the armed forces had been good for him, for from what he could remember back in the varsity days he had always been an untidy bugger.

Putting his cases down, he noticed a holdall placed just outside the spare room on the ground floor where Marcus had slept. Marcus had mentioned in the phone call that he would not be hanging around for long once Barnaby had returned. True to his word it looked like his old friend was already packed and ready to make his departure. He briefly entered the kitchen and poured himself a glass of water. He took one exhausted look at the pile of letters that Marcus had presumably stacked on the table, before wearily trudging up to his bedroom on the first floor. As far as he was concerned at that precise moment, not only the letters but indeed the whole world could wait. After barely summoning up the energy to undress, he sank blissfully onto the bed and within seconds was deep in slumber.

*

Steve Harmer waited patiently on the phone. He had been going through Joe Loxley's list of priority suspects and some of them had opened up some promising lines of enquiry. There had been three names on the list that had connections with the armed services and he was now completing what he thought would be a routine call to Aldershot Barracks.

A woman's voice crackled faintly on the line, 'Can I help you, sir?'

The poor sound quality of the line felt like it was more New Zealand than Aldershot. 'Good afternoon, this is DS Harmer from Scotland Yard. I am making enquiries regarding a Marcus Varney stationed with 3 Para?'

Responding to her request to spell the name out, he heard the woman reply, 'Could you please hold for a minute, sir?'

'No problem.' Harmer tapped his fingers on the desk as he waited for a further two minutes before the crackly voice returned.

'I'm sorry, sir we have no one listed with that name.'

Harmer rolled his eyes to the ceiling as he wondered silently to himself why you could never seem to get the staff nowadays. 'I think you will find that he should be listed somewhere, I have him indexed on the 1984 register which I have in front of me.'

Once more the crackly voice requested him to hold. Finally, after a further couple of minutes the voice came back, 'Hello, sir, we have found the name. Marcus Varney was medically discharged in April 1985.'

Harmer sat upright in his chair. 'Does it say what the problem was?'

'Nothing has been detailed, sir, though he was discharged with distinction.'

Harmer looked at the notes in front of him. 'I take it that must be a reference to his outstanding service in the Falklands.'

'Yes, sir.'

'Do you have his last known address?'

The line crackled irritatingly for a further thirty seconds before the voice announced, 'Number 9 Skeldergate, York.'

Harmer noted the address and thanked the lady, before putting the phone down. Taking a few seconds to absorb the possibilities of this new information he picked up the phone again and rang the headquarters of Yorkshire Police, Northern Division.

*

'Where we off to tonight, Simone?' It was the usual question that Steve Laker would be asking as the day's trading drew to a close.

Simon Llewelyn was studying the closing positions on his screen and he liked what he saw. It had been another profitable day for the desk. 'I have to see someone at the *City of London Club* in Old Broad Street; you can tag along if you like.'

Laker pulled a face. To him the club was far too old school; he could think of much livelier places to spend the evening. 'How long you going to be?'

'About an hour; after that the world is my lobster.'

'Meet us in the 'Temple of Doom.' Laker was referring to the *Mithras* wine bar, a popular drinking location situated in a side street off Cheapside.

'I will be there.'

Laker went on enthusiastically, 'We can go on to the *Arbitrage* afterwards, it should be rocking by then.' Noisily he rounded up his fellow traders on the desk, before they all exited the trading floor in animated conversation.

Llewelyn thought to himself that for the past few weeks it had been pretty much the same routine on most evenings. Every night had seemed to be an excuse for a party, with the excited young traders eager to celebrate and let off steam. Their trading team were known within the company as the 'Marzipan Set,' because they were regarded as too young for partnership level which was termed as the icing, but rated highly enough to be above the cake which represented the majority of plodders without serious prospects. As a consequence they had been generously rewarded financially in order to ward off head hunters from rival companies. One of these head hunters was the reason for Llewelyn's rendezvous in the *City of London Club* that evening. Though he did not have the slightest intention of leaving DJZ he did like to keep his finger on the pulse regarding his market value. Besides which, he found it all tremendously flattering and a useful boost to his ego. After making his now routine phone call to Catherine telling her he would be late home, he hurriedly grabbed his overcoat and left the office.

*

Detective Inspector Ben Hazlewood of the Yorkshire Constabulary, Northern Division, cursed silently to himself as he was forced to slow the car and take his place in the growing queue behind a chugging tractor. He was on the A168 Thirsk road on his way to York after being instructed to make a detour on his way home in order to make a house call. As he sat there looking out at the cold rain and darkening skies, he could not help thinking it was bloody inconvenient, especially as the directive had come via a telephone call from that lot in New Scotland Yard. After leaving the police station in Northallerton, his police radio had burst into life to give him the glad tidings. He was to pick up a PC Tom Wallington at York Police Station in the Fulford Road before going on to an address in Skeldergate. It seemed it had something to do with the two recent murders in London which had been making all the headlines. You would have thought that they would have sent up one of their own super-sleuths instead of getting North Yorkshire Division to do all the legwork. It would often be the case that a county chap did all the hard-grind only for the London lot to come in and reap the benefit when the case was close to being cracked. The 'Yorkshire Ripper Case' on which he had worked diligently for months back in the early Eighties, had been a perfect example of Scotland Yard being called in at the death as if they were the only people clever enough to solve it.

He gave a little cheer as the man driving the tractor finally acknowledged the huge queue that was forming behind him and moved off the road to let them pass. Many years ago in the early part of his career, he'd had the misfortune to be posted for six months with the Met in

London. He had hated every second of it. He could not get used to the sheer size and diversity of London, not to mention the phony role-playing and clever-dick conceit. He remembered he had counted down the days to his return so that he could get back to the grassy fells and wide valleys of his native Yorkshire. Above all he preferred his own people - at least you knew where you were with them. He also resented the fact that everything that was considered to be so important to the country was based in London. From Scotland Yard and Whitehall to the Houses of Parliament and Buckingham Palace, it all seemed so stacked against the north of the country. Now it even looked as if the bloody economy was booming down there compared to everywhere else. Though he was far from left-wing in his politics, even he harboured serious doubts as to whether the Tories' radical policies were ever going to be of benefit to anyone living north of Nottingham. His Rover SDI 3500SE V8 accelerated smoothly as the road opened up appreciably in front of him; he calculated he could be in York in thirty-five minutes given a clear run.

*

Loxley had needed no second invitation when James Cumber had popped his head around the door of his office and invited him to sample the fish and chips in the canteen. He had spent a long day repeatedly mulling over small-print data and detailed paper work; he felt he needed to get away from his desk and have a good stretch.

After being served at the counter, Loxley and Cumber carried their trays towards a table already occupied by Bob Norton and Brian Parrish. 'Room for a little one, Bob?' asked Cumber cheerfully as he squeezed in beside him.

Pointing to the empty plate in front of him Norton replied, 'Yes, okay, we are all but finished here.'

Loxley parked himself next to Parrish before asking more in conversation than in hope, 'Don't suppose there are any promising developments, Bob?'

'Nothing yet though we haven't quite finished confirming the alibis of those with the left-handed signatures.'

'It certainly won't do any harm to make doubly sure they are all watertight.'

'A few of the alibis appeared to merit a little further digging and we've since gone over them again. At least DS Parrish has.'

A look from Loxley was enough to prompt an answer from Parrish. 'Have almost finished checking them again, sir, but I would not hold out too much hope, unfortunately they are all looking to be rock solid.'

'Shame,' said Cumber.

Parrish went on, 'On the positive side DS Harmer has told us he is following up on some interesting leads.'

Thinking of the recent list of names he had passed on to Steve Harmer earlier in the day, Loxley replied, 'That sounds encouraging. If anyone can come up with something crucial to crack this case I would put my money on the old 'Bloodhound.'

Not long afterwards Norton and Parrish left the table, leaving Loxley and Cumber to tuck eagerly into their fish and chips. Loxley had noted with satisfaction the more relaxed body language that appeared to exist between Cumber and Parrish. He could not help commenting, 'Do I detect a little easing of tension between you and DS Parrish?'

Cumber's forkful of chips was paused halfway to his mouth as he answered, 'Let's just say that we understand each other a little better.'

Loxley was pleased to hear it. 'Good. It can only be for the benefit of the team. I know he can be a surly cuss at times but I think he is a good copper; I would not want to lose him.'

They ate in silence for a while before Cumber, with a slightly concerned look on his face, asked, 'Are you still confident that the murderer is in the class of 76?'

Shaking some more vinegar on the remainder of his chips Loxley answered, 'I can't say I was ever overly confident; sometimes you just have to go with your gut feeling.'

'Where does the investigation go if the St Benedict's connection is a dead end?'

Looking serious Loxley took a swig of his tea before answering, 'That is something I have been asking myself and if you want the truth the answer is I just don't know.'

Pushing away his empty plate, it was Cumber's turn to look serious. 'You don't think that there is a danger we've focused too much on the St Benedict's lead?'

'Possibly we have,' Loxley answered thoughtfully. 'But I don't think so. As I say it is just a feeling but I sense we are getting close.'

'Hearing you say that gives me a tad more confidence than I was actually feeling a minute ago.'

After washing down his last mouthful of battered cod with a swig of tea, Loxley managed only the slightest of smiles. 'Let's hope for both our sakes that my instincts are correct and your confidence in them is not misplaced.'

*

As DI Ben Hazlewood slowly brought the car to a halt outside a block of modern flats in Skeldergate, York, he noticed that they were parked directly opposite the *Lady Anne Middleton's Hotel.* It was an establishment he was well familiar with. He and his wife Joan had used it on the odd occasion in the past when they had fancied a weekend break in York. He made a mental note that they should do it again sometime. He had made up good time after the holdup with the tractor and had been pleased that PC Tom Wallington had been ready and waiting when he had arrived at the Fulford Road police station. Hazlewood had vaguely recognised the young police constable standing before him, but this would not have surprised him as in the course of his daily duties he would have had dealings with most of the North Yorkshire Constabulary at some time or other.

Before they exited the car, Wallington handed him two A4 sheets, one of which was the interview sheet while the other contained some brief details of the man they had been sent to question. Hazlewood first noted approvingly that Marcus Varney was a Falklands hero, for he had always held a great admiration for the armed services. He then read of the possibly significant Oxford connection in the London murders and the recent discovery of Varney's medical discharge. In the small print there was an explanation of the significance of the signing of the interview sheet to establish if the interviewee was left-handed. Alighting from the car, they walked briskly towards the entrance of the flats as a steady flow of freezing rain continued to fall out of the inky black sky.

He pressed the buzzer displaying the number nine and there was a short delay before they heard a woman's voice on the entry phone speaker. Hazlewood introduced himself, 'Hello, this is the Yorkshire police, does a Marcus Varney still reside at this address?'

Hazlewood detected a concerned tremor in the woman's voice as she enquired, 'Is he in trouble?'

He was quick to reassure her, 'Not at all, we just need to speak to him in order to help us with our enquiries. Can we come up Miss…?' He left the question hanging.

There was a noticeable pause before she answered. 'Sorry, I am Pamela Varney, Marcus's wife; please come up.'

They were greeted at the door by a woman Hazlewood judged to be somewhere in her late twenties. After displaying his ID she led the two policemen into a small sitting room. 'I must tell you that Marcus no longer lives here as we split up about six months ago.'

Before Hazlewood could respond a man entered the room from the kitchen area. There was an awkward silence as a slightly flustered Pamela Varney introduced him. 'Sorry, this is Bob Turner, he is a good friend.' The man smiled self-consciously but did not venture too far into the room.

After his initial surprise at the man's sudden appearance Hazlewood sat down on a small divan alongside PC Wallington who opened his notebook. Glancing around the room, Hazlewood thought that the décor looked a little like a showroom from a DIY store, unnaturally free of clutter with plenty of light-coloured wood on show.

Accepting the offer of a cup of tea he asked, 'When was the last time you saw Marcus?'

She paused on her way to the kitchen. 'It must be a couple of months at least since he came to see our daughter Melanie.'

As if on cue a small girl entered the room carrying a colouring book. Mrs Varney walked towards her and gave her a reassuring hug. Momentarily wondering who else might suddenly show up in the flat Hazlewood got back to his questions. 'Is it unusual for him to leave his visits for so long?'

'Not recently. Marcus and I have had big problems so it is probably for the best. He has spoken to Melanie a couple of times on the phone in that time. I believe he is down at Totnes in South Devon with his mum and stepfather. He said he wanted to spend some time down there as he needed a break.'

Though her features were showing signs of strain and her hair was tied in a tight bun, Hazlewood could see that she was not unattractive. 'Do you mind me asking how long you have been married, Mrs Varney?'

'Three and a half years.' She carried on into the kitchen to put the kettle on. Meanwhile the man introduced as Bob Turner kept his head down and busied himself browsing the magazine rack in the corner of the room. Hazlewood made some polite attempts to engage the small girl in friendly conversation but these were unsuccessful as she stared back at him unsmilingly. He felt some relief when Pamela Varney eventually re-joined them carrying a tray of tea.

After taking a sip of his tea he asked, 'I see that Marcus was medically discharged from the army last year. Can you tell me what the problem was?'

She suddenly looked distressed as if the recent memories were still too raw and painful. 'You probably already know that he was a Falklands veteran who served with distinction.'

Hazlewood nodded. 'I do.'

She went on, obviously having difficulty with her thoughts, 'He started to get problems about a year after we were married. They said it was a classic case of Post-Traumatic Stress Disorder and that with the right medication and therapy he could be treated. Unfortunately his condition also led to a drink problem which sent him further downhill. His enforced discharge from the army made things much worse. He seemed to lose all his self-esteem. He had a few job interviews that led to nothing.

He used to say that once the employer heard you were a war veteran, they would label you mad, bad and sad. It was around this time that I began to realise that our marriage was in big trouble.'

'Did he try to get further help?'

'Oh, there was always some token help on offer, but like many of the men who served in the army he was too proud to admit that he needed it. He was afraid that people would see it as a sign of weakness. He did eventually get prescribed some medication but it did not seem to help him with his drinking, in fact it seemed to make it worse.'

'Do you have his parents' telephone number?'

She rose from her chair. 'Yes, I have it here.' She retrieved a piece of paper from a small unit of light wooden drawers and gave it to him.

'Would you mind if I use your phone, Mrs Varney?' asked Hazlewood, motioning towards the telephone in the corner.

'No, go ahead.'

Hazlewood rose from the chair and picked up the phone. After dialling the number he let it ring persistently but there was no answer. Either there was no one home or someone wasn't picking it up. 'Do you have the parents' address?'

She again went to the unit of drawers, retrieved a small address book, and gave PC Wallington the details which he noted down.

As Hazlewood stood up to leave he looked across at the man introduced as Bob Turner. 'Do you mind telling me what you do for a living, Mr Turner?'

The man looked uneasy as he self-consciously answered, 'I'm a plumber, sir.'

Pamela Varney was quick to add her support in order to ease his obvious awkwardness. 'Bob works locally. He's very good,' she added with a faint attempt at a smile.

Hazlewood gave her a contact number. 'Thank you for the tea, Mrs Varney. If Marcus gets in touch please don't hesitate to give us a ring.'

'I will. I don't suppose you can tell me what it is about?'

He did not want to add any more to her obvious anxiety. 'Just routine stuff, Mrs Varney, nothing to worry about.'

As he moved towards the door Hazlewood again tried to engage the little girl in some friendly banter, but there was still no response, not even a flicker of a smile.

As they walked back towards the car PC Wallington remarked, 'I didn't get the feeling of a happy household, sir.'

'Aye, lad, unhappiness certainly, but also something else.'

'Like what, sir?'

'Fear and despair. You thought that the Falklands war ended four years ago, didn't you lad? Well, there is your evidence that the fall-out goes on for years afterwards. When you get back to Fulton Street do a check on the plumber Ben Turner, make sure he is legit.'

Wallington made a note. 'Will do, sir.'

An hour later Hazlewood was pulling up outside the *Blacksmiths Arms* in the small village of Westow. Situated in the Ryedale District not far from the Howardian Hills, it had long been one of his favourite pubs when he fancied a pint on his way home. Just off the A64 it was a perfect stopping point between York and his hometown of Malton. After being diverted when returning home earlier, he was now in no rush, as Joan had reminded him when he had phoned about his delay, that she was having a night out with her local darts team. As was usually the case when he entered the bar a few of the grizzled locals turned and stared. A couple of them registered some faint recognition in their expressions before turning their attention back to their pints. That was the way he liked it, with no one feeling obligated to make idle chatter. Ordering a pint of Tetley's and a steak and kidney pie, he retreated to a table as far from the bar as he could get. His keen appetite ensured that he made short work of the pie, before returning gratefully to his beer.

As he sat admiring the exposed beams and appreciating the warmth of the roaring log burners, he began to think back to the flat at Skeldergate. Though it was now officially out of his hands, he could not help thinking of the silent plumber Turner, the anxious face of Mrs Varney and most haunting of all, the vacant, slightly despairing expression on the face of the little girl. He had briefly updated the team at the Fulford Road station when he had dropped off PC Wallington and they would have no doubt kept New Scotland Yard informed regarding Varney's whereabouts. Though he did not want to believe that a Falklands hero could have had anything to do with the London murders, he kept thinking back to the atmosphere in the flat and it started to make him feel uneasy. Though he was sure that the boys in Fulford Road and New Scotland Yard would continue to try contacting the parents in Totnes, he nonetheless reached into his pocket and pulled out the piece of paper which had their details. Making use of the pub payphone he rang the Totnes number once again in an attempt to put his mind at rest- but still there was no answer. Putting the paper back in his pocket, he resolved there and then to ring the number again first thing in the morning.

*

Simon Llewelyn looked across at his trading partner Steve Laker and allowed himself a wry grin. As was usually the case when these party evenings were coming to an end, his friend would invariably be locked in a passionate embrace with some like-minded female. It had been a good night. After his discussion with the head-hunter in the *City of London Club,* he had caught up with his trading colleagues in the *Mithras Bar* before going on to the *Arbitrage* in Throgmorton Street. It had been the usual wild party atmosphere in the *Arby* with loud music, flowing champagne and dancing bar staff. Now nearing the end of the evening, they had ended up in the hot sweaty dive bar of *Dirty Dick's* in Bishopsgate. Having had enough partying for one night, Llewelyn was trying unsuccessfully to make himself heard above *True Blue* by Madonna as he tried to get Steve's attention. Before he left he wanted a quick chat to discuss the strategy regarding a couple of securities that were expected to be extremely volatile when trading opened the next morning. Finally giving up after seeing no possibility of Laker disengaging from his new-found friend, Llewelyn shouted his goodbyes to any remaining traders that were still listening before mounting the stairs to the exit.

Crossing the road into Liverpool Street, he appreciated the crisp cool air refreshing his face after the hot stuffy environs of the pub. He felt a little light-headed but he had been careful enough not to drink too much as Catherine did not appreciate him coming home incapable. He felt his step quicken at the thought of getting back to their flat in the Barbican and seeing her. It was still early enough to order in a Chinese and watch an episode of *Blackadder* which he had videotaped earlier. He crossed Blomfield Street and made his way towards the entrance of Finsbury Circus. The small oval-shaped garden area was a handy cut through to Moorgate. As was his usual practice when entering the park, he took the right hand path and passed through it in an anti-clockwise direction. From a nearby bar he could hear the distant strains of *Don't You Forget About Me* by Simple Minds. He sang along softly with the catchy chorus as he walked through the gardens. It would have been difficult for him to know which came first, the slight movement he detected in his peripheral vision, or the strong, muscular arm that suddenly clamped like a vice around his chest and pulled him forcibly backwards. Surprisingly he barely felt any pain as the knife sliced incisively across his throat, though he did manage to catch a horrifying glimpse of the shimmering steel blade. Almost immediately, he felt a sensation of something warm and liquid around his neck, swiftly followed by a dulling of the senses as if being suddenly shut in a sealed and darkened room. He was vaguely aware of falling to his knees as his breathing began to come in agonised gulps. As the distant melodies of Simple Minds reverberated on the wintry evening breeze, Simon Llewelyn finally collapsed face down on the path – engulfed by infinite oblivion.

CHAPTER TEN

A FALLEN HERO

Ben Hazlewood stirred restlessly in his bed. He must have fallen into a fitful sleep at some stage because he had only been vaguely aware that Joan had joined him in bed after returning home from her darts night. But now he was wide awake, his mind filled with haunting images of the expression on the little Varney girl's face, the brooding, awkward presence of the plumber Bob Turner - and was it his imagination or did he detect a subtle cry for help in the eyes of Mrs Varney? He propped himself up and looked at his alarm clock - it had just gone half-one in the morning. His troubled thoughts were sharply interrupted by the sound of his bedside phone buzzing. Joan stirred beside him and mumbled something in her sleep as he picked it up.

'Aye, Ben, it's Mike, sorry to disturb you at this time in the morning but I think it's something you should know after your earlier visit to Skelderdale.'

It was DI Mike Galloway from Fulton Road. Hazlewood rated him highly both as a detective and a valued loyal friend. 'Aye, Mike.'

'It seems there's been another murder in London.'

Hazlewood had a sudden awful foreboding of what was coming next, 'Go on.'

'Thing is we did finally manage to get through to Varney's parents; it seems they had been out all evening at a bridge club.' There was a slight pause. 'The bottom line is they have not seen their son for well over a month.'

Instantly filled with thoughts of Mrs Varney and her daughter, Hazlewood replied with a note of urgency in his voice, 'Mike, I may be wrong on this but I think you should get a squad car around to 9 Skeldergate immediately.'

'Don't worry, Ben, it's been done. New Scotland Yard issued the same instruction when we informed them.'

'That's a relief, I have felt uneasy about that family ever since I left the flat yesterday.' There was no way he would get back to sleep now. 'I'll be over within the hour.'

*

Marcus Varney appreciated the near empty road as he drove smoothly along the newly constructed M25. He felt exhilarated, as if a large weight had been lifted from his shoulders. No more would he have to live in the shadow of his more successful peers. No more would crippling jealousy and twisted envy cast its miserable and demoralising shadow over his existence. It had been his original intention to drive back to York to finish off that devious, cowardly bastard Bob Turner before handing himself over to the police. But for the first time that he could remember in a long while, he felt free of all anger and resentment. Besides he had already given Turner a bloody good hiding for trying to get his feet under the table with Pamela. More importantly he did not want to cause any further distress to his daughter by risking her witness yet one more traumatic scene on the domestic front. As a consequence he had decided at the last minute to drive past the A1 junction that would have taken him to York, deciding instead to spend his last day of freedom in Oxford. Where better than iconic Oxford with its dreaming spires, a city where he had spent some of the happiest days of his life and some of his most miserable. He was sure that Francis would not mind him borrowing his Land Rover for just a little longer. He had returned to his friend's house the previous afternoon with the intention of collecting his belongings and bidding Francis farewell, but he had found his old college friend lying on his bed in a deep jet-lagged sleep. Not wishing to disturb him, he had quickly written a thank-you note, before leaving the door keys on the hook and taking the holdall which he had packed earlier. Good old Francis, he was a true friend, someone he could always rely on. It was a shame that they had lost touch for so long after leaving Oxford. He turned off the M25 at junction 16, picked up the M40 and pointed the black Land Rover towards Oxford.

*

'So we at least now have a name and a major suspect who is out there somewhere,' declared Superintendent Bill Kemp as he poured himself a glass of water. The New Scotland Yard murder team were again assembled around the long polished table with Bill Kemp sitting at its head.

Loxley responded, 'Yes, we have a nationwide manhunt underway, with all units around the country actively involved in the search.'

It was now five o'clock in the morning. In little more than an hour the country would again be waking up to the horrific news of another London slaying. The events in the early hours of that morning had seemed to Loxley as if he was in the grip of a recurring nightmare. Once again he was standing out in the freezing cold, accompanied by the space-suited SOCOs, their white overalls illuminated brightly in the powerful spot lights. Most chillingly of all he was having to look at yet another young man lying lifeless in a London public garden, before the ambulance eventually carted him off to a hospital morgue.

Momentarily having trouble forgetting the mental image of Simon Llewelyn's lifeless body, Loxley had to make a conscious effort to focus his full attention as DC Bob Norton rose from the table and stood in front of the information board to deliver his presentation. 'Llewelyn was on his way back to his flat in the Barbican after a night out with his chums. It seems his fiancé Catherine was there waiting for him and she has since been informed of his death. Not surprisingly she has taken it pretty badly.'

A pale-faced DS Parrish drew deeply on his cigarette as he nodded his confirmation, for it had fallen to him to be the one to inform the young lady of the tragic news. He was still shaken up at the memory of her almost hysterical reaction, as she struggled to absorb the reality of what he was telling her and the crushing of her future happiness and plans.

'From what you say it's pretty obvious that Llewelyn must have been stalked for most of the evening,' said Bill Kemp.

Bob Norton agreed. 'We will put out an appeal for anyone who saw anything suspicious in the area. The good news is that this time we do have a name in the frame. Everything we know so far points to Varney being a major suspect.' Norton used a ruler to underline the incriminating evidence; 'Marcus Varney, age 32, last known address was in York, now separated from his wife Pamela and has a four-year-old daughter, graduated from St Benedict's College 1976, a Falklands hero, he was discharged a year ago with PTSD; parents have already confirmed that he his left-handed. His whereabouts over the last month is completely unknown. Also significantly in view of the Tyler debacle, his physical description reads 5ft 6" of stocky build.'

Bill Kemp let out a loud curse, 'I just knew our small stocky man had to make another appearance in this case. So the hooded man seen walking up Essex Street by our drunken newspaper hack could have been the murderer.'

Norton agreed, 'Yes it's possible, sir, that the man that spooked Arthur Thorn outside *The Edgar* could have been Marcus Varney leaving the crime scene.'

Bill Kemp looked across to Dr Tom Conway for confirmation. 'No doubt that it is the same hand again, Tom?'

The Doc answered, 'Same efficiency, only difference was that this time the victim was allowed to fall forward.'

'The killer probably felt he had less time to hang around; the evenings can be quite lively in the square mile these days.' suggested Cumber.

Bill Kemp looked thoughtful. 'That probably explains it. The fact that it was a Tuesday this time is probably because of our blanket operation on the Monday night.'

'I make you right, sir,' Loxley agreed. 'It's just a tragedy we could not have saved young Llewelyn last night.'

'I know what you are saying, Joe, but how could we have done anymore?'

'Unfortunately, sir, knowing that to be the case does not make it any easier,' Loxley answered. 'I have been informed that when Llewelyn was interviewed last week at his workplace he showed no outward signs of alarm or anxiety. The only thing we can do now is ensure there are no more victims. We have Yorkshire Division looking after Varney's family in York, while the Devon and Cornwall police are watching the parent's house.'

Bob Norton added, 'Early television and radio broadcasts will give out a description of Varney first thing this morning, with the strong advice that he is not to be approached or confronted in any circumstances. Unfortunately, in the most recent photo we have of him he is sporting a military crop, so we cannot be sure how close the image relates to his present look.'

Bill Kemp rose from his chair. 'Well, short and stocky will do for a start. As per usual I will handle the press conference this morning.' With the sound of scraping chairs the meeting was brought to an end.

*

The early morning air was crisp and cold when Marcus Varney arrived in Oxford and parked Barnaby's Land Rover in Cardigan Street, a small turning in the Jericho district. The earliness of the hour ensured that the street was still dark, eerily quiet and devoid of people. He had avoided the motorway for the most part on his route to Oxford, even managing at one stage to get a couple of hours sleep in a quiet byway near Pangbourne Railway Station. After turning off the engine he took off his hooded track suit top and removed his trainers before stuffing them into a large holdall. He then placed the ignition key into one of the zipped compartments. He pulled out a dark blue tie with an Oxford crest, then, adjusting the rear view mirror, he tied it neatly around his shirt collar with meticulous care. Reaching over to the seat behind him, he picked up a pair of shiny brogues and three quarter length Crombie overcoat. He felt it was important to look smart if he was to enjoy his last day of freedom. Looking out of the car window he noticed the watery, winter sun was beginning to rise in the east, illuminating the bright pastel paintwork on the attractive terraced houses. One of those houses had been the student digs, which he had once shared with Francis Barnaby back in their carefree days. It still looked remarkably unchanged; could it really be all of ten years ago? What great times they had shared back then. What a streak of good fortune it had been when he had bumped into him in a London pub. After going back to Francis's house they had talked long into the night. He could not remember exactly when it was that his malevolent plan for Rupert Buxton and Timothy Galton began to formulate, but after hearing of Barnaby's planned excursion to Australia and the offer of looking after his house for a few weeks, everything had suddenly seemed to fall into place. He remembered Francis had taken great pride in showing him his collection of surgical scalpels, neatly set out in a small tin box. He recalled them having a drunken discussion on the merits of a rifle bayonet or a scalpel, as an effective murder weapon. Varney chuckled softly at the memory; that surely would have been the moment his plan began to crystallise.

Buxton and Galton: how he had resented them, so arrogant, so superior, so damn sure of themselves. He could remember that there had been a brief time when he had not felt such crippling resentment towards them. In the early days at St Benedict's when he and Buxton had been studying law, he could recall their relationship being cordial enough, though never warm. Like himself, both Buxton and Galton had been outstanding athletes. At that time he had felt that this shared natural ability would lead to a joint camaraderie but that had never proved to be the case. In fact as time went on he was made to feel that he was undoubtedly the inferior outsider. The fact that they were both much taller and looked down on him, seemed to reinforce their utter disdain for anyone they deemed to be a lesser mortal. In his time at St Benedict's he lost count of the times they would take the opportunity to remind him that he was judged to fall very much into this inferior category. He grinned to himself. Well, not any more. Now mercifully they were no longer around to torment him, he had seen to that. He felt almost euphoric at the thought. He left the Land Rover carrying a small holdall and walked briskly along Walton Street towards the city centre.

*

Francis Barnaby rose slowly from the bed and scratched his head. His clock on the bedroom wall told him it was approaching eight in the morning. He had slept solidly for over twelve hours. He slipped on his dressing gown and visited the bathroom, before slowly shuffling his way downstairs. Feeling that he was still in need of a little more acclimation time, he was thankful he did not have to report to Bart's hospital until the evening. As he entered the kitchen he noticed that the holdall that Marcus had left in the hallway the previous day had gone. It was then that he saw the note left on the kitchen table and picked it up. Reading it to himself it said.

Sorry to have missed you old chum did not have the heart to wake you up. Thanks once again for the loan of your house, will catch up later on. Did not think you would mind me hanging on to the landrover for a little longer, rest assured you will get it back.

Varnish.

Shaking his head ruefully, Francis heard himself say under his breath, 'The cheeky bastard, he had better return it by tonight otherwise there will be hell to pay'. He went into the kitchen and put on the kettle for coffee before dishing out some cornflakes. He had to admit that 'Varnish' had done a good job in keeping the house tidy and ensuring there was still a plentiful food supply. With some reluctance he picked up the pile of unopened letters, went through to the lounge and switched on the television. As he sifted the letters into the usual separate categories of bills, junk mail and the more interesting, he became vaguely aware of the breakfast telly news in the background reporting a murder that had taken place in the City of London. But it was only when he heard the name of the victim that his attention became fully fixed on the screen. He felt his stomach lurch as he realised that they were talking about his old university colleague Simon Llewelyn. It could only been a few months since he had seen him at a mutual friend's barbecue. On that social occasion Simon had seemed happier than he could ever remember him. He recalled that he could hardly keep the grin off his face that day as he spoke enthusiastically about his new career in the city whilst standing alongside his attractive new girlfriend. Now in direct contrast to that most recent memory, the news reporter on the television was solemnly describing how he had been mercilessly slaughtered in a London Park. Still unable to fully comprehend what he was watching, the news report went on to connect the killing to two other murders that had taken place that month. With a sense of emerging horror he recognised the names of the two other victims and the connection to his old college in Oxford. In the case of Timothy Galton, he now had a vague recollection of a placard headline reporting the murder of a London MP when he was in Perth. At the time he had not bothered to follow up on the story, as he had made the conscious decision whilst on holiday to cut off all contact with the world he had left behind.

Feeling he needed that coffee, he walked unsteadily into the kitchen to make it before returning to the screen. The next image that confronted him caused a sick feeling in the pit of his stomach. The idyllic holiday he had just experienced in Perth, the park, the sun, the contented relaxation, became a distant memory as he looked incredulously at the image of the named suspect. It was Marcus Varney, admittedly looking somewhat different with a close cropped military haircut, but it was undoubtedly Marcus. With his head reeling, he recalled the conversation with his secretary when he had rung her from Perth. It could not have been a coincidence that New Scotland Yard had rung the hospital enquiring as to his whereabouts. As he frantically searched through his hand luggage for the telephone number he had jotted down, he could hear the voice of the news reporter in the background. The announcer was warning people that his old friend was not to be approached in any circumstances. Finally retrieving the Foster's beer mat with the scribbled number, he felt his hands trembling as he picked up the phone. Listening anxiously to the ringing tone at the other end of the line, his gaze fell upon the tin box with its lid wide open - a scalpel was missing.

*

Loxley and Cumber studied the features of Francis Barnaby very closely as they sat opposite him. After his phone call to New Scotland Yard they had wasted little time in getting around to his house in Bedford Row. Though the surgeon's face now in front of them was lightly tanned from his recent jaunt to the southern hemisphere, his lips were noticeably pale.

Loxley waited patiently for Barnaby to compose himself before asking, 'So until you bumped into him in the pub you had not seen Varney for the best part of ten years?'

There was a slight tremble in Barnaby's hands as he picked up his mug of coffee. 'That's correct. I had popped into my local for a swift pint on my half-day and there he was as large as life. We recognised each other immediately.'

'What pub was this?'

'*The Old Nick,* just around the corner from here in Sandland Street.'

'Did you think he had changed much?'

Barnaby thought for a second. 'Not really, a bit more manly perhaps and maybe a touch more thoughtful in his responses. I put it down to maturity. Of course I had already heard all about his heroics in the Falklands. Which reminds me, he looks a bit different to the image shown on the television, his hair is now considerably longer.'

Cumber noted this detail in his notebook as Loxley went on, 'So you came back here afterwards?'

'Yes. We talked for hours. In view of our friendship back at Oxford I suppose it was not surprising. We had a lot to catch up on.'

Loxley leaned forward slightly. 'Thinking back to those conversations, can you remember him at any time mentioning any of the victims?'

'Certainly not Buxton or Galton, but I do remember at one point telling him how well Simon was doing in the city. It's only now in view of what has happened that I can recall him reacting slightly curiously to the news.'

'In what way?' Cumber enquired sharply.

'Well, he did not seem overly pleased, nothing obvious, just strangely indifferent.'

'Whose idea was it regarding the house sitting when you were away,' asked Loxley.

'No one in particular, we both seemed to come to the idea jointly. It certainly suited me as I have never liked leaving the house empty for any length of time.'

Loxley motioned towards the open tin box positioned prominently on a highly polished wooden unit. 'So you first noticed that a scalpel was missing this morning?'

Barnaby's face looked distressed at the memory. 'Yes just after hearing the news about the murders. I could not believe what I was seeing.'

Cumber picked up Varney's written note from the glass coffee table in front of them and studied it before asking,

'When you returned home yesterday he was nowhere to be seen?'

'The house was empty. The only sign that he was still around was his holdall, which was already packed and standing in the hallway. He must have returned and written that note soon after I crashed out on the bed.'

'I notice he has ended the message with the name 'Varnish,' Cumber said.

'Yes, that's right, it was his nickname at St Benedict's.'

Cumber looked across to Loxley, 'Remember the shopping list that fell out of the newspaper at Galton's flat?'

Loxley remembered it very well. 'The additional item with the question mark.'

Cumber confirmed the item loudly, 'Varnish. Galton could have been idly speculating on who murdered Buxton.'

'Very likely,' agreed Loxley, before turning to Barnaby and asking the obvious question, 'Mr Barnaby, from what you know of Marcus, could you ever have imagined him capable of such crimes?'

Barnaby did not hesitate in his answer. 'Not the Marcus I knew, not in a million years, but who knows how he might have changed after his experiences in the Falklands?'

'Did you know that he was discharged from the army with PTSD?' Cumber queried.

Barnaby looked surprised. 'No I didn't, he never said.'

Loxley got up from the chair. 'Well, Mr Barnaby, hopefully it should not be too long before we track down your vehicle. In the meantime, I would appreciate you staying put while we continue with the search. I also think it would be wise for you to be accompanied by one of our officers if that's ok with you.'

Barnaby looked slightly taken aback at the thought that his own life might be in danger, but he accepted the restrictions without protest. As he accompanied the two policemen to the door he had a sudden thought. 'What I can recall from our days at Oxford was that though a lot of fellows admired Buxton and Galton, they were not particularly liked as people. Certainly, Marcus was never particularly keen on them. This animosity would usually come out when he was a bit drunk, nothing too sinister just a bitter resentment, that's all. I can also recollect there being a situation with Galton over a girl that Marcus thought a lot of. At the time it went quite deep with him.'

Loxley looked interested. 'How deep?'

'To the point where afterwards he began to drink heavily, causing him to lose serious focus on his law studies.'

Loxley smiled politely before turning to the door. 'Thanks for the info, Mr Barnaby, we will be in touch.'

*

DI Ben Hazlewood thought it best to give Pamela Varney some time to compose herself as he sat opposite her in the flat. She was wiping away her tears with her handkerchief, her daughter Melanie standing expressionless beside her. After the phone call in the early hours Hazlewood had not wasted much time in travelling to York and joining up with the police protection team. Outside the Varney flat in Skeldergate, there were two unmarked cars parked across the street. Inside the vehicles there were armed officers keeping a watchful eye on the main entrance.

Hazlewood turned his attention to Bob Turner who was standing next to Pamela Varney with a comforting hand placed tentatively on her trembling shoulder.

'Had Marcus Varney ever physically threatened you?'

Turner hesitated for a second, seemingly looking down at Pamela Varney for guidance before answering, 'All the time.'

'Did he ever get an opportunity to carry out his threats?' Hazlewood prompted.

Turner hesitated once again, only answering after the slightest of nods from Pamela Varney. 'There was one night when he attacked me as I left the flat after he had been drinking heavily. He punched and kicked me repeatedly. Fortunately for me he was confronted by some guests who were leaving the hotel across the road and I got the chance to drag myself away from him.'

Pamela Varney had stopped crying for the moment so Hazlewood addressed his next question to her, 'So Marcus was fully aware of your relationship with Mr Turner.'

'Yes. Bob has been a great support for me, a true friend.'

Hazlewood glanced at Bob Turner, 'Just a friend?'

Pamela Varney looked across at Turner. 'Yes. Bob has said he would like it to be more but I have told him I am just not ready for another relationship.'

'I realise it might be painful for you to answer this, Mrs Varney, but I have to ask. Did Marcus ever assault you?'

She was quite definite in her answer, 'Never.' She glanced towards her daughter, 'We did have violent rows and there were times when the furniture was damaged, especially when Marcus was drunk. I regret them now because they were often in front of Melanie. But he was only aggressive to me in his language, never physical.' She went on tearfully, 'I just cannot believe that he could have had anything to do with these murders.'

It was clear to Hazlewood that despite everything, Pamela Varney still held very strong feelings for Varney. He so wanted to believe that she was right about him not being the murderer. But he was also well aware that his own personal admiration for anyone who fought heroically in the Falklands had the potential to cloud his professional judgement. His thoughts were abruptly interrupted by the buzz of the phone. Hazlewood motioned for Pamela Varney to answer it. She slowly walked over to the phone and tentatively picked up the receiver.

For one split second there was a palpable air of tension, before her body language noticeably relaxed and she handed over the phone to Hazlewood. 'Hello, Ben.' It was DI Galloway from North Yorkshire Division headquarters.

With Pamela Varney staring at him intently, Hazlewood did his best to look impassive as Galloway informed him of the latest dramatic developments that had been relayed from New Scotland Yard. Replacing the receiver thoughtfully, Hazlewood turned to Mrs Varney. 'Scotland Yard have interviewed an old friend of Marcus who says he has just returned from a holiday in Australia. It seems he has been allowing Marcus the run of his London house while he was away.'

Pamela Varney looked agitated. 'That doesn't mean he had anything to do with the murders!'

Hazlewood went on calmly, 'Unfortunately that's not all. It seems the friend was a surgeon at Bart's hospital and certain incriminating items have gone missing from the house.'

Pamela Varney's features crumpled into a look of desperate desolation as she instinctively drew young Melanie towards her and sobbed.

*

As he waited to cross the busy high road, Marcus Varney was pleased to see that Oxford had altered little in the ten years that had passed. Sure the fashions had changed and there were a few different shop-fronts, but the collegiate atmosphere that he remembered so fondly was still very much in existence. With everything feeling comfortably familiar, he was quietly enjoying himself. He had briefly paused to glance at his old college which had looked exactly the same, before spending some time in the nearby covered market. He was now heading towards Merton Street and the meadow of Christ Church beyond. The day was bright and clear with the sort of chill air that gave an edge to a man's energy. He was enjoying the nostalgia, with each small memory triggering another fond recollection.

His world seemed a much happier place now that he had rid it of Buxton and Galton. The more he had heard of Buxton's increasingly successful law career the more tormented he had felt. It had reminded him on a daily basis of his own personal failure. He thought back to a moment in his time at Oxford when Buxton had openly ridiculed him in front of a crowd of fellow students after hearing that he had dropped out of his law course. It was a defining moment that in time was to burn ever deeper in his heart.

The planning and execution of Buxton's murder had gone perfectly. He had chosen a Monday night for the killing because it was usually the quietest evening of the week, but also if he was honest because the word Monday had always held its own personal significance to him. Ever since that devastating day in 1966 when he had returned home from the Lords cricket ground after a day out with his Dad. They had enjoyed an idyllic day watching England play the West Indies. After finishing a pleasurable conversation discussing the relative merits of Garfield Sobers and Colin Milburn, his father suddenly adopted a serious expression and put his arm around him. In a hushed and sombre tone, he told Marcus that he and Mum had not been getting on too well recently, with it probably being best for everyone if he left home for a while.

Marcus remembered being struck dumb with shock, for up to that point his childhood had been one of total happiness and security. As he had stood there slowly comprehending that his cosy world had started to crumble about him, the hit tune of the day *Monday Monday* by the Mamas and Papas was playing on the radio. He had been

241

haunted by the song and its title ever since. Only a few weeks after that traumatic day his mother had tearfully told him that his father had fallen in love with another woman and had chosen to live a different life. From that point on his father was to play an increasingly minimal part in his existence, with this unhappy circumstance becoming even more entrenched when his mum met someone else and moved on with her life.

The gardens in the Temple had been the perfect location for the first kill, though with hindsight he realised that he had been a little incautious in risking being seen by members of the public. The similar physical description of the Tyler kid had been an unexpected stroke of luck and a useful diversion for the police. In the days leading up to the killing he had become increasingly aware that he was not the only one keeping a close eye on Buxton's movements, as on more than one occasion he had spotted Danny Tyler in the vicinity of the Temple.

Passing through Merton Grove, he entered the wide expanse of Christ Church Meadow. It had always been one of his favourite locations, even before he had met Julie. He had been introduced to her in the *Turf Tavern,* by a mutual friend. Beautiful Julie: how wonderful those times they had spent on the meadow in that blissful summer of 1985. Often just talking of their hopes and dreams, somehow seeming to know what the other was thinking and feeling. In that summer when time appeared to stand still, he really felt that he need look no further for his lifelong soul mate. He stood for some time contemplating the meadow and thinking of her beauty. He remembered the soft lustre of her hair, those laughing eyes and her effortless sexuality. Finally he slowly turned away and retraced his steps back to the High Street.

*

'It's looking increasingly like Varney is our man,' declared Bob Norton. 'We have just had it confirmed that a traffic warden slapped a ticket on Barnaby's Land Rover in Finsbury Circus last night.'

The murder team were in the incident room at New Scotland Yard, conducting an impromptu midday progress meeting after the dramatic developments of the morning. With the manhunt now in full swing, the case was getting blanket coverage on both radio and television.

Steve Harmer added some further information. 'Not only that, we also have two sightings of a man meeting Varney's description seen loitering in the city last night. One sighting was in the early evening in front of the arched entrance to Austin Friars, which is just across the road from the *City of London Club*. We know from talking to his workmates that Llewelyn was in there around that time. The second sighting was much later in the evening when a man answering the description was seen hanging around the Liverpool Street entrance to the arcade. Again this is just around the corner from the *Dirty Dicks* pub where we know Llewelyn ended up.'

Looking determined, Bill Kemp said, 'It can only be a matter of time. We'll soon have him cornered.'

'All units countrywide are on the lookout for the vehicle,' said Loxley. 'A black Land Rover should stick out like a sore thumb.'

'The SOCOs also came up with something extra,' added Bob Norton, 'seems they found some clothing fibres on a warped railing behind the bush adjacent to where Llewelyn was killed; they matched the ones found in the other murders.'

Cumber suggested, 'Looks like Varney bent the railing deliberately beforehand in order to squeeze through and get a quick getaway after the deed.'

Norton agreed, 'Very likely.'

'So he prepared the ground before he struck?' said Bill Kemp.

'Exactly.' said Loxley.

'How very military,' Kemp concluded with a wry smile, before adding, 'keep by the phones, lads, we should get a call anytime.'

*

Marcus Varney browsed the shelves in *Blackwell's* bookshop in Broadway. It had always been one of his favourite venues. He found the smell and presence of the books comforting, as if he were among friends. He had just enjoyed a leisurely pint and a pasty in the *Turf Tavern,* while not feeling in the least conspicuous in the familiar surroundings. The pub had been comfortably busy with tourists, students and even some early Christmas shoppers. It had pleased him to see that it was little changed from ten years previously, still possessing the discreet corner furnished with a small table and two chairs where he had spent such pleasurable hours in conversation with Julie.

Now comfortably installed in the warm interior of *Blackwell's*, he reached up for a sizable volume that had caught his attention. He read the title with a smile; *The Complete History of St Benedict's in the Turl* by Francis Lightfoot. Well, his old history master appeared to have kept himself busy. 'Lecher Lightfoot'. Who would have thought it? Back in the Seventies Lightfoot had appeared to spend most of his time chasing the attractive female students. He had a serious crush on Julie – how they used to laugh about it. He recalled that Lightfoot would invent situations just so he could be alone with her. Julie would always be one step ahead, as she knew his game only too well. He could certainly remember feeling Lightfoot's resentment at the time when he and Julie were going out together.

Of course it just had to be Lightfoot who informed him with barely hidden delight that he had seen Julie and Timothy Galton canoodling on the riverbank together. It was the day that Julie had told him that she could not see him that afternoon as she was busy with an important essay. He remembered wandering over to the riverbank in a disbelieving daze, not wanting to contemplate the awful possibility that Lightfoot was telling the truth. Then he saw them sitting together by the river, talking, laughing and caressing. Immediately feeling a gut-wrenching ache in his stomach, he had headed straight towards the *Turf Tavern* with tears in his eyes and a heavy heart. To dilute his outraged anger and deaden the pain of the betrayal on

245

that ground-hog day, he must have drunk close to ten pints of cider. Of course the relationship between Galton and Julie was only to last the time it took for Galton to move on to his next conquest. It really did appear that Galton had taken Julie away from him for no other good reason than the pure fact that he could. There was a brief time afterwards when he and Julie did try to pick up the pieces of their shattered affinity, but the bond that had existed between them had been broken, with the relationship damaged beyond repair.

He was to spend the rest of his university days in an alcoholic haze, literally pissing up the wall any chance of his planned future career in law. He could still see the smug faces of Buxton and Galton at that time, not even attempting to disguise their obvious amusement at his self-destruction. At least now he would be spared the torment of having to read newspaper accounts telling of Buxton's brilliance and glowing reputation in the legal profession. No more would he have to endure television images of Galton at Westminster basking in the reflected glory of the Falklands victory.

Feeling as if a huge weight had been lifted off his shoulders, he carefully returned old Lightfoot's volume to its rightful place on the shelf, before moving on to browse the military section.

In the year after university he had drifted aimlessly, with his life mainly revolving around alcohol. He had always enjoyed a drink, but it was in this period that he began to realise that he had a serious problem. Every evening he would start out with the intention of having a couple of pints in the pub, but more often than not he would end the night lying in a field or a gutter, with a concerned bystander occasionally coming along to help get him home. It was around this time that his estranged father died suddenly from a heart attack. He had been in no fit state to attend the funeral, not that he would have recognised any of the fellow mourners if he had. For the truth was that since that dark day back in 1966 when his father chose to shatter their comfortable existence, their lives had taken a very different path. His stepfather had never come close to replacing him, not that he would ever had wanted him too.

Fortunately his anxious Mum never totally gave up on him. Revealing her fears for his future to the wider family, it had been a distant relative that had come to his rescue. He suggested that Varney should seek a career in the armed forces before he wrecked his life completely. Once he was recruited it had been the making of him. At that critical time in his life he had needed a situation where everything was structured and organised for him. It gave him a purpose and, more crucially, opened up a more promising future than the one he glimpsed regularly in the bottom of a pint glass. Once he was in the army he did not have to grapple with everyday decisions or risky life choices; all he had to do was obey orders and be the best soldier he could be. They would look after him. It was why a life in prison held no fears for him now. Once inside its institutionalised walls he would be protected from both himself and the outside world - what could be better?

Blackwell's had a decent selection of military books and in amongst them were a couple of volumes relating to the Falklands conflict. He selected one of them and leisurely browsed it. How proud he had felt that day to be a part of the 3 Para Battalion that set sail from Southampton aboard the Canberra. It was only in the long voyage south that the true realisation of what was occurring began to sink in. At first many of his fellow Paras had been convinced that the Argentinians would soon back off once they realised the Brits were coming, but the nearer they got to their destination the more intense and real the situation became. Perusing the pages of his selected book, he realised that no prose or images found within its cover could ever come close to reflecting the intensity of what he had experienced. He thought back to the raw fear he had felt for the first time standing at the base of Mount Longdon, the unforgiving terrain, the freezing temperatures, but most of all the horror of the long savage battle that followed. Surrounded by hostile fire and the dying cries of both fallen comrades and feared enemy, it was the night he discovered that he had what it took to be a real soldier warrior. He found he was good at it. It seemed that the fear that he felt in the kill or be killed scenario of the close-quarter combat could be every bit as addictive as the most seductive drug. The strange absurdity was that when the fighting was at its most intense he had never felt more alive, even though there was death all around him.

He remembered the triumphant return to Southampton and the tears of pride in his mother's eyes at the Falklands

Victory Parade in the City of London. He reflected on the sense of achievement that he felt at that time. That so special feeling that he was valued and important. Looking back it now seemed like another life. Where did it all go?

Unbelievably things were to get even better when he met Pamela. She had approached him at a social function arranged by the military wives. Vivacious and attentive to his conversation, he had felt an instant attraction to her. Through the course of the evening she revealed that she had just ended a long term relationship and by the end they had exchanged phone numbers. From that point on it had been a whirlwind romance ending with her soon falling pregnant with Melanie. Within the year they were married with a baby girl and living in York. For a few idyllic months everything had seemed perfect but then out of the clear blue sky; the nightmares began. At first they were not too intense, but gradually they would become more frequent and real. He would wake up sweating and shaking, unable to speak coherently. Eventually the horrific images started to appear in his waking hours as the memories of Mount Longdon came back to haunt him with a vengeance. He knew his army career was in serious trouble when he began to find himself cowering in secluded alleyways in broad daylight. When the army finally discharged him on medical grounds it was the worst day of his life. He remembered crying like a baby on the long journey back to York. Once he had returned home he became overwhelmed with feelings of failure and worthlessness. In the following nightmare weeks he began to increasingly withdraw into himself and away from his family - worst of all he began to drink heavily again. At first the drink had seemed to help him with the anxiety attacks and gruesome flashbacks, but all too soon the alcohol took over his moods and reinforced his feelings of failure, depression and impotent rage.

He was sharply brought back into the present by the loud laughter of the *Blackwell's* shop assistant as she shared a joke with a customer. Deciding he had browsed enough, he promptly returned the Falklands book to the shelf, picked up his holdall and left the shop. His watch told him it had just gone two in the afternoon. He knew that there would not be too many hours of freedom left, as it could now only be a matter of time before Barnaby's Land Rover would be discovered. He walked briskly down Catte Street, pausing only briefly to glance at the imposing structure of *Radcliffe Camera* - he had always thought it one of Oxford's more impressive buildings. Turning left into the High Street, he headed in the direction of *Magdalen Bridge* – he had one more place to visit.

*

It was early afternoon in the squad room at New Scotland Yard and the murder team were gathered once more in an informal meeting. Brian Parrish had just entered the room with a tray full of coffees as Chief Superintendent Bill Kemp did his best to keep up morale. 'Should not be too long now, lads, it's purely a waiting game.'

'Barnaby's Land Rover has got to be on the road somewhere,' said Bob Norton. 'Why else would he have made off with it?'

Cumber speculated, 'I suppose he could have had some sort of London lock-up organised.'

Loxley was doubtful. 'It's possible but unlikely. With Barnaby back from Australia he knew he had lost his London residence. It looks very much like it was his intention to quit town.'

Bill Kemp agreed, 'I make you right, Joe.'

They all paused to take their drinks as Parrish offered them around.

Bob Norton took a grateful sip of coffee before saying, 'We have searched all the official parking areas near airports, train stations and docks, but so far they have all drawn a blank.'

The door was suddenly thrown open by an excited looking Steve Harmer holding a sheet of paper. 'They have found Barnaby's Land Rover in the Jericho district of Oxford.'

Bill Kemp was the first to react. 'Oxford, well bugger me, he has gone back to where it all began.'

'Was there anything found in the vehicle?' Loxley asked.

Harmer looked at the writing on his sheet of paper and read it out with a hint of drama. 'A holdall containing the ignition key to the Land Rover, a blood stained tracksuit top, a pair of trainers, thick woollen gloves, a scalpel and a claw hammer.'

There was more than a hint of emotion in Bill Kemp's voice as he turned to Loxley. 'Go get him, Joe.'

CHAPTER ELEVEN

THE LAST POST

Roy Field unlocked the door leading through into the small office high up in the main stand of the Iffley Road Athletics Stadium. He was there to pick up some papers relating to athletic meetings scheduled for the coming summer of 1987. He had been associated with the stadium for the best part of thirty years. Ever since those hazy nostalgic days of the Fifties when, as a youth, he had been one of the privileged few to witness at first hand Roger Bannister's successful attempt to break four minutes for the mile. Being Oxford born and living around the corner, he had always had easy access to the stadium and on that momentous day he had been in the right place at the right time. From that moment he had felt a passionate connection to both athletics and the stadium. First as a competent club athlete, then as a ground-staff maintenance and administration man, the stadium had been his life for as long as he could remember. Going to the drawer of the desk, he retrieved the folder he was looking for and sat down briefly to check over a couple of items. After a few minutes he rose from the desk with a grunt of satisfaction and went over to the large panoramic window that overlooked the track. It was a view he never tired of, even on cold winter days like this when the stadium was empty and deserted. As he stood appreciating the view that evoked so many personal memories, a slight movement out of the corner of his eye drew his attention to a man sitting alone on the grass verge next to the track. The man seemed to be lost in his thoughts, with only the occasional movement of his head confirming he was not some sort of still-life model. Normally he would have gone outside and engaged the man but there was something about the stranger's demeanour that urged caution. He had seen the lunchtime news bulletins reporting on the nationwide manhunt relating to the London murders. He was also well aware of the Oxford connection regarding the victims, reading with interest the newspaper accounts reporting the links to St Benedict's College. Though smartly dressed in a long overcoat, the physical build of the man who the police were looking for seemed to bear more than a passing resemblance to the stranger he was now staring at. Realising it was probably advisable not to hang around any longer than he had to, he picked up the papers he needed and swiftly left the office. Within ten minutes he was back at his home and ringing the Oxford police.

*

Marcus Varney sat lost in thought and perfectly still by the side of the athletics track. Though the stadium was deserted and eerily quiet, in his mind's eye he was back in the summer of 1975, to a time when alongside Buxton and Galton, he had been one of the glory boys of the track. His thoughts went back to a time when the stadium was packed with spectators, the sun was hot and the taste of victory was sweet. At that time he thought his life was always going to be like that, satisfying, successful, feeling acclaimed and valued. In the case of Buxton and Galton that had proved to be the case, but sadly for him that fleeting feel-good factor he could now remember so well had proved to be a wicked, deceptive illusion. For the disappointing reality was that apart from his time spent in the armed forces, his life since those halcyon days spent on the Iffley Road running track had felt like one big relentless descent to the bottom of the steepest hill. As he stared at the empty track he could still see the grinning, triumphant figures of Buxton and Galton. For them it had been just the beginning of a life that was going to get even better.

After his medical discharge from the army, unemployed and with his life and marriage falling apart, he had written to Timothy Galton on several occasions pleading for help. The arrogant bastard had not even bothered to reply personally, eventually fobbing him off with a secretarial letter advising him to get medical assistance. This had led to a few drunken confrontations with him in the street in which Galton had pretended not to remember him. It was after the final encounter on Westminster Bridge, when Galton, accompanied by one of his parliamentary toadies, had totally ignored him that something far more sinister began to formulate in his brain. It was not long after that confrontation that he had bumped into his old friend Francis Barnaby, giving him the opportunity to plan a strategy to accommodate his increasingly darkening thoughts.

As in the case of Rupert Buxton, he had stalked Galton for several days. Getting to know his habits and movements, he had made sure that he was more cautious this time after the eyewitness descriptions in the aftermath of the Buxton killing. He made the decision to make himself less physically conspicuous by making more use of Barnaby's Land Rover when out on the streets. St John's Gardens in Westminster had been an obvious choice to carry out the killing. It had been Galton's regular practice to stop off at *The Marquis of Granby* on his route home from Westminster, before passing through the gardens on the way back to his flat. On that Monday evening he had watched Galton enter the pub with his colleague, before driving around to St John's Gardens. After what he thought to be a suitable time lapse he had left the Land Rover and taken up his position behind a bush in the gardens. Spending a good deal longer in the location than he had anticipated, the whole exercise had been given an extra edge of enjoyable frisson when the uniformed beat-copper passed by a few minutes before Galton appeared. Varney found himself grinning at the memory. The kill when it came was clinical and efficient. His old army captain would have been proud of him. Searching deep into his holdall he extracted a Mars Bar and took a bite, his thoughts slowly turning to his third victim, Simon Llewelyn.

*

Accompanied by two beacon flashing squad cars, Loxley's Audi had reached the outskirts of Oxford. Loxley was pleased to see that they had made good time. During the journey Cumber had picked up a radio message telling them to urgently divert to the Iffley Road Athletics Stadium. It seemed someone who answered Varney's description had been seen acting suspiciously in the vicinity. The shot of adrenaline that this news had instilled in Loxley had motivated him to drive even faster, with Cumber having to remind him on more than one occasion of the two accompanying squad cars. Loxley had allowed himself a slight smile as he made the conscious effort to slow down a little in order for the escort to catch up – driving fast had always been one of his favourite recreations. They had been told to liaise with DI Dennis Sugden of Oxford Division when they got there. It was a name that Loxley knew well. He had worked alongside him some twenty years before when he had served his stint in Oxford as a uniformed constable. He remembered that Sugden had turned down a posting to London at the time, preferring the steadier pace of Oxfordshire to the more hectic buzz of the metropolis. Remaining in Oxford, he had gone on to build a steady reputation as a highly capable and reliable detective. Loxley had always liked him and they had kept a distant eye on each other's career path through the ensuing years. Loxley thought that it would be good to see him.

Arriving in the locality of the Iffley Road Stadium, Cumber let out a low whistle. 'Looks like we've got the whole of the Oxfordshire police force on the case.' The area was a mass of flashing blue lights and uniformed police.

Getting out of the car they were approached by an officious-looking officer in a black combat jacket. 'Excuse me, sir, you can't park here.' Loxley did not bother to reply; he took a deep breath and flashed his New Scotland Yard badge.

There was an awkward moment before the officer answered, 'Sorry, sir, just doing my job.'

With Cumber struggling to keep a smile off his face, Loxley answered politely, 'No offence, constable, very commendable of you. Now can you impress me further by pointing us in the direction of DI Sugden?'

Still looking a little flustered the constable answered, 'He is about a hundred yards down on the right by the side entrance gate, sir.'

The whole area was thronging with uniformed police and squad cars, but as they approached the small gate Loxley recognised the voice of Dennis Sugden before they had even set eyes on him. Easily heard above the general hubbub, Sugden was in the middle of imparting some strategic information to a group of officers. As he waited patiently for him to finish, Loxley thought to himself that Sugden had not changed much physically in the twenty years since he had last seen him. Though he remembered him as always being a big lad Loxley detected a little more thickening around the waist, but other than that and the beginnings of some distinguished greying around the temples, he was wearing well.

Not wishing to waste too much time on the wistfulness of youthful nostalgia, Loxley greeted him, 'It's been a long time, Dennis.'

Sugden looked both pleased and relieved to see him. 'Am I glad to see you, Joe. Heading this operation all feels a bit above my pay grade.'

Loxley allowed himself a chuckle. 'You are doing just fine,' he said. 'So what is the situation as it stands?'

Looking pleased with the initial compliment, Sugden answered, 'Well, we strongly suspect that it is Marcus Varney inside the stadium so we have ring-fenced the surrounding area and reinforced it with marksmen from the Armed Response team.'

'Is he saying or doing anything?'

'Most of the time he has been sitting down in front of the track; you can see him from the road.'

Looking around, Loxley was annoyed to see a sizable gathering of television and newspaper men. 'I think we can push them back fifty yards for a start. How the hell did they get here so soon?'

'News travels fast nowadays. It seems you only have to have one big mouth giving the scoop away.'

Loxley answered, 'I am beginning to think that real life news drama is the new entertainment,' before adding, 'Let's take a look at Varney.'

They were led to a low fence that skirted the stadium in Jackdaw Lane. Sugden handed Loxley a pair of binoculars and told him to look at a small clearing in the trees. Though he was smartly dressed, Varney cut a forlorn figure as he sat motionless in front of the main stand.

'You say he has been sitting like that since you got here?' asked Loxley

'Yes, apart from the odd occasion when he has stood up to stretch his legs.'

Scanning the binoculars wider afield Loxley said, 'Probably will be a good idea, Dennis, if you take command on the main gate area. I take it the rear of the stadium is well secured. We do not want our rabbit finding a bolthole now we have him cornered, do we?'

Sugden was quick to reassure him. 'He is well and truly snared, believe me he has nowhere left to hide.'

Passing the binoculars over to Cumber for him to take a look, Loxley said, 'Good. Well, I think it's about time that we established contact with him, try to get some sort of a rapport going. In the meantime let's get this media circus pushed back.'

Sugden responded immediately. 'I will get a loudhailer.'

*

After his thoughts had turned to Simon Llewelyn, Marcus Varney's mood had begun to change. The feelings of relief and liberation that he had felt so euphorically after he had left London were beginning to fade like the burnt-out embers of a blazing fire. For try as he might in his own tormented mind, he could find no justification for why he had killed Simon Llewelyn. Unlike the obsessive malevolence he had felt for Buxton and Galton, there was no good reason to hate or resent such an inoffensive chap as Simon. If anything Simon had made a bigger mess of his law studies at Oxford than he had done. At St Benedict's, Simon had been known as the poor eccentric misfit, a dreamer, a no hoper. Despite knowing this, when Francis Barnaby had informed him that Simon had been doing really well with his new career in the City of London, he had felt a furious resentment and a deep sense of envy. The unpalatable truth had to be that he had found it impossible to accept the fact that even a fellow drop-out like Llewelyn should now be enjoying a better existence than him.

He now realised that he could have found any number of excuses to pull out of the third murder. From the moment when the policeman delivered the police letter requesting Francis get in contact when he returned from holiday, or equally on the Monday evening when the police had swamped the streets of London. Why didn't he? Instead he had waited till the Tuesday evening to complete his brutal mission. Slowly and horrifically, the truth began to dawn on him. The harsh reality was that he had enjoyed the game, everything from the planning and stalking, to the execution and getaway. From the selection of Finsbury Circus for the final grisly act, right down to the purchasing of the claw hammer at Robert Dyas hardware store in order to buckle the park railing - he had loved every second of it. He remembered the mounting excitement he had felt as he followed Llewelyn from the *Dirty Dicks* pub to the Finsbury Circus entrance, before running around the perimeter and squeezing through the fencing. After taking up his position behind a bush opposite the bandstand, he recalled the almost bestial anticipation that he had felt as

Llewelyn's footsteps drew near. For the truth was in that moment he had possessed no more feeling for Simon Llewelyn than a chicken farmer would have felt for a trespassing fox. The slow comprehension of the magnitude of his atrocities began to sink in ever deeper. Increasingly filled with self-loathing, he grappled with the grim realisation that his mind had become wickedly warped by a lethal mix of trauma, disappointment, twisted jealousy and alcohol. In that precise moment and for the first time, he was starkly confronted with his own irrational psychosis. With crystal clarity he could now see that the delusion that he could somehow go on to live a contented life free of the crippling hatred of his former graduate colleagues while securely encased within the confines of a prison wall, were nothing more than the cruel trick of a twisted and damaged mind. For the harsh truth was there was no future. How could there be?

He was brought back into the moment by the raucous cry of a solitary crow hovering on the distant skyline. For that brief moment as he watched it gliding peacefully over the treetops, he found himself yearning for the apparent simplicity of the bird's existence. The watery winter sun was beginning to sink in the west, causing a grey, misty gloom to descend upon the landscape. What little breeze there had been had died to nothing, bringing a tranquil stillness to the trees as if in a picture.

The peaceful calm was abruptly interrupted by the sound of an amplified voice calling his name. From what he could make out, the voice was warning him that he was totally surrounded by police marksmen. He looked to his left and noticed for the first time a mass of blue lights flashing insistently in the distance. The amplified voice was now repeatedly informing him that it would be best for everyone if he gave himself up and walked slowly towards the assembled police with his hands held high above his head.

He heard himself utter softly under his breath, 'Better for everyone, really?' Those were the exact same words his father had used all those years ago when he had chosen to walk out of his life. With a deep empty sigh of resignation he reached for his holdall and pulled out a small photograph. He studied the image for a good few minutes before the features on the faces in the picture began to blur as his eyes filled with tears. He carefully returned the photograph to the holdall before taking out an army issue LA91 Hi-Power Browning pistol which he had kept as a souvenir from the Falklands conflict. With steady deliberation he placed it in his overcoat pocket and rose slowly to his feet and raised his hands. Leaving the holdall behind him, he started to walk purposefully towards the flashing blue lights. He had approximately got to within a hundred yards of the massed police activity, when he felt a compulsion to break into a run. He was back on the summit of Mount Longdon with the biting South Atlantic wind blowing in his face. For one more time he was the valued and admired Falklands hero of the nation. He reached deep into his pocket for the Browning.

Loxley was watching intently as the distant isolated figure of Marcus Varney walked towards them. Initially he had felt relief that Varney had appeared to respond to his request to come quietly, but there was something about Varney's body language that made him feel uneasy. Though his hands were above his head his walk looked too swift for the circumstances, too resolute. Loxley's rising fears were made reality when Varney suddenly burst into a run.

Hearing the rattling of gun barrels as the police marksmen raised their rifles, Loxley lifted the megaphone to issue one more desperate plea, 'Marcus, I repeat you will be shot if you do not obey our instruction. I order you now to stop running and put your hands in the air.'

If Varney heard the instruction he showed no sign of obeying it. To Loxley's mounting alarm Varney increased his pace while appearing to be waving what very much looked like a gun. There was a depressing inevitably about what followed as the police marksmen opened fire. Varney stumbled before appearing to recover slightly, only to fall once more in a hail of gunfire. For a few seconds the echoes from the shots reverberated around the vast expanse of the Iffley Road Stadium, eventually replaced by a stunned, solemn silence. The inert form of Marcus Varney was rapidly surrounded by police marksman as Loxley and Cumber started walking slowly towards the spot where he fell. Varney lay on his front with his head turned to one side. His eyes were wide open, unseeing but strangely exultant. The Browning handgun lay a few feet from his outstretched arm.

One of the marksmen picked it up for examination before presenting it to Loxley with the empty chamber. 'No cartridges, sir.'

Loxley was not surprised. Right from the start this case had somehow had the feel of an unfolding Greek Tragedy.

Cumber spoke first. 'It looks like he decided to go out in a blaze of glory.'

Loxley was quick to reply. 'There's no glory to be found here, James, only death.'

*

After returning to the Saint Aldates police station and ringing New Scotland Yard to give Bill Kemp the dismal details of the grim conclusion, Loxley was grateful for the chance to shut himself away from all the commotion, and concern himself with the forlorn task of rummaging through the contents of Varney's holdall. As he sorted through an assortment of neatly folded garments, he felt something hard and metallic in one of the zip compartments. Loxley was soon looking at a shiny silver medal adorned with a blue and green striped ribbon. The ribbon was studded with a small silver rosette. This had to be Varney's Falkland military medal. At the bottom of the holdall there was also a small photo of Varney holding a child. Loxley assumed it must be his daughter. With both of them laughing and gazing lovingly at each other it looked a happy picture. In view of the morbid realities of what had transpired in Varney's life since and the tragic climax which he had just witnessed, Loxley felt he was looking at an image that existed in a parallel universe.

A little surprised to hear himself sigh heavily, Loxley returned the contents to the holdall before making his way to the canteen to join Cumber for a much needed mug of tea. The canteen was busy, packed with excited police staff discussing the dramatic events that had unfolded. It took a little time for Loxley to eventually spot his junior partner sitting in the corner with DI Sugden. Collecting his tea at the counter he went over to join them.

As Loxley took his seat, Sugden confirmed the general consensus. 'So it looks like it was definitely a case of a highly efficient serial murderer with an unsound mind?'

Loxley took a deep swig of his tea before answering. 'No doubt about it, a classic case of a good egg turned rotten. Name your reasons; festering long time grudges, jealousy, envy, disappointment, all fuelled and triggered by a combination of twisted rage, alcohol and the mental trauma resulting from his experiences in the Falklands.'

Cumber paused thoughtfully for a few seconds as he finished off what remained of his chocolate Penguin, before saying, 'Tragic, from hero to zero in four years.'

'I think you have just about summed it up, James,' said Loxley, still struggling to put the poignant memory of the contents of Varney's holdall out of his mind. Catching both Cumber and Sugden by surprise, he unexpectedly stood up from the table. 'Much as it's been good to see you, Dennis, and much as I like Oxford, I feel it's time for me to go home.'

*

On the drive back to London there was very little conversation. Cumber had tuned the radio onto a cup match in which Spurs were playing away to Cambridge, whilst Loxley had just been lost in his thoughts. Normally

Loxley would have been interested in the fortunes of his favourite team, but the case had troubled him in a way like no other he could remember. Arriving back at New Scotland Yard, he had not been surprised to learn that the 'Super' had already left for home after yet another hurriedly arranged and stressful press conference. It occurred to Loxley that maybe his own low mood could be partly explained by the Super's proposed retirement plans. All through his career Bill Kemp had always been there for him, the protective older brother he never had. After ordering in a Chinese takeaway he and Cumber had spent the next hour bringing Brian Parrish and Bob Norton up to speed with their case notes.

At least the lateness of the hour ensured that when Loxley eventually left to make his way home from New Scotland Yard, the roads were appreciably clear of heavy traffic. The traumatic events of the day had left him feeling flat and exhausted, with none of the feelings of euphoria and satisfaction that usually went with the conclusion of a challenging high-profile case. In what had been a difficult investigation, he had been left feeling cheated at the conclusion. The harsh truth was that the whole affair had been a tragedy which could and should have been avoided. He wondered how many other tortured army veterans were out there, people like Varney, tormented and twisted by their thoughts while feeling abandoned and ignored by the country for which they had fought so bravely. In an attempt to lighten his mood he turned on the car radio and tuned into a late night music station. The song that emanated through the speakers seemed fittingly appropriate to the moment. Humming along with *I'll Find My Way Home* by Jon and Vangelis, he found himself thinking warm thoughts of Janet and his daughter Clare and counted his blessings.

THE END